Mark the Galactinaut

NOEL STEVENS

iUniverse, Inc.
New York   Bloomington

iUniverse books may be ordered through booksellers or by contacting:

iUniverse
1663 Liberty Drive
Bloomington, IN 47403
www.iuniverse.com
1-800-Authors (1-800-288-4677)

Because of the dynamic nature of the Internet, any Web addresses or links contained in this book may have changed since publication and may no longer be valid. The views expressed in this work are solely those of the author and do not necessarily reflect the views of the publisher, and the publisher hereby disclaims any responsibility for them.

ISBN: 978-1-4502-2596-0 (sc)
ISBN: 978-1-4502-2764-3 (ebook)

Printed in the United States of America

iUniverse rev. date: 04/09/2010

AUTHOR'S NOTE

Scientists tell us our universe is not alone – "branes" or "curtains" hide us from other, unseen dimensions, other universes.

Incredibly tiny holes fill these "branes".

But Heisenberg's Uncertainty Principle tells us we cannot tell beforehand the size of the holes.

Farmers disappear from fields and no one ever sees them again.

A hole can grow to the size of a man, for an instant, and suck a man into another dimension, another world we can never see from our world.

KEYNOTE STATEMENT

A pterodactyl danced towards him with a comical jumping step, and Mark blew off its head. Three more came at him, in comical, dancing steps, and he cut holes into them.

"Come on!" the ten year old shouted. "Come on! Here I am! Come and get me!"

...and he saw the alien "Naomi" in a nest of big sticks... she had picked up a stick and was fighting a baby pterodactyl, ten feet long, with a wicked beak...

His laser fired... Naomi scrambled out of the nest.

"Keep behind me!" he yelled...

BOOK ONE

Mark got out of bed feeling grumpy. There was nothing – but nothing – to tell him that night he would be sleeping a zillion miles away in space, and if you'd tried to explain it to him, he wouldn't understand what you were talking about.

So Mark got out of his warm bed, feeling cold and sleepy, with his mother calling him, and went to the bathroom for a quick shower. His mother kept telling him that after the warm water, he had to turn on the freezing cold before he came out of the shower, but at ten-years-old he wasn't *that* silly.

The bathroom had warmed up a tiny bit with the steam, so he dressed in there and went downstairs to breakfast.

One look at his mum's face told him she was in another of her days of feeling really down. Try as he might, he couldn't think of anything to cheer her up. He sat down to his cornflakes with hot milk, without saying anything, and then ate his bacon and fried eggs, with toast.

Mum worked on a computer in a stock room, and the screen showed where everything had gone or had to go. Mark didn't know whether that made her feel blue or whether he, Mark, was to blame too.

Mum's name was Jane, so he tried to cheer up saying, "Last night I dreamt of this beautiful lady and her name was Jane…"

He glanced quickly at his mother. She gave him a sort of smile and then went back to having a set face. That wasn't going to work.

Mark was scared to go to school, because Clive the Club, Paul the Pug and Harry the Hatchet were out to get him. Mum gave him his packet of sandwiches and one pound note, and he wondered desperately how he could get them to school without the Club, the Pug and the Hatchet punching him up and stealing his food and money.

His mum looked at the clock, and said, "We've got to get going." Then she did smile, and said, "Mark Clough…" Then she smiled some more, and said, "Mr. Mark Clough, you be a good boy today and watch it."

A big smile spread all over Mark's face and he hugged his mother hard. But he had a knot in his stomach thinking of the bullies.

* * *

Outside, thank goodness, it wasn't raining. It was an April day in England, with low scudding clouds, and when Mark got on his bike, the wind blew him this way and that. His hands felt cold and he cycled behind the factories till he got on the wider road. He rode for a half a mile and turned through streets of small houses with gardens. Then he pedalled through office blocks, and as he got near Milton Mudwallop School, three bikes shot out behind a building and careened into him. Mark crashed onto the roadway, on his side, taking skin off his face and hands. The Club, the Pug and the Hatchet jumped off their bikes and kicked him in the chest and stomach, pulled his bag off the handlebars and emptied it. They found his sandwiches. Hatchet went through his pockets and found the pound note.

"Hey," he shouted. "You little thief! This money's mine," and they all laughed like mad. Hatchet kicked him in the leg, as he struggled to his feet, and Mark fell over again.

They rode off. Mark put his books and things back in his bag, checked his bike for damage, and got on it, aching where they had kicked him. He rode to school slowly, feeling a bit thick-headed and dopey.

In the school yard, he locked his bike into the rack, and Naomi came running over.

"Mark, you've got blood on your face!" she cried in fright. "What happened to you?"

He told her, mumbling.

"Those scrapes are all dirty," she exclaimed. "You've got to see the Matron! Quickly, come with me."

Mark wanted to hang back, but she caught his hand. He glanced around to see other kids looking, so pulled away his hand and grumbled, "I'm coming."

The Matron asked him what had happened, and he said he had swerved to avoid a car.

"Oh, the traffic," wailed the Matron. "And you small children on bikes! It's wicked, it is."

Naomi listened to him with her lips tightening. Suddenly, she turned away and marched off without a word, tossing her head in the air. The Matron glanced after her, and said, "Now we've gone and upset that one, haven't we just."

When the Matron finished with him, Mark went up to his classroom. He would be late, but he had an excuse this time, and the Matron would back him up.

As he walked in the door, the teacher said, "The Head wants to see you, Clough. Off you go."

Mark wasn't going to leave his things unprotected on one of the desks, so he took his bag with him.

He knocked on the Head's door, and heard the Head say, "Come in."

Mark went in, and the Head said, "Ah, it's you, Clough. You've been all patched up?"

Mark nodded, his lips pressed together. "So you were waylaid by those three, eh?"

"It was a car, sir," stuttered Mark.

"A car, my eye. Don't you dare give me that. They rammed you side-on, did they? They took your lunch and money, eh?"

Mark stared speechlessly. How did he know all this?

Naomi!

That little... that... He couldn't find the words. That snake in the grass. Grrr. Always telling him that he was special. And now telling *on* him.

The Head stared at him, then took up his pipe, slowly stuffed it with tobacco, lit it with a lot of sucking, and puffed, watching the smoke, and then turning his eyes back to Mark. He didn't say anything. He stared at Mark, puffed contentedly, and brought his eyes back to Mark.

"That's right, isn't it?" said the Head.

Mark looked at him dumbly.

"THAT'S RIGHT, ISN'T IT?" roared the Head, and Mark jumped half out of his chair.

He nodded ashamedly... well, half nodded, sort of nodded.

The Head sat unmoving, smoking.

Suddenly, they heard a loud knock on the door.

"Come in," called the Head.

A burly policeman came in, and the Head nodded at Mark.

The policeman studied him.

"Right proper mess they done of your face," he decided finally. "They stole your tucker and they stole money, that's right?"

Mark sat unable to move or speak.

The Head gave him an alarming glare, and Mark nodded quickly.

"May I sit?" asked the policeman. "Have to fill out this form."

The policeman wrote carefully, concentrating on each word, and then said, "Young man, please write your name down here."

"What does it say?" quavered Mark in a voice that didn't sound his own.

The policeman handed it to the Head.

The Head looked sternly at Mark. "It says they knocked you off your bike, caused you injuries, stole your lunch packet and. stole money to the value of one pound."

Mark twisted this way and that, the Pug, the Club and the Hatchet would *murder* him, cut him up in little pieces…

"Write down your name," commanded the Head.

Mark wrote down his name.

The Head pressed a button, and after a couple of minutes two teachers came in with Pug, Club and Hatchet. The teachers made them stand by a tall bookcase, with a tapestry hanging on one side, showing knights in medieval armour. Mark looked enviously, hungrily at that armour that protected all their bodies.

The policeman said solemnly, "Mark Clough, is this them…?"

Mark sat, struck dumb.

"…what did it?" said the policeman impatiently.

The three looked at Mark with expressions that said – 'just you wait'.

Mark nodded.

"Say 'yes'," said the policeman.

Mark said, "Yes."

The policeman said to the Head, "I'll take them down to the Police Station and lock 'em up. You'll make the phone calls."

"Most certainly," said the Head warmly. "And thank you for removing these individuals from my school."

They left, and Mark took three or four careful breaths.

Mark asked, "How long will they be locked up?" He looked hopefully at the Head. "Many years?"

The Head laughed. "Until the school day ends. Then the policeman will send them home."

Mark thought about that with a knot of fear in his tummy.

"As soon as that?" he said to the Head. "And what are the phone calls, then?"

"To their parents. To tell them".

The Head sighed. "Then the parents will complain and protest to the newspapers and the television. We'll see what the parents say about their poor darlings…"

A knock on the door interrupted him.

A teacher came in with some lunch packages, and an envelope.

4

"Ah," said the Head. "Thank you."

The teacher left, with a nod, but didn't say anything.

The Head opened the envelope, and took out a pound note.

"Boy, I believe this is yours. Take it," he commanded. "Which is your lunch ?"

Mark pointed mutely, and thought, How did he know about the pound note! Naomi! Naomi told him! She betrayed what he had told her in secret!

The Head handed him his lunch, and smiled. He swept the other lunches across the table, and with a short laugh said, "Take them all and share them out with your friends".

The good news was that the Pug, the Club and the Hatchet would be very hungry.

But Mark supposed that the hungrier they got, the more terrible their rage.

He put the pound note back in his pocket, and carried the lunches outside and went to the lockers, where he put the food away in his locker.

With heavy, dragging feet, he went back to the classroom, and spent the morning, hardly able to hear or understand what his teachers said.

At lunch time, Naomi ran up to him in the corridor and said, "You can share my lunch, and two of my girl friends too…"

Mark could see other boys looking at him. They had probably decided he wouldn't put up much of a fight and were wondering to have a go at him.

Mark had to tell Naomi that she had betrayed him, but he couldn't.

He told Naomi, "I got my lunch back, and I've got three lunches more."

Who could he share them with? No one.

It was only months since he and his mum came to Milton Mudwallop and it was the worst thing that had ever happened to him in his life. He had no friends. He sometimes talked to other boys, but often he had to run away from them for his life. Often, they surrounded him and began pushing him, with a few punches…

"Three more lunches?" asked Naomi in amazement.

"They've taken those kids to prison," said Mark.

"Oh, goody!" shrieked Naomi.

Two other girls joined them.

He would look a sissy if he sat eating his lunch with three girls.

"Come with me," said Mark, and he grabbed a couple of lunches from his locker and handed them over.

He felt for his bag, and knocked his lunch into it. There was a park near the school, and he'd ride there on his bike to eat his sandwiches.

"But where're you going?" cried Naomi, running after him. He hurried away.

"Gotta go somewhere on my bike," he mumbled.

Naomi stopped in disappointment, and watched him as he vanished around the corner.

* * *

He sat on a seat in the park, and opened his bag. He had two lunches inside, not just his own. He opened his lunch, and ate a sandwich.

A dog hurried over, and stood in front of him, wagging its tail, its head on one side, looking at him wistfully. Mark decided it was a stray and wondered how it hadn't been picked up. It was a bit dirty and its coat was unruly.

He took out the second lunch, and began feeding the dog, which wolfed the food hungrily.

Did this lunch belong to the Pug, or the Club, or to the Hatchet? Whoever it was, he was going to kill Mark either today or tomorrow.

Mark felt very sad. Would he die where he fell, or die in hospital? He could see his mum crying. Who could she turn to when he was gone…? Who would love her?

Once on TV, Mark watched a film where a man ate his last meal, before they killed him.

He swallowed the last of his lunch with a lump in his throat. Now he knew what that man felt like. He looked at the dog. A policeman or someone would pick it up as a stray and a vet would put it down. Likely as not, it was eating its last meal like Mark.

* * *

Mark rode back to school, and sat through the classes in the afternoon.

When school was out, he hurried to his bike, and saw about eight kids heading for him and closing in. He slipped into a crowd of boys and girls, and as they pushed through, after him, a fight broke out. They turned around, got into the fight, and then bashed and punched each other.

Mark scrambled to his bike, unlocked it with trembling hands, and pedalled away furiously.

He heard Naomi calling him, and looking back, saw her on her bike behind him. He let her catch up, and she said,

"Where are you going?"

"I want to be by myself," he told her, and her face crumpled, and she let him ride on ahead.

Near his home, he turned down a side road beside some workshops, then wound through high brick walls, and came out in front of fenced fields.

He rode through the fields to low hills, and at the top of the hill, he got off and opened a gate in the fence, that gave onto a dirt track that went across a moor.

The bike bumped badly on the track, but he got out further into the moor, the track following high ground.

The track curved around to an outcrop of big rocks, and as he approached it...

He was spinning dizzily. Everything was grey, shot with pale light. He kept spinning, then suddenly stopped.

He was lying on a vast, cloudy landscape, with his bike beside him. The clouds stretched so far he couldn't believe it was possible. They were grey and pink, with great twisting sweeps of orange and gold and blinding silver.

He blinked and blinked. It wasn't right. He pinched himself, but his fingers went through his arm. His body and bike were sort of misty. He got to his feet and tried to walk on the cloud downhill. He couldn't. He could walk only on the flat. He wanted to look downwards to see where the moor was.

Far, far away, he saw a big opening in the clouds. He thought, I'll walk over there, when he found himself racing across the cloud tops and was there in a flash.

He looked down, and saw only more clouds.

"Mummy!" he shouted, but no sound came out.

Then he got more frightened than ever in his whole life.

He squeezed his eyes closed, very hard, so that when he opened them he'd see the moor around him. He opened his eyes, and saw only these beautiful colours.

So he squeezed them even harder than before. But when he opened them, nothing had changed.

He cried, and then, ashamed, looked around to see whether anyone had seen him crying.

There was no one. NO ONE. Nothing to eat or drink. He would starve to death, or die of thirst like people in the desert.

He wanted his mummy.

Far away, the clouds rose in high columns. I want to go over there and look, he thought, and suddenly he moved with amazing speed.

At the foot of the towering cliffs of cloud, he willed himself to rise. But he couldn't. He could move on the flat, that was all.

His bike!

He looked around, and it was with him.

He wanted to go back. He wanted to go home. He wanted to be on the moor again. Tears coursed down his face. Someone had to tell him what to do, and there was NO ONE.

He sat down, but it made no difference whether he stood or sat. He didn't get tired.

I'M BY MYSELF, he thought, in utter terror.

Then a thought pushed into his head from outside. SHUT UP! I CAN HEAR YOU! STOP ALL THIS FUSS.

He looked around everywhere, and saw only greys and pinks, and orange and gold. Very beautiful, but empty.

He turned frantically this way and that, looking and looking.

Then he saw a small black dot about a million miles away, moving towards him with the speed of lightning.

It *was* heading for HIM. Mark cried out with relief, but no sound came.

It slowed down suddenly, and came closer and closer, then stopped beside him.

The starship was immense; it must have measured several miles across. And it turned slowly around.

He "heard" in his brain, "FIVE MILES ACROSS."

A long platform slid out of its side, and the edge stopped at his feet. He willed himself to move up it slowly, and as he drifted up, he saw an open doorway. Inside, a barrier of light with sharp dancing sparks, that roiled and boiled and blocked him, but he was so scared to stay outside he willed himself into it. He felt thousands of small jabs, and then was through it, and he heard his bike clank as it hit the metal wall of the passage way. He realised he was standing, had stopped floating. He had to hold his bike, or it would have fallen. He pinched himself, and felt it! He had gone solid again. He took a deep breath... he could breathe the air. Where was he? He was in a curving metal corridor, the walls a shiny, copper colour. He stopped in wonderment, Suddenly, he wasn't afraid.

"GET A MOVE ON WITH IT, WILL YOU!" he "heard" in his brain, although he felt the words more than heard them.

He hurried forward, and the corridor stopped curving. The corridor was curving around something – he could hear a big thumping behind the inside wall. Then it ran straight, so he got on his bike and rode about fifty yards to a big green door, which opened by breaking into four parts and withdrawing into the wall.

He braked his bike, got off, and walked into a large room, the walls covered in banks of blinking lights.

In the centre, rose a large grey snake, one half of it coiled on the floor, the rest rearing up towards him. Beneath its head, it had four arms with hands and fingers.

He "heard" in his head, "What a racket you made. I could hear you millions of miles away."

Mark stared at the eyes of the snake. They were large and brilliant and clever. It had no nose, but a big mouth and ears.

He heard a singing in his ears, and felt himself going dizzy. In all his life, he had never known what real fear was till this very second. He tried to keep on his feet by clinging to his bike, but he knew he was going to fall over.

"Do I look as horrible as all that?" he heard inside his head. "You ought just to see yourself. You are ugly as sin. Bits and pieces all over the place. You've got a head that doesn't belong to your body, and arms and legs sticking out in every direction. Your nose looks awful, sticking out like that, and you've tried to cover everything up with bits of cloth all over, and leather on your feet. People in glass houses don't throw stones."

"Who are you?" gasped Mark weakly.

"I am a young girl, on my school holidays", he heard.

The snake went over to a keyboard, and her fingers ran over the keys.

"I thought so!" she "sent" mentally to Mark. "You're talking and thinking in English! It says so here. You're from the planet… er… let me see, yes… from Earth!" she finished triumphantly.

She turned to a big solid, silver box, that rolled forward, and said, "Clackety Hobo, we're over the Solar System. We're over the star called Sun."

"Clackety Hobo?" whispered Mark.

"Don't you like my name?" said the silver box in a metallic voice, in English, advancing in annoyance upon Mark.

"It's a marvellous name," shrieked Mark, swinging his bike between himself and the robot.

"I'm so pleased," said Clackety Hobo. "So we're going to be friends, then. I don't have any friend who's a human. I know all about you, because your television programs escape from the surface of your planet into space. We have a satellite that picks them up, and beams them into this dimension, where we receive them about an hour later on our world."

"Your *world?*" whispered Mark, weakly. "*Dimension?*"

Another robot glided forward. "I'm Hettie Hobo," she announced. "How did you live out there, in the open, in this dimension?"

The snake said, "I can't go out there. I'd disintegrate in an instant."

9

"Disintegrate?" said Mark. "What does that mean?"

The three looked at him pityingly. "Don't you go to school on your world?" asked the snake.

"Of course, I do!" said Mark bravely. "But we don't do big words."

"Well," he amended, "I don't do very well at them."

The snake moved towards him, and he bounded back.

"Isn't he rude!" exclaimed Clackety Hobo.

Mark felt someone interfering in his brain, and suddenly rose high off the floor. He looked down and saw he had been turned into another snake with arms. He gave a despairing cry.

"What have you done to me?" he wept.

"Nothing," said the snake. "It's all in your head. You're just imagining what you see. It's the idea I've put into your mind."

Mark suddenly popped back to his human self.

"See!" said the snake.

The snake looked thoughtful, and said, "What about this?"

She turned into a pink rabbit.

Mark shook his head hard. "That's no good," he said.

She turned herself into a yellow, fluffy koala bear.

"I'm sorry," said Mark in a very determined voice, "But I don't think I like that at all, not at all."

She changed into a an eleven-year-old girl, in a white dress that came down to her feet, with a big pink ribbon, and another purple ribbon over her blonde hair.

Mark began to laugh. "Girls don't wear ribbons…"

The ribbons vanished.

"And the dress should only come down to – oh, I don't know. Well, your knees, maybe."

The dress shortened to her knees.

"That looks sort of better," Mark admitted. "You need pockets on the dress."

Pockets appeared all over the dress, about twenty of them.

"About four pockets," said Mark , after a great mental effort.

The dress showed four pockets.

She was barefoot.

"You need shoes."

Shoes appeared.

"What is your name?", an amazed Mark asked her.

"Ethelinda," the beautiful, smiling young girl said.

"ETHELINDA!" cried Mark. "Nobody's called *that*. It's not English."

"It is English, and it means 'noble snake'. It's in our computer banks. It comes from the German."

"German has nothing to do with English. Germany's another country altogether, "said Mark, loftily.

"Hundreds of years ago, a lot of German entered the English language."

"We're not taught that at school," said Mark, sulkily.

Hettie Hobo said, "Ethelinda, you look lovely. But how did he... what is your name?"

Ethelinda said, "Mark. He's called Mark... Mark Cough, no, Mark Clough."

Hettie Hobo said, "How did Mark get into this dimension?

Mark said, "I was riding, my bike along a rough trail across a moor, when suddenly I found myself up here..."

"It's not 'up'," said Clackety Hobo. "It's another dimension which is contiguous with your own."

"What is contingous?" asked Mark in a whisper.

"*Contiguous!*" snapped Ethelinda. "It means the two dimensions occupy the same place, but are invisible to each other."

"What are 'dimensions'?" asked Mark, in a voice that quavered.

"Dimensions are different worlds, silly," said Ethelinda. "Look, you live on Earth, that goes around the Sun in space, that right? You look up at night and you see the stars. All of that is our universe, *our* dimension. I live on the planet Xiucheu –"

"Excuse me," gulped Mark. "Choo Choo?"

Ethelinda said seriously, "That's not a *very* good pronunciation, but I suppose it will do..." She looked extremely doubtful. "I live on Xiucheu and you live on Earth, and our Galaxy is the Milky Way."

Mark protested, "At our school, when you're 10 years old, you haven't got up to the Galaxy yet. What is the Galaxy?"

Ethelinda said airily, "It's about 100 thousand million stars, all stuck together by gravity in a big wheel hundreds of thousands of light years across –"

She frowned. "That's not right." She tapped the keyboard. "Oh, bother, I can't find it. Well, it's thousands of light years across, or something, and the whole Milky Way slowly spins and all the stars keep their places in the wheel. Well, let me say, I'm glad I wasn't born on Earth. You kids don't know nothing!"

"Don't know *anything*", Mark corrected her.

"So, this dimension has nothing to do with the dimension our universe is in," ventured Mark, after some thought.

"It's completely different," Ethelinda agreed, straightening her dress, and moving over to a mirror to look at herself. "Am I pretty?" she asked him.

"You're the prettiest girl in the whole world," said Mark sincerely. "You're the prettiest girl in this dimension, and in our own dimension too, and I know of no other girl clever enough to pull me out of all those clouds and wake me solid again."

"Am I your best friend?" Ethelinda asked him wistfully.

"Oh, yes!" cried Mark eagerly.

"And me!" cried Clackety Hobo and Hettie Hobo in unison. "Don't you love us?"

Mark blushed. "That's sissy," he complained. "But," he admitted, "I like you all better than anyone in the whole world except my mum, because I love her too."

Mark felt it was all right to say he 'loved' his mum. But Ethelinda saw through his trick. "Ah!" she exclaimed, "So you do really love us too."

Tears came to her eyes. Clackety Hobo and Hettie glided over to him and held his hands with their metal hands.

Mark swallowed a couple of times.

After all, he was the *man* here.

"How did I get into this dimension?" he said, to change the subject to something not so soppy. "I was just riding across a moor."

"You cycled into a vortex," said Clackety Hobo. "This dimension invaded ours, in a sort of funnel that was spinning around very fast."

"And that's a... 'vortex'?" said Mark, uncertainly.

"That's a vortex," said Hettie firmly. "There's lots of them. You ask your teachers at school. They will have read about people – farmers and so on – suddenly vanishing in the middle of open fields."

"But," said Mark, "I've ridden along that path before, and nothing ever happened."

"Vortices only last a few minutes. They can stay in the same place, or they can move around. Then they vanish, from the bottom up. If they strike a tree or a building, that breaks up their whirling around. But you can never see them."

"Can we get back to our world?" Mark asked.

"Oh, yes," said Ethelinda. "This starship is equipped to move from one dimension to another. We'll take you right back."

"Why is this ship five miles across?"

"They put in this ring just inside the edge – it's got to be more than 15 miles around. Particles whizz round and round and we speed up their vibrations to trillions and trillions of times a second. Then they go to a big cavity, where we make a vibrating force field with them to burst through the brane between our world and hyperspace."

"What's a cavity? Like in a tooth?"

"An empty space – can be tiny. Ours is ten storeys high."

"And what's 'vibrate'?"

"To bounce fast as lightning, to shake, to shiver, to quiver, to throb – you know."

After a long pause he said, "And where are you going next?"

"We re going to a planet about 15 light years from here. We're going to visit other planets too."

"Will police and customs let us in – just kids?"

"They won't, so we don't go to those places. Lots of other planets only let you land at the Trading Fields. No one has ever seen the rest of those worlds. From the air, you sometimes see cities, sometimes trees. With infra-red, you see millions of 'people' under the trees. You can see their cities, if they have them. They usually have amazing bodies, like you.

"But I love the way they have made you," she added warmly, and Mark was uncomfortable – that was soppy again. Well, he did feel fonder of Ethelinda than anybody else in the whole world – except his mum.

"Lots of planets have no technology, but you can't land. They're ferocious. Kill you and eat you. Some of those planets – they live in huts, all close together. They devour you, just the same.

"I'm on holidays, Dad's lent me this old starship to visit the planets I like going to."

"Your school holidays," supplied Mark, "How far away is your planet from here?"

"About 40 light years."

"And why don't you travel in our universe?"

"Because it would take us about 160 years to get there," said Clackety Hobo impatiently. "Don't you know that?"

Mark shook his head miserably.

"I've only got three months school holidays, see?" explained Ethelinda. Although, in that time I could go right to the other side of the Galaxy – of the Milky Way – but my dad doesn't like me going very far from home. He makes me promise not to go more than 100 light years away."

"And this starship is yours?"

"It's an old cargo ship."

"But how many people are there on board?"

"Just us three. Well, there's the shipboard computer, Dumpledoo. He's *awfully* clever, but he's bolted in to the ship."

A deep booming voice filled the big hall.

"HELLO, MARK. IT'S A PLEASURE TO HAVE YOUR COMPANY."

Mark looked everywhere at once.

"It's a pleasure to make your acquaintance," said Mark, looking nowhere specially. He was sure that is what his mother would want him to

13

say. "I'm sure we'll be very good friends, Dumpledoo," he added, off his own bat.

Dumpledoo boomed, "We should try to make more friends with humans."

Ethelinda said, reproving him, "We are *never* allowed to go to Earth, except in an emergency."

Dumpledoo boomed, "Perfectly true, and no doubt wise."

Mark thought that his home planet did not sound very popular. He hurried to change the subject.

"And what about the other people who have stepped in a vortex. They just stay up here till they die of hunger and thirst?"

"If you can live in this dimension – and I see you humans *can* – you never feel hunger or thirst. No, someone on a starship would hear your thoughts and come and take you on board. Our planet has tens of thousands of starships travelling through this dimension." Ethelinda took a deep breath after saying so much.

"You only have starships on Choo Choo?"

"Choo Choo, as you call it, has starships, and lots of other planets too," said Hettie. "Poompkieuon is one."

"Pumpkin?" said Mark in wonder.

"*Poompkieuon*", said Clackety Hobo with exasperation. "We deal with them a lot."

"Yes," said Mark, anxious to please. "I've got it. *Pumpkin*. Some of these words are really strange. *Pumpkin*."

Clackety Hobo made a noise as though a tin of nails had spilled inside him.

"This dimension outside of our starship," asked Mark, "What is it made of?"

Dumpledoo boomed, "It's made of the same stuff as our own universe – fields of energy and particles. But in our universe, harumph...! Let me see, the lowest sound you can hear with your human ears vibrates at 16,000 times a second."

"That's an *awful* lot in just one second," said Mark doubtfully.

"Now, in our universe, X-rays, they vibrate... oh, dear, the last time we landed on Xiuchen – I'm sorry, on Choo Choo - they took out my circuits on human beings and put in updated knowledge on human beings AND on the planet Earth, and they've left out the X-rays. But if I remember right, X-rays vibrate at 3 million times a second – or is it more? Choo Chooens always try to be so exact, and look what they've forgotten to put in!"

Mark felt his head whizzing. That many times in ONE SECOND? He was going to say what he thought, and then decided to shut up.

Dumpledoo said, "Now in this dimension we've got outside, the particles vibrate at thousands of millions times a second, or millions of millions times a second."

Mark just gaped.

"Mark, can you hear me?" demanded Dumpledoo irritably.

"Thank you, Dumpledoo," Mark managed to get out. "What are particles?"

"Earth sounds awful," said Hettie Hobo. "What *do* they teach the children there?"

"Particles are the tiniest bits of stuff that go to make up atoms, and atoms make up matter."

"So I'm made of atoms?" said Mark.

"Of course you are!" boomed Dumpledoo. "Whatever did you think you were made of?"

"Well, legs and arms and skin and head, you know," said Mark feebly.

Ethelinda smiled at him sweetly, and put her arm around him. "And you're the handsomest boy in any dimension," she told him, making him blush. "But all your bits and pieces are made of atoms."

"What funny ways you have of thinking," said Mark, thinking out loud. Then he realised that he had criticised them, and shrank.

He hurried to say, "So all the school kids on Choo Choo travel to far away planets."

Ethelinda looked unhappy. "I'm by myself," she said. "Everyone else wants to stay at home. They say travelling is for cargo pilots, merchants, transport drivers – that it's boring and dangerous and dirty."

"It's not dirty," cried Mark. He looked around him. "This is one of the cleanest places I have ever seen! It's not boring! I'd love to go to visit other planets."

Ethelinda's face lit up. "You mean that? Truly and truly?"

"More than anything in the whole world," Mark said solemnly.

Clackety Hobo and Hettie Hobo said together, "Can't he come with us?"

"Then it's decided," said Ethelinda, with a happy smile on her face.

Dumpledoo boomed, "A ship approaching, 20 million miles away. Five seconds… it's stopped beside us."

On a big screen, Mark saw a serpent head, old and grizzled. .When he first saw Ethelinda, he had been so shocked that be didn't notice, but now he realised the head was massive, making the thick neck look skinny. Inside his head, he heard a fast give and take of thoughts he couldn't understand. Then the huge serpent head turned, and glared at him.

Mark felt chilled to the bone.

The screen snapped off.

"What was that?" he asked.

There was an uncomfortable silence.

Dumple Doo said, "That was a long-distance trader. He even goes to the other side of the galaxy, of the Milky Way. He said, well... er." Mark realised that Dumple Doo was *two* words.

"Let Mark hear the conversation," commanded Ethelinda.

Dumple Doo boomed, "This is what was said:

Trader:	Ethelinda, my little girl, why have you stopped? It's wonderful to see you, but is something wrong with your ship?
Ethelinda:	We stopped to pick up an Earthling. He was caught in a vortex.
Trader:	AN EARTHLING! On board. He'll murder you in your sleep!
Ethelinda:	He's very nice.
Trader:	Haven't you seen the TV programs they transmit? They're always killing each other. They reckon time by years, and in the last 100 years they have murdered 175,000,000 people in wars, and so on, on their planet.
Ethelinda:	Mark is different.
Trader:	They're all the same. In their TV shows, they try to imagine what aliens are like, and they always show *us* as killing and treacherous. They show US as being like THEMSELVES.
Ethelinda:	But Mark is different and he's my best friend.
Trader:	Madness! All the way through the Milky Way I haven't seen a planet as dangerous and violent as Earth.
Ethelinda:	You're being a fuss-pot.
Trader:	If you say so. Is he very strong?
Ethelinda:	He's so weak, you'd feel sorry for him.
Trader:	What sort of bar of iron could he bend?
Ethelinda:	He hasn't got the muscles to bend *anything*.
Trader:	And he's unarmed?
Ethelinda:	We found him with empty hands.
Trader:	Well, there's nothing like travel to learn about planets and the weird people who live on them. All my love, and enjoy yourself.

That's the end of the conversation," said Dumple Doo.

Mark's face crumpled, and he looked as though he was going to cry.

"Is it really that violent where you come from?" Hettie Hobo asked him, gliding over to him with some clanks inside her.

16

"What's that cloth on his face?" asked Clackety Hobo.

Ethelinda stepped over to him, and touched it.

"Oh! That hurts," said Mark, pulling back.

"What happened?" asked Ethelinda. "Did you hurt yourself?"

"Three boys attacked me!"

"ATTACKED YOU!" roared Dumple Doo. "You mean deliberately?"

"Deliberately?" echoed Mark, confused.

"ON PURPOSE!" roared Dumple Doo. "They tried to cause you harm ON PURPOSE?"

"Yes," whispered Mark.

Dumple Doo boomed, "This starship weighs a million tons. We'll go down there and squash them with it like disgusting bugs!"

Ethelinda said anxiously, "Dumple Doo, you have to keep your temperature even! If you burn any circuits, it's an awful job to fix them up."

"That's very true," grumbled Dumple Doo. "A very wise warning."

"So it IS as bad as that down on Earth," said Hettie Hobo, amazed. "Just as well they can't get off world."

Clackety Hobo said, "Just as well they're stuck down there and so ignorant."

Mark felt Ethelinda searching his mind. She said, "Pug, Chop and Hatchet?"

"Club," Mark corrected her.

"Let's go down to Earth and fix them, what do you say?" Ethelinda asked the three robots.

The three robots cried in one voice, "Let's!"

"Oh, no," said Mark. "Listen…"

An enormous hum filled the spaceship, and Mark saw colours swirling before his eyes.

On the screen, appeared a close-up image of Jupiter.

Dumple Doo asked, "Were you walking in the other dimension? You walked all the way to Jupiter. You should really learn not to move around so much."

"Will we go to Earth through the Solar System?" Mark asked them.

Ethelinda said, "No, it'll take us weeks. We'll have to accelerate and we'll be pressed so hard against our seats for days, we'll hardly be able to breathe, besides, there are asteroids all over the place."

A dazzling light filled the screen.

She said, "Look, our force-field has just hit one. We're moving so fast, we atomised it. Turned it all into light and heat. Dumple Doo, let's get out of here."

Again the sickening hum filled Mark, and on the screen, he saw the coloured clouds of the other dimension. They moved for a couple of seconds to a distant cloud, then everything hummed, and then Mark saw the Earth on the screen.

Ethelinda searched his mind. "Dumple Doo, find Milton Mudwallop in England."

The starship moved so fast, the Earth appeared to roll over under them.

"Got it," said Dumple Doo, highly pleased.

"We mustn't really squash them…" began Mark.

"We'll go down in a canoe," said Ethelinda, quite excited.

"A *canoe!*" exclaimed Mark.

"It's a small landing craft," said Clackety Hobo. "It's really got a roof and windows."

They went out another door.

"Bring your bike," said Ethelinda. "We'll leave it at your house."

"It depends on the time. My mum might be back home."

"When does she come back?"

"About six o'clock."

"What time does it get dark?"

"About six."

"It'll be all right."

They were in a bright metal corridor that rose steeply, and it went on and on.

Mark worried "It must have been after half-past-four when I got into the vortex…"

"While we are in this dimension, time goes amazingly fast."

Mark's jaw dropped.

They hurried on.

A six-sided door opened by withdrawing into the walls.

They went through, to a cigar-shaped ship, about fifty feet long.

Clackety Hobo held out his hand, and a door opened in the side.

They went inside, and Ethelinda said, "You're used to seats. I can read it in your mind. We'll build you some, but now you stand against that wall."

Mark stood there, and arms came out and held all of him.

"Hey!" he cried. "I want to look out of the window."

The arms released him.

"Turn around and face the window."

The arms gripped him again.

The door closed with a sucking sound, and they glided through another door into an enormous hangar.

At the other end of the hanger, part of the wall rose up and lay against the roof. They went through, and the wall closed again.

Hettie Hobo said, "We're in an air lock. They're sucking out all the air and storing it in a tank."

An outside hatch opened, and Mark found himself staring down at the Earth. To his left, it was dark, with lights from the distant Middle East. Below him, the light was paling, and to his right, the sun was stronger.

"Why does time go so fast in the other dimension?"

Clackety Hobo said, "Because things change very fast."

"My watch goes very fast?" wondered Mark. He said eagerly, "If I make my watch go more slowly in the morning, it would take ages till I had to go to school."

"Now that's no good at all," said Hettie Hobo severely. "Because everything else would have to slow down too... the Sun in the sky, your mum, the cars outside. Your mum would have to move so slowly, it would take her an hour to get down the stairs. In the other dimension, we were talking and talking, and before that, there was all the time you were by yourself before we found you. But down on Earth, only about one minute passed."

Mark decided that was silly, and that they didn't know what they were talking about. But when they came low over the roofs of Milton Mudwallop, he saw it hadn't begun to get dark, and his watch showed only quarter-to-five. And it had been well after half-past-four when he rode into the vortex.

Hettie Hobo said, "Now, if you fly in a space ship in this universe at one-third the speed of light, time would go incredibly slowly on board, and after a year, when you came back home, years and years would have passed in Milton Mudwallop."

This alarmed Mark. Once you got off the ground, watches went mad!

Ethelinda told him, "Concentrate on a picture of your house so we steer there."

Mark pictured his house, and was thankful that Ethelinda had forgotten about Pug, Club and Hatchet.

She read this thoughts, and said sharply, "I haven't forgotten about them. I've reached their minds, and now they're getting on their bikes and coming to your place."

Mark got a clutch of fear in his stomach.

Hettie Hobo said, "If your mum went on a spaceship at one third of the speed of light, and you had a screen at home so you could see inside the cabin, and if your mum walked across the cabin, on your screen in Milton Mudwallop she could take from sunrise to sunset to make those few steps. As you watched the screen, you mightn't see immediately any movement at all of her feet until minutes had passed."

Mark blinked.

He said, "But we're going to my place?"

19

"To leave your bike."

"To put it away in the shed?"

"That's right", said Ethelinda. She told Clackety Hobo and Hettie Hobo, "You must film everything… everything."

"What for?" exclaimed Mark.

"Because back on Choo Choo, I want to try and win the Blue Medal for Science with my report on life and physiology of Earthlings. No one has ever dared land on world here, it's far too dangerous."

Mark cried anxiously, "We can't land the canoe in our garden because it's too small. And we can't burn mummy's flower beds!"

"We'll use our anti-gravity. Up in our starship, our robots plug in the energy for our anti-gravity to top it up, but we don't have much of it, anti-gravity burns up energy like mad. So, we use it for the very last bit of all. Then we put down long legs to stand on. Usually we use the anti-gravity to land the canoe flat, but it'll flatten all the flowers. We'll land with the canoe pointing straight up.

"Clackety Hobo and Hettie Hobo have some anti-gravity of their own, so they'll float us down to the ground."

Mark thought of a ladder.

"What a marvellous idea!" Ethelinda cried. "We'll make a ladder for the canoe to push out, and fix another to the inside wall, to reach up your seat when we put it in."

"When everyone sees this, there'll be thousands and thousands of people," Mark protested.

"No there won't, because I'll set up a mind block over the whole town."

Mark thought about that.

"But if you Choo Chooans can do that, why are you afraid to land here?"

"Only a few families can do it," said Ethelinda loftily.

"Ah! That's why you go to other planets on your holidays and other kids stop at home!"

Ethelinda gave him a bad-tempered look. "If you want to look at it that way, I suppose you could say that," she sniffed. "But I've got a much more lively spirit than the other kids, don't forget that!"

"I think you're the most fantastic girl in the whole world," cried Mark. "I just knew you were, but now I can see why!"

An enormous smile filled Ethelinda s face. "You're my best of bestest friends, and I'm happy as happy that you're coming with me!" she said in delight.

Mark looked down and saw his garden. It was a long, long way down.

"We can't jump that far. You don't know what it's like jumping on Earth."

Clackety Hobo picked him up with one hand and grabbed his bike with the other. The hatch opened and they floated down slowly. He saw Ethelinda riding piggy back on Hettie Hobo.

They landed in the garden, and Ethelinda said crisply, "Put your bike away."

Mark put it in the shed and came out. Clackety Hobo went in and said, "What are all these lumps of metal for?"

"They're gardening tools."

Ethelinda took a little metal cap from Clackety Hobo and put it on her head.

"Mark, picture in your mind someone using the gardening tools."

Mark did that and sparks ran from the metal cap to Clackety Hobo.

Ethelinda told him, "Afterwards you must print out all of this for my All Schools' Blue Medal for Science."

She marched to the door. "We must get busy, because those three monsters will be here soon, on their bikes."

Mark got the key from its hiding place under his belt and opened the back door. He switched on the light and they all went in.

Hettie Hobo looked at the light bulb. "Electro-magnetism," she sniffed.

"What is this place?" demanded Ethelinda.

"This is the kitchen. This is where we eat. And I'm *hungry*," he wailed.

Ethelinda explored his feeling and sparks flew from her metal cap to Clackety Hobo. In fact, sparks hardly ever stopped all the time they were in the house.

"What do you eat?"

Mark opened the fridge, and Clackety Hobo snipped tiny bits of meat, fish, lettuce, green pepper, bread, butter, jam, potato and cucumber which he put in thimble sized containers. He took an apple, orange, raisin, biscuit, a square of chocolate, a piece of pineapple, some milk, an egg and a tomato, which he put away in his side.

Mark said, "A lot of this has to be cooked."

He went to the gas stove, and lit it.

"Picture the food cooking, Mark."

He pictured meat and fish cooking., and potatoes baking, and his mouth watered.

They went into the dining-room, and he sat at the table, holding knives, forks and spoons he took from the sideboard, then sat in an armchair, and then on the sofa.

Ethelinda sighed. "What a scieitnitif report this is going to be!"

Hettie Hobo said sharply, "*Scientific!*"

"And the physiology."

There was that word again! "What is physiology?" Mark asked her.

"All about how your body works."

Mark looked himself up and down doubtfully.

In the bedroom, he lay on the bed.

Clackety Hobo said, "We've seen those on some planets. We'll make you one on board our starship."

In the bathroom, Mark showed them the washbasin and the shower, and Clackety Hobo snipped a piece of soap and toothpaste.

Mark put his toothbrush in his pocket. "Can you make me toothpaste to clean my teeth with, on the starship?"

"Right away," Ethelinda promised him.

She looked at the lavatory. "What's that for?"

Mark blushed red, then pictured himself using it.

"Ah," said Ethelinda. "When you go red in the face, you know you need to use it? Very interesting physiology."

"No!" stuttered Mark.

Clackety Hobo snipped a tiny piece of the plastic cover. "We'll make you one of those when we get back. How does it work?"

Mark pulled the chain.

He said," Would you all leave, please? I need to use it."

They left him, and fanned out through the house.

After Mark washed his hands, he came out with a piece of toilet paper. "I'll need a roll of this," he said, handing the paper over.

He said, "My mum will be getting back. We won't have time for Pug, Club and Hatchet."

"They'll be here in a couple of minutes," said Ethelinda comfortably, "And it won't take long for you to make mincemeat of them."

"I thought you were going to squash them with the ship."

"Now, don't you worry. Come into the bedroom here."

It was his mum's room, and the wardrobe had full length mirrors in the doors.

Clackety Hobo fixed a silver box under the wardrobe where no one could see it, then stretched out his hand, and violet sparks rippled and played all over the glass.

Ethelinda explained, "This glass is now a galactic screen. Your mum will be able to see and hear you almost instantly from hundreds of light years away. The signal will travel straight into the Second Dimension – that's where we're going back to now after you've beaten up Pug, Club and Hatchet – and come out again here on the mirror… ah! The boys are outside. Off you go."

Mark shook his head violently, and suddenly a sort of current in his brain propelled his legs forward without his being able to stop them.

He opened the front door, and his legs hurried him down to the front gate into the street.

The three bullies saw him, and gave an exultant shout, and ran towards him.

His head seemed to rise higher and higher in the air, and three skidded to a halt, looking at him in terror. He strode towards them, and couldn't stop himself. He punched them and knocked them over. He kicked them, and they got to their feet, and ran, looking over their shoulders. Flames came from his mouth and roiled along the roadway. They jumped on their bikes, and rode off, screaming.

Suddenly, Mark felt himself again, sweating and trembling.

"When I go back to school one day, they'll KILL me," he wept.

Ethelinda and the two robots were in the roadway with him.

"I've put a mind block on them," said Ethelinda. "Whenever they see you they'll scream in terror."

Mark shook his head.

"But the other kids'll get me," he despaired.

"Aren't there special ways of fighting? I saw something on your TV once."

"Well... there's Ju Jitsu, and Judo, and Taekwondo, and Kung-Fu, Aikido, and Karate..."

Ethelinda concentrated very hard.

"The masters of those arts are very far away," she said. "Down in London. Let's get in the canoe, and hover over London, while I get it all out of their minds."

Hettie Hobo picked him up, and they rose swiftly through the air, into the canoe.

When they were ready, the arms in the wall held Mark, and they sped through the air over England, to London.

They hovered over London, while Ethelinda entered the minds of the martial arts masters, and sparks flew from her cap to Clackety Hobo.

Then the arms held Mark flat, instead of up and down, and they rose swiftly to the starship.

* * *

After the change into the other dimension, that made Mark feel a bit sick again, he said, "I want something to eat. My legs are shaking..."

He felt the bag he carried, put his hand inside, and found the rest of some lunch.

He pulled out a cheese sandwich and took a big bite. Then he broke off a little bit of cheese and gave it to Clackety Hobo. "This is called cheese. Did you get any down in the kitchen?"

Clackety Hobo said, "We should have finished synthesising in about thirty minutes."

"What is *sinnysising*?" Mark asked him, worried. "I rather need to have something to eat."

Hettie gave an impatient sigh. "Suppose you have a wall. You knock it down and find it's made of bricks. Then you put the bricks together again, and build the wall as it was."

"Bricks aren't any good," said Mark sharply. "We *never* eat bricks. We can't."

Ethelinda said, "It means to separate your food down to its smallest chemical parts, and then you've found out what they are, you know how to make more food."

"Ah," said Mark, in relief.

Ethelinda had the metal cap on, and sparks were flowing to Dumple Doo.

"Have you got it all?" she asked.

"Very good, very good!" boomed Dumple Doo. "I'll make a rubbery robot to teach him Kung Fu, Judo and the rest of it. Mark, after you eat, how long does it take you humans to digest?"

"I don't know," said Mark. "I've never thought about it."

"But after a big meal, a scrumptious meal, how long would it be before you could do something violent and get puffed out?"

Mark thought about it very carefully. "About an hour and half, I suppose."

"Oh, very good," said Dumple Doo. "Pertinent and concise. Thank you."

Mark looked puzzled.

Hettie Hobo said, "To the point and in very few words." A robot came in with a chair, and Mark sat down thankfully.

"Where are we going?" he asked.

"To a planet about 15 light years from here. We should be there in about twelve hours. It's called Bt'Ngh Bt"Ngh Bt'"Ngh."

"Bingo Bango Bongo?" said Mark, astonished.

"No!" said Hettie Hobo, disgustedly. "It's Bt'Ngh Bt"Ngh Bt'"Ngh."

"That's right," said Mark eagerly. "Bingo Bango Bongo. And what are people who live there called?"

"Bt'Ngh-nlc."

24

"Ah! Bongoes!"

"I don't know how you earthlings manage to communicate," said Hettie Hobo, annoyed.

"Communicate?"

"Talk to each other. Understand each other."

Mark asked, "And you can't travel 15 light years in our home universe in twelve hours... I mean, the universe where our homes are?"

Ethelinda said, "Don't be silly. Our universe is awful!"

"What's wrong with it?" demanded Mark.

"It's full of hard edges. You bump into asteroids, you can smash against a planet. It's freezing cold, or thousands and thousands of degrees hot. It's full of gravity wells you have to avoid. It's got mass. And radiations that can kill you. And it would take us 15 years to get there if we could travel at the speed of light, which we can't."

"Why can't we?"

"Our ship would need so much fuel, it would be as big as a... oh, I don't know, as a star. We would use all our push just trying to move the fuel. We might be able to get to one-third of the speed of light, which would take us 45 years, but when we got back, hundreds of years would have passed on our planet, and everyone we know would be long dead."

"I can't understand all this business of time changing, that I can't trust my watch."

"Because of mass, silly."

"Mass is something big?"

"Mass is like... well, heavy." Ethelinda shook her beautiful golden locks in exasperation.

"Down on Earth, you stick to the floor or to the ground. You weigh whatever you weigh. If you climb up something and jump, you'll land and hurt yourself if it's too high. That's because the Earth – or the Sun – or a star – are sending out gravitons which enter your body and draw you to the centre of the Earth. But you can't go to the centre of the Earth, because the ground stops you."

"This is complicated."

"Look, if you can't understand all of this, you'll have to stay at home in Milton Mudwallop and you can't go off world. Do you want us to take you back?"

"No! No!"

"Now, suppose you're in the cabin of a spaceship, way out in space, so far away no gravitons from a planet or star can reach you – well, *hardly* any. Then what happens? You float in the cabin. You're weightless. But suppose you're floating without moving. You can't move unless you get a PUSH. Because although you're weightless, you still have *mass*. If we stop our starship in ordinary space, it doesn't weigh a million tons any more, but it still has almost a million tons of *mass*. So we have to fire huge rockets to get moving again. On Earth, you say that mass is caused by Higgs boson particles, which are different to gravitons. Higgs particles are *intrinsic*."

"What is intrinsic?" asked Mark, now scared to ask so many questions.

"That means the particles are already in you, are part of you wherever you go."

Mark looked down at himself doubtfully. He couldn't see anything like that.

"Why aren't we floating in here?"

"Artificial gravity holds us to the floor," said Dumple Doo in a soothing, friendly voice. "Here comes Scrumptious Mumkish with something to eat."

A robot glided in, carrying a table, which it set down. "Hello, Mark," she said in a lady's voice. "I'm the ship's cook,"

A door opened in her side, and she took out plates and cutlery.

"Just you set yourself down there, child," Scrumptious Mumkish said.

First she served a vegetable salad, with lettuce, cucumber, tomatoes, olives, pepper plant, cheese and raisins. Mark finished it all off, and then she served roast beef, with baked potatoes, gravy and peas. Then he had an apple and orange.

He sat back, contented.

"How did you know how to make all of that?"

Ethelinda said, "Really, we have taken all your food and made a sort of very nourishing sludge. But I have put all this into your mind, so that you will eat it with a good appetite. I'm picking all your best meals out of your memory, even though you mightn't remember some of them any more."

"It was *wonderful*."

Clackety Hobo wheeled in an armchair.

"Now you can make yourself comfortable. But first come with me, because we've built you a bathroom, and you must clean your teeth."

Ethelinda didn't come to the bathroom with him; the toothpaste had the strangest taste, but it made a lot of froth and cleaned his teeth perfectly.

He went back and flopped thankfully in the armchair. What an afternoon! He'd never been so tired in all his life. Everything was happening all at once, he couldn't take it in. He couldn't be sure it was all happening, or that he was dreaming. But he *knew* he wasn't dreaming. And he *knew* he understood practically nothing. Had they taught him this at school and he didn't understand? No – they hadn't taught him anything about this.

He stretched in the armchair. He ached all over. The chair was wonderful.

Ethelinda went on, "Now, planets are all different sizes, so their force of gravity changes. On really big planets, where we don't land, you'd have to go on hands and knees, you'd be so heavy. Choo Choo is only three-quarters as big as Earth, so we feel heavier on Earth, but if you come to Choo Choo, you could jump much higher than on Earth, or run much faster.

"If you're in a car on Earth that's driving fast, you weigh one or two tons. You don't notice it, because it's your mass that's changed. If your gravity weight changed, you'd break the springs on the car seat. You understand? If the car hits something, you are flung forward with two tons of force, you smash through the windscreen, and you're dead."

"Suppose I'm wearing a seat belt?" said Mark, heatedly.

"Then you're all right, because the seat belts are made to hold on to four tons. If you travel at one-third the speed of light, you weigh hundreds of thousands of tons *mass*, and as you just have your muscles, it takes you all day to take one step. But you don't notice. Only somebody watching from Earth would notice. In the same way, you don't notice your mass has gone to two tons when your car does 60 mph."

Dumple Doo made a noise like a cement mixer mixing cement with stones in it.

Ethelinda whirled around, with her hands on her hips, and said, "You shut up, you hear me?"

Dumple Doo made a noise like a washing machine, and was then silent.

"How do you know all this?" demanded Mark suspiciously.

"They taught me at school."

She glared at Dumple Doo.

"Of course, what I've said may need a few delicate brush strokes to fill it out."

Dumple Doo was silent.

Mark said triumphantly, "If the Higgs particles are inside us always, why don't we have a huge mass now. Why doesn't it take us years to get to Bingo Bango Bongo?"

"Because back in our universe there's an energy field you humans don't know about. The Higgs particles push it ahead of them, and it tries to stop them. So the faster you go, the Higgs particles are pushing up a bigger and harder wave in front. It's a field with particles so tiny, it's as though there aren't any particles at all. With our Higgs particles, it's as though we're wading through treacle.

"But in this dimension – the field doesn't exist. No Higgs particles. We can go as fast as we like. Well, really, we are going at about only one-fifth as fast as we could. Daddy doesn't like me speeding, and he doesn't like me playing too far from Choo Choo – I've had to promise him I won't go more than 200 light years away."

Mark asked, "How many stars are there in 200 light years?"

Dumple Doo complained, "I don't have that in my program! For an earthling who's never been in space, you ask some hard ones. Well, doing arithmetic – 200 light years out in every direction from Choo Choo or earth, I get about 15,000 stars like your Sun you see on earth. Maybe, between 12,000 and 18,000 suns. Then there are all those other stars."

"And what sort of engine have you got?"

Ethelinda glanced at Dumple Doo, who boomed, "We used liquid hydrogen. We fill it with shock waves till it's about 2,000 degrees hot, then mix it with liquid oxygen, and – BOOM!"

Mark was lost. "How hot is boiling water?"

"One hundred degrees. This is 20 times hotter. And when the liquid hydrogen turns back into a gas, a lot of energy escapes too. You know?"

"Oh, *everyone* knows that," said Mark.

Then he asked, "So how fast are we going?"

"About 11,000 times faster than the speed of light. Suppose we could *just* manage to go at one-third the speed of light in our own universe, then we're going about 33,000 times faster."

Mark pursed his lips and nodded as though he found that the most natural thing to do.

He asked, "We can't travel in our universe because gravity wells are everywhere. What are they?"

Clackety Hobo said, "It's like riding a bike across a field full of mine shafts. You fall down one of them, you're in trouble."

Mark shuddered.

"The Earth, the Sun, all the planets and stars are trying to pull a passing starship down on to them. Suppose we *are* down on the surface of the Earth or Choo Choo, then it's like we're at the bottom of a well."

Mark looked at him blankly.

"Imagine you're out in the middle of a desert and some Arabs take you to a well that's a hundred feet deep. Suppose it's got a ladder. You climb down with a goatskin, fill it up… then you've got a devil of a job climbing up that ladder again. At the top, everything's flat, and then you're all right. So, our starship has to make its rockets blaze away until we climb up out of the gravity well that is the Earth, or Choo Choo, and we finally pull away so far we're free."

Mark nodded wisely. "That's very true."

He felt sleepy with all this space-talk. He wasn't used to it. He wasn't even sure it wouldn't really be simpler to stay in Milton Mudwallop and ride his bike to school every day.

But then he decided that wasn't a very good idea. He decided this was still better.

He thought of Milton Mudwallop, and remembered his mum.

"Can I say good-night to my mum?"

"Of course you can," boomed Dumple Doo.

A large screen lit up brightly.

On it, Mark saw his mum's bedroom.

He heard his voice shouting out, "Mum! Mum! Come into your bedroom."

Nothing happened. He heard his voice roaring this time, and then he saw his mum's head peering timidly around the edge of the screen.

"Stand in front of your wardrobe mirror, mum," he heard his voice say.

He saw his mum stand in the middle of the screen.

"Mark!" she screamed, reaching her hands forward and touching the glass, so that Mark could see the palms of her hands. "Where are you?"

"It's all right, honestly. I'm on a starship and we're going to a planet called Choo Choo."

"Chew Chew?" whispered his mum, and he saw she was going to faint. She suddenly straightened up, and stared fixedly.

"I've had to enter her mind," said Ethelinda, from behind him.

"I'm on a starship," repeated Mark.

Dumple Doo projected a full view of their starship on the screen.

"I'm inside that," said Mark. "I've just had roast beef and baked potatoes."

"You've been kidnapped?!' said his mother, shrill.

"No, I'm here with friends," said Mark. "I'm with Ethelinda, who's on her school holidays, and she's taking me too."

Ethelinda filled the screen, with her golden locks, a beautiful smile and her dress with four pockets.

"Mark, you come straight back home, right this minute. You've got to go to school tomorrow."

"I can't, mum, honest."

Dumple Doo boomed, "He's now about one light year away. About 57 thousand million miles away. We are travelling at about 2 million miles a second."

Dumple Doo worried, "I *hate* these human figures. I hope I've got that right, because with this updating they gave me, I don't know *what* mistakes they've programmed into me. Is it 5.7 thousand million miles? Alien numbers – bah!"

But his mum couldn't hear that bit.

"But you've *got* to go to school."

"They're teaching all sorts of stuff you don't learn at school. And we're only going to visit a couple of planets and then I'll come back."

"Oh, Mark! Mark! You've fallen into the hands of ALIENS! You must escape. They'll tear you to bits, they'll torture you! Oh! my poor darling little boy."

Hettie Hobo appeared in the screen and shouted, "How dare you!"

His mum saw the robot and screamed, "A monster!"

Hettie Hobo turned to Ethelinda and said disgustedly, "Please do something, young lady, right now!"

"Yes," said Ethelinda meekly.

A shiver ran through his mum, and then she looked out from the screen, woodenly.

"Oh, Mark. I'm so proud of you. I can't believe it. You're marvellous. I can't wait for you to come home. How long will you be?"

"Only a few days," boomed Dumple Doo.

"Is that another robot?" asked his mother. "That's an awful cold he's caught. He should look after it."

"Thank you, "boomed Dumple Doo.

"What do you think of the starship?" asked Mark.

"It looks awfully advanced. How big is it?"

"About five miles across."

"Goodness me!"

"You mustn't tell anyone about this."

"I promise," she said. "I love you. Have a good sleep. Goodnight."

* * *

Mark went back to his armchair. He was worn out, and felt sleepy. It was only eight o'clock.

"I'll have to go to bed," he said unhappily. *No one* went to bed at eight o'clock.

Clackety Hobo said, "Before you go to sleep, we need to photo your insides, for Ethelinda's All Schools' Blue Science Medal."

Mark followed him down a long corridor, into a side room, where he lay down and pushed into a short tunnel. They pulled him out, and swung a huge, shining disc over him.

Dumpty Doo began clicking and rattling, and then boomed, "Look at this!"

"Goodness!" exclaimed Hettie Hobo. "When he breathes in, the air goes to these enormous lungs, and his lungs take out the oxygen and put it into his blood. Mark, you need air to live. Without air, you'd suffocate."

30

Mark was too taken aback to speak. Then looking in fright at Ethelinda, he said, "Everyone's like that."

Ethelinda said, "We have tiny little lungs, just for enough air to let us speak. What an inefficient, environmentally dependant way to live," she said, with a superior look on her face.

"What is *inefficient?*" asked Mark humbly.

"Doesn't work properly," snapped Ethelinda.

"And environmentally dependant?"

"Means you're at the mercy of the air around you, at the mercy of the world around you. You can't get air, you die. Well, oxygen, actually."

"Is there oxygen on Choo Choo and Bingo Bango Bongo?"

"That's no problem there," said Ethelinda impatiently. "An oxygen-breather, for The Great Snake's sake! Never heard the like."

"How many planets can I go to and breathe all right?"

"About a dozen. But half of them are huge, so you'd be at the bottom of such a deep gravity well you'd weigh so much you'd have to go on hands and knees, or wriggle along, flat on the ground."

"How many planets are there?" Mark asked, suddenly curious.

"Millions, I suppose, but with life that we have visited, a few thousand. With intelligent life, *that we have visited*, about a hundred. But on most of them, we have to wear space suits, because their air is poison. If it got into our lungs, it would burn holes inside us. And if *you* breathed it – oh, you'd carry it straight into your blood all over your body and you'd shrivel up like a dead autumn leaf."

Mark nodded energetically, to show he understood.

Clackety Hobo gave him a pot. "Please pee into it. We need a sample."

"With Ethelinda looking!"

Ethelinda stared at him in amazement, then turned around.

Then Clackety Hobo led him to his bedroom, with a big bed.

"We've just built this for you," he said proudly. "Now come next door."

He showed Mark a bathroom, with a washbasin, a bath and shower, and a lavatory.

"Mark, the first time you use the lavatory, please don't pull the chain. We need a sample. We'll pull the chain, but in future you pull the chain."

Mark turned very red. They weren't being rude, but –

"Look," cried Hettie Hobo, "He's turned all red. He's going to have to go…"

Mark grew angry. "Will you go, please! Leave me alone!"

* * *

Pyjamas lay on the bed. The bed was firm and cool. Mark fell straight asleep.

* * *

Clackety Hobo was shaking him.

Ethelinda stood behind him.

"Time to get up."

Mark looked at his watch. It was four o'clock!

"We are arriving in about three hours, and you have to do a lot of training."

Mark stumbled out of bed, rubbing his eyes. They led him to the big room, and on the table he saw two fried eggs, bacon, slices of toast, butter and jam.

He ate hungrily, then went to the bathroom, and later, got dressed.

Clackety Hobo said, "We'll wait an hour for you to digest your meal. You can have a class while you're waiting."

"Oh, no!" cried Mark. "I hate classes, and there's no teacher here."

"Put this cap on," commanded Hettie Hobo.

With the metal cap on his head. sparks flew, and Mark saw tens of thousands of galaxies, all forming bubbles around balls of dark matter. A voice explained everything.

Then he saw the Milky Way, and saw it slowly turning, and then he seemed to go up close, and see tens of thousands of stars. Then he saw all different sorts of stars, and the voice went on explaining. Then he saw dust clouds in fantastic colours, and the voice went on explaining.

It all vanished, and he saw Clackety Hobo with the cap in his hand.

Mark followed the robot to another large room, and Ethelinda and Hettie Hobo stood against the wall, watching.

"We're going to teach you martial arts, so that when you go back to school they can't bully you again. It takes years to learn this properly, but we'll teach you in about an hour."

He put the metal cap back on Mark's head, and a rubber figure looking like Mark himself came in from a side door.

The rubber figure attacked, and, suddenly, Mark knew how to throw it. For an hour, they fought, using Aikido, Judo, Ju Jitsu, Karate, Taekwondo and Kung Fu. Mark's arms and legs ached, but they attached clamps to him, and he felt electricity coursing through him, and all his tiredness went away; energy filled him.

At the end of an hour, Clackety Hobo said, "You're at the level of brown belt in all the arts, so that will look after you when you have to go back to school."

Mark felt his stomach drop. He'd have to go back to school. He was millions of miles away, but this wouldn't last. He'd have to go back, and he couldn't see any way out of it.

Clackety Hobo gave him a long spear. "On Bingo Bango Bongo, the Bongoeans sometimes have to go outside. There are giant devils, who feed on mineral mud from nearby hot springs, but if they can grab a Bongean, that makes a tasty dish. For some reason, they're frightened of snakes, and Choo Chooeans can block their minds. But they might find human flesh and blood very appetising, so you'll have to carry several spears out in the open. Let's go to the hangar."

In the hangar, a long way away, a black target darted back and forth.

"You've got to learn to throw hard, because they've got thick pelage."

"What's pelage? "

"Fur, pelt, hair…"

Mark put on the cap, and while the sparks flew, he threw spears till his arms ached. They put clamps on his arms, to give him new energy. Soon, he never missed, and could throw farther and farther.

It was almost seven o'clock. His mum would be getting up. None of the kids would have got to school yet.

In the canoe, Mark found they had built him a seat. He got in, with six spears tied together. With Ethelinda and the two robots came Scrumptious Mumkish.

"We won't be able to eat their food?" Mark asked.

"Unless you want a tummy-ache," laughed Scrumptious Mumkish. "Don't you worry, I'm here to look after you and Ethelinda."

Mark felt the awful humming. It stopped. They must be back in their universe, their own universe. The canoe moved into the airlock; it shot out into a black sky, with stars everywhere. It curved, and then Mark saw a huge red sun, and a planet below them with two pink moons.

They dropped very fast, and as the planet rose to meet them, Mark saw it was not well lit. One half had a reddish glow that was nothing like bright daylight back on Earth. He saw two pink moons. This was a strange place. The canoe tipped, and he gazed into the skies, into the cold, far reaches of space, and he wondered in what direction lay the Sun, and whether he could even see it from his window. Somewhere, out there, among those thousands of stars that turned the whole sky yellow, was his house, and his mum getting up to go to work.

They closed in on the surface of the planet, and Mark gasped. Mighty grey sheets of rocks rose steeply everywhere, gigantic grey slabs, with clouds swirling among them. Then he saw dozens of flat bits, about half mile wide, clothed in dark green. Where the flat bits came up against the walls of merciless rocks, he spied pinpoints of light. High and low on the slopes, plumes of steam rose thickly, twisting and snapping in the wind.

They hovered over a wide green platform, shaking in the wind, and Clackety Hobo said, "Mark, we've made some thermal clothing for you. Take off all your clothes and put this on."

Mark put on a thermal singlet and long underpants, then a thermal shirt and trousers, then a thick anorak with a hood and gloves hanging to it, and thick, tall boots.

He asked, "What is thermal?"

Ethelinda told him, "Thermal clothing is clothing that keeps you specially warm."

At the bottom of the cliff, was a light. The canoe drifted towards it, and landed.

"Look out for devils," warned Hettie Hobo, "We are getting out and going straight into that cave. The opening's very low so that devils can't get in. Clackety Hobo and me will stay with the ship, because we can't fit in the doorway of the cave."

Mark followed Ethelinda out, grasping his spears, and looking around him. Ethelinda got down on her knees, and went through the doorway, while Mark watched.

What Mark saw froze the very blood in his veins. It was an eight-foot tall devil, just like he had seen in books and illustrations. It had wide, curving horns, round pointed ears sticking far out the side of its head, and a long, goat-like face, huge teeth, long hairy arms, and animal hoofs. Its red eyes looked mad, its mouth was wide open and drooling spit, as it raced towards him.

He couldn't believe this was Mark Clough. He seized one of the spears and threw it as though he had practised every day for all his life. The spear flew true and buried itself deep in the devil's chest. The devil reeled back, clutching the shaft.

Mark whirled, pushed his spears into the cave and wriggled inside as fast as he could.

After a short tunnel, which was freezing and wet, he came to a wide, tall sort of room, with ragged rock walls and roof, lit with a soft red light. He got to his feet.

Ethelinda looked at him in admiration.

"Thank goodness, I'm with you," she gasped. "Aren't you brave and strong."

Mark was shaking all over, and his hands were trembling.

He looked at her dumbly. He was panting as though he'd been running. He tried to get control of himself, and first he couldn't.

I was *scared*, he thought to her.

I know, she thought back, but it's all right now. Follow me.

He tried to walk along behind her, but he felt sick to his stomach.

Her thought came into his mind. It's all right now. Your stomach feels perfectly well. You're perfectly well. Relax.

And he felt all right again.

"We have pictures of those devils back on Earth. How did we humans find out about them?"

"Perhaps some evil Pumpkin trader captured some, and let them loose on Earth, a long time ago."

"I thought only humans were evil."

"The Pumpkinoneans would never kill, but they like playing jokes, and they don't realise some of the jokes are nasty."

They went out of the red-lit room into another passageway lined with dark, shining glass, and a golden light came out from the glass.

"Where does the light come from?" asked Mark, amazed.

"The Bongeans have trapped the heat from underground thermal springs to make electricity, to drive generators."

After about four minutes, they entered an enormous, domed hall, brightly lit. The glass walls, with glass columns rose to the top of the high dome, with intricate patterns worked into the glass. Mark had never imagined anything so marvellous.

It was full of Bongeons. They had four legs, on a body about the size and colour of a lion, with a trunk growing out in front straight upwards with four arms and a head like a big owl's. Their heads were about a foot taller than Mark's. Some of them pulled wooden carts, with wooden wheels, a harness strapped around their middle between their legs. Others carried big baskets hanging on each side of the back parts of their bodies.

They all stopped, and suddenly Mark's mind was a crazy confusion of thoughts of "Welcome!", "Hello!", "We haven't seen you for a long time."

Then they all turned their eyes on Mark, and his mind was overcome with thoughts, "Hello! Who in heaven's name are you?" "What planet have *you* come from?" "My God! He's got two legs and a body like a devil." "My God, he looks like a devil but he's much smaller and he's got a different sort of head!" "Are you a devil?"

Ethelinda's thought was like a great shout. "He's just killed a devil outside, when we were coming in. With his spear."

Then Mark heard a medley of voices in his head.

"He's carrying spears! Look! He's killed a devil! It must still be lying there outside! No! Other devils will have carried it off to eat it."

Mark stood beside Ethelinda and asked, "Don't they speak?"

She told him, "They don't have noses to breathe with and they don't have voices, so they can't talk. They're telepathic, like so many races on so many planets."

"What's *telepathic?*"

"Sending thoughts straight from one brain to another."

"On Earth, I've seen pictures of creatures –" Mark began. He checked himself, and thought he wasn't polite, " – of people like this."

"On Earth, you call them centaurs."

"*Centaurs.*" Mark rolled the word around his tongue. But they didn't have four arms, he remembered.

"On Earth, the centaurs were supposed have the body of a horse and the torso of a man."

"What is a torso?"

"The trunk – the part of the body from the waist up."

A centaur-Bongean pushed through to them.

"Lynette!" cried Ethelinda.

"Welcome!" said Lynette. "It's been so long. We have missed you. You still have that rattle-trap of an old cargo ship your dad gave you?"

"The same," said Ethelinda. "This is Mark."

Lynette looked doubtfully at Mark.

"You look like a watered-down devil. Where are you from?"

36

"I'm from Earth."

"Oh, you poor, poor boy. We don't have television, but we have heard stories from planets which do. That's a horrible planet you come from, killing each other. A trader came through the other day, and told us what he had seen. Part of the Earth is desert, isn't it? A family of 'Arabs' had built a tank to collect water, and some soldiers came and broke it up. I don't remember who the soldiers were, but they were another colour. You have different coloured people, he told me. Is that *really* true?"

Mark nodded dumbly.

"Mark killed a devil, when we were coming in."

Lynette looked at him with admiration. "Devils kill so many of us. We carry spears when we go outside – well, the men do. We women aren't strong enough to throw spears properly. You're so young! Our youngsters can't throw spears."

"Why do you go outside?" Mark asked.

He thought of the rearing walls of dark rock.

"We pick the fruit off the trees. The fruit grows quickly and ripens in about two days. Then it rots. We would die if we didn't eat it. We have to eat all we can, and we have to pick it before it goes off."

Mark got the feeling again that all of this wasn't happening, that he would blink and find himself back in his classroom. Lynette really had *said* nothing – it was as though she was talking. All her thoughts came into his head as though she had really spoken, and he had to *think* his answers and questions. He glanced at his watch. Back home, he'd soon be wheeling his bike out of the shed, to ride to school. But the shed with his bike in was millions and millions of miles away. Or had he imagined all that about his bike and school... he shook his head.

"Come with me," said Lynette.

They walked along a tunnel with beautifully green and gold glowing glass, then turned into another side tunnel that was pale blue, the glass richly traced with designs, and came into a huge cavern, lined with shining white and blue glass. About a hundred small centaurs were playing, or swimming and splashing in an enormous pool of water, lit green from below.

Lynette said, "I'll leave you here to play with the children, until the Elders are ready to see you."

Ethelinda asked, "Could you allow Scrumptious Mumkish to enter? She has our food."

"We'll go and fetch her," promised Lynette.

Lynette left, and Mark saw that all the children were clustered around them, staring.

A girl about Mark's age sent him a mental message.

"Ethelinda is a Choo Chooean, but you don't see her as a snake. You see her as an Earthling."

"That's right," said Mark.

"She's dressed differently to you. Is that because she's a girl?

"And do girls always have four pockets?"

"I suppose they can have more," said Mark, uncertainly.

The centaur suddenly changed into a lovely, black-haired girl, in a blue dress, with five pockets. Her hair was lustrous and straight, and she wore a fringe across her forehead.

"The hussy!" hissed Ethelinda.

Mark's mouth dropped open.

She said, "My name's Naomi".

"Naomi," repeated Ethelinda.

"Naomi? Why... you knew that hussy Naomi back at your school." Her eyes flashed in anger. "That Naomi creature offered you her lunch," Ethelinda sputtered.

An adult centaur appeared.

"Ethelinda, could you come with me? The electricians want to consult with your wisdom."

Ethelinda glared at Mark and Naomi, and went off.

Naomi asked him, "Do you know how to swim? Let me take off your clothes."

Mark blushed furiously.

"I'll undress myself," he stuttered.

Naomi pulled off her dress and stood naked.

Mark looked away as he undressed, and then dived into the water. It was warm and transparent.

Naomi dived in beside him, so Mark swam fast, to show off. But Naomi kept up with him easily.

Finally, he stopped, treading water, and the other children clustered around him.

"Do you have many friends, back on Earth?" "Who are your friends on Earth?" "What are they like?"

He felt them inside his mind.

Then they cried, "You're lonely! You don't have any friends, except Naomi and boys aren't supposed to have girls for a friend! You're all alone! What a hard place!"

In the swimming pool, Naomi put her arms around him and pressed him tightly with her earthling body, as Mark saw it.

She said, "We're all your friends, and always will be. Here, everyone loves everyone else. You shall be a Bongean, and one of us."

He heard them all chorus, "Mark is one of us. Mark is Bongean, like us."

They fell silent, and Mark saw an old centaur dressed in a long brown cloak standing at the edge of the pool.

He sent the thought to Mark, "I grieve for you, Mark. You live on a cruel world. Here, you shall always belong. This shall always be your home."

He paused.

"Some of us must go out to collect the fruit. Will you go with them, with your spears?"

"You bet!" He swam to the edge of the pool.

"Can I go too?" begged Naomi. "Mark will protect me."

"Children *never* go outside," the old man warned her. "Why are you so willful?"

"Please," she begged.

"You know you can do as you wish."

The centaur looked away, twitching his tail.

Mark and Naomi climbed out of the pool and got dressed. Mark went over to his spears, and picked them up.

The centaur led them back through the tunnels. Mark carried his anorak over his arm, and when they came to the freezing, wet rocky entrance, he put it on again, and pulled the hood over his head.

The centaurs didn't feel the cold.

Outside, he saw a dozen of them, spreading out among the trees. They carried panniers over their backs, and they put the pink fruit into them.

Naomi carried a basket and she went eagerly to a tree and picked the fruit.

She said, "It's got a lovely taste, but it mightn't be a good idea for you try it."

She froze when she heard shouts.

Four devils appeared among the trees, and the centaurs hefted their spears.

The devils kept their distance, then disappeared.

While Naomi picked the fruit, Mark kept one spear in his right hand.

With shocking suddenness, a devil raced out of the trees at him. Mark didn't have time to throw. He rammed his spear into its chest, and it pulled back spurting blood. Three others appeared, and Mark launched the spear which flew, deadly, into the throat of the second devil.

The first devil scooped up a screaming Naomi and raced off. Mark's second spear caught him between the shoulder blades. He staggered, and the third devil caught Naomi, who screamed, "Mark! Mark!"

Mark pelted after it, and saw four more devils blocking him. He hit the first devil in the belly, and the others fled.

Running out of the trees, he saw the devil carrying Naomi, sprinting up the steep rock, its cloven feet sure. He launched a despairing spear with all the strength and fury in his ten-year-old body – and it fell short, clattering on the rock.

He heard Naomi's cries, and stupefied, watched the devil swiftly scaling the wall, higher and higher.

Centaurs surrounded him, and seized him. "Quick! Back into the cave!"

"No!" he cried, struggling against their arms and hands.

"You can't climb up there! Back into the cave!"

They lifted him bodily, and carried him back to the low opening.

Inside the tunnel, he collapsed, moaning and crying, then doubled up with his arms across his stomach.

They picked him up, and carried him through tunnels and tunnels, to a hall with soft lighting, where the Curers waited for him.

Mark lay there, doubled up, as stiff and unmoving as a statue moulded from glass.

Ethelinda came in, and knelt beside him, calling his name.

An Elder came in, and they all stood aside. "This is not a thing for the Curers," he said. "It is not his body that must be cured."

He sent a powerful thought into Mark's mind. "Stand up!"

Mark heard it as a distant whisper, through his agony and numbness.

His body unfolded, without his having anything to do with it. He got to his feet, without his legs obeying any command from himself.

Another powerful thought-shot through him.

"Come, child! Follow!"

Like a glass doll, Mark walked behind the Elder.

They walked, and walked.

Then they entered a wide, low ceilinged temple, with rich, dark glass walls.

Mark felt himself coming to.

He smelt incense. Then he saw a score of centaurs in long red robes, standing in a big circle, chanting and humming.

They led Mark to the middle of the circle, and the beautiful chanting grew louder and deeper.

An old centaur stood before him, dressed in a rich golden robe.

Mark sneaked a look around him, and saw Ethelinda beside him.

The man in the gold robe spoke.

"I am the High Priest. You are in the Temple of the Highest Mysteries. Welcome. You have been accepted into our people. You are one of us. You have risked your life to protect us. Welcome."

He looked at Ethelinda.

"Ethelinda, you know this Temple. You have been shown the Mysteries. Welcome."

He turned back to Mark.

"Mark, who are you?"

Mark was so astonished he could not speak.

"Speak!"

"I'm Mark Clough."

"But the words 'Mark' 'Clough' tell us, tell you, nothing. Are you *you* because you are *you*? Or are you what other people think you are? Your mother thinks you are her son, your teachers that you are their pupil."

"Yes," admitted Mark, screwing up his brain hard, to think. "I'm a son and a pupil, but really, I'm me."

"And what do you mean by 'me'?"

Mark looked around the chanting; .slightly swaying figures, staring at him.

"Well, I think about my bike… about not getting beaten up…"

"But are you more than that?"

Mark considered the High Priest, looking at his enormous eyes.

"I suppose I'm *me*… I suppose I think about what other people think about me."

"The truth is that you are *you*."

The High Priest paused, and Mark listened to the chant, that seemed to tremble through his whole body. He saw all eyes were on him.

"I will now tell you the biggest secret in the universe.

"Everything you have, you will lose, One day, your body will decay, and then die. Naomi now is being devoured by devils. But that *you* who you are will never die, as Naomi has not died.

"The present moment never changes. Everything that happens, flows into the present on the one side, to vanish forever on the other side, as though it never was. You remember it as the past, but it never was. Time is a stream that carries everything away, but the Present stands outside time. The *you* in this very present instant lives forever, because this present instant is forever.

"*You* have been *aware* for thousands of millions of years. Those who are aware in the present are aware as long as the present lasts, which is forever. You will put on new bodies – Naomi now will put on a new body – on new planets, but *you* are *aware* now and always."

The chant now was faster. Mark looked at the robed figures.

"What is 'aware'?" asked Mark, confused, very confused and worried. He could understand the present was always the present. Also, that the past had long gone away, but that was about all.

"You are aware of the floor of the temple. The floor is not aware of you. You are aware of your hands, but your hands are not aware of you. You are aware of the colour red. Many races on different planets cannot see red, but *you* can. But red is not aware of you. You are aware of your feelings, but your feelings are aware of themselves, not of the real you. You are aware of your thoughts, which usually you can't control. But your thoughts are aware only of themselves.

"Consider Clackety Hobo and Hettie Hobo. They have thoughts and feelings, but they are not aware of themselves. They were built, they flow into the present. But one day, they will be switched off. Your awareness that you are *you* is the blinding light of your spirit, your spirit that lives, undying, in the Present, in the eternal Now."

"Thank you," said Mark, politely.

The High Priest gathered his robe about him.

"Mark," he said, "you have never lived one minute in the past. You will never live one single minute in the future. You live *now*. Only that. Can you remember your past lives?"

Mark thought.

"Not one," he said firmly. "Can you?"

"All of them. So, you earthlings cannot. The Choo Chooeans can."

Mark turned to Ethelinda, unable to believe what he had heard. Ethelinda nodded. "We all can on Choo Choo."

He said to the High Priest, "You can remember back – how far?"

"Thousands of millions of years."

Mark twisted that around in his mind.

"I can't understand that," he said.

"It's your human brain. On many planets people remember, on others, they don't. All brains are different. Think for a moment. Over the last seven years, you have lived each five minutes, twelve of them in each hour. All those five minutes must add up to 25,000 or 30,000. Do you remember them all?"

Mark shook his head, very decidedly.

"But sometimes something important happened, and then you remember. Or someone reminds you. Tell me, were you *alive* in every one of those five minutes you can't exactly remember?"

"Oh, yes!" said Mark. "I was alive. I didn't miss out a single five minutes."

"Well, it's like that thinking about our past lives."

"I hope Naomi doesn't get the idea of being born now on Earth," he worried.

"What she will do, she is doing," the High Priest said.

"They don't teach us about that at school," complained Mark.

42

"Humans have human brains. All brains are different. You have cars, and tractors, and lorries… all sorts of things, all different."

"Why do you – er, why do *we* – go back to getting born?"

"To live in love, goodness and truth,"

Mark couldn't think of anything to say.

The chanting rose, loud and triumphant.

"You have been taught the Mystery of Mysteries, you have been initiated, you are an Initiate in the Mystery of Mysteries."

The High Priest stepped forward, and laid a brown robe over Mark's shoulders.

The light faded from the walls slowly, the temple darkened. Ethelinda led him outside.

Lynette appeared, and told them to follow her. She walked ahead, her rump swaying and her tail swishing. On the side of a corridor, she opened a door and led them into a room lit by pale green light from the glassy walls. There was a bench against the wall where Mark could sit.

"Rest, and think. Then you can go back to the children's hall, and the swimming pool."

Mark flopped on the bench, and stretched out.

"That fruit," he said angrily.

"They must eat it," Ethelinda told him patiently.

"What else do they eat?"

"Mushrooms. They've got miles of rocky tunnels, without any glass, but with overhead lights, growing mushrooms. They're special mushrooms full of minerals and whatnot."

"Don't they need grass?"

"It's as though one mushroom is the same as a sack full of straw or grass."

"And when do they sleep?"

"They lower the lights. They fold their legs underneath them, and rest their necks against the wall somewhere."

"Their *torsos*."

Ethelinda said *very* carefully, "I wasn't quite exact. The torso is really the part between the waist and the neck, leaving the head out of it."

"Ah!" said Mark, rolling to his side.

He couldn't get comfortable. He rolled onto his other side. He was all het up.

He got up, put his hands in his pockets, and walked up and down, his head bent.

"It's Naomi?" said Ethelinda, without sympathy. "Isn't it?"

Mark kicked the door. He was trying to *think*, very hard.

He swung around, and didn't seem to be just ten years old.

"Lead me back to the outside. Call up the canoe, because we must talk to Clackety Clack."

Ethelinda was taken aback. She'd never seen him like this – well, sort of grown-up. "Clackety Hobo," she corrected.

Then she snapped, "What for?"

"We've got to go up to the spaceship. I want Dumple Doo to make a laser gun. Spears! Spears! That's crazy. Spears!"

He had opened the door, and was walking along the corridor.

"Come back!" cried Ethelinda. "That's the wrong way, silly!"

Mark hurried back, and Ethelinda demanded, "What on Choo Choo are you talking about? What laser?"

"Come into my mind, and I'll make pictures." He felt Ethelinda in his mind, and he imagined different sorts of pistols and revolvers. Then he imagined a big hand gun shooting out a laser ray and cutting a tree trunk in half.

"Ah!" said Ethelinda. "Follow me. That is an idea."

Mark said excitedly, "I want one gun for me, and another made of glass, so that the Bongeans can take it to pieces and learn to make their own. Do you want Dumple Doo to make another one for yourself?"

Ethelinda said firmly, "No. If my father found out I had a weapon, he'd never let me go out to play by myself again."

They hurried through the underground caves and passageway, greeting the centaurs they passed.

"You *do* know what a laser is?" Mark asked her.

"What a silly question," said Ethelinda, loftily. "I made one in Handiwork class at school. I seem to remember I used a full mirror at one end of a tube and half a mirror at the other."

"What did you do in Handiwork?" Mark asked her, as they hurried along.

"It was a lot of kids' stuff. Sewing, carpentry, making things – I made an apparatus for measuring deep space attenuated gravity waves –"

"What's *attenuated*?"

"That's weak, worn out, toned down, you know."

She thought.

"I made an apparatus for measuring cosmic ray bursts…"

"What are *cosmic ways*…?"

"Cosmic rays! They haven't taught you that at school! You're ten years old."

Mark hung his head.

"Well, you know what's in the nucleus of an atom?"

Mark kept dead silent.

"Well, they're very high-speed bursts of protons. They hit the air, and knock electrons and mesons out of the oxygen and nitrogen in the air. Mesons, of course, go through *anything*. They're not an atomic particle, but a *sub* atomic particle."

Mark said humbly, "Sub-atomic, of course."

Ethelinda said, "Of course, we get gamma rays from space too, so I built an apparatus for Cerenkov radiation. That's a bluish light. When certain substances are hit by gamma rays, electrons are freed which give you this light."

She was trying to remember.

"I built this electricity circuit, with a gap, and sent gas through the gap, to make a plasma of the gas. The gas plasma was about 30,000 degrees. That was real fun."

"How hot is the Sun in my solar system?"

"About 5,000 degrees."

At the entrance cave it was freezing and damp. They put on their anoraks and pulled up their hoods.

"Hold your spears ready," warned Ethelinda.

There was *no* need for Ethelinda to remind him.

Using a metal band around her wrist, she summoned the canoe, which hovered near the entrance about four minutes later.

They stepped outside, fearfully, Mark with a spear ready, then rushed inside the canoe.

"Take us up to the spaceship," Ethelinda told him.

"What's happened?" asked Clackety Hobo.

Ethelinda put on the metal cap and sparks flowed to the robot. Her thoughts came into Mark's mind, and he saw she was picturing the death of Naomi, and then the laser gun.

Clackety Hobo said, "I'm going to radio that up to Dumple Doo." He paused. "Mark, that's very good. It's much better than a spear, truly."

Dumple Doo's voice greeted them when they came into the big living-cabin.

"What a terrible business. The robots are in the workship making the laser guns. On the second gun, they're using a dark glass, but the Bongeans will be able to make it you'll see. Mark, you suggest a laser ray as thick as a pencil, but I think one as thick as your wrist would be better. We have a gas on Choo Choo that you can't find on Earth, and it should be perfect for the laser ray. I don't suppose on Earth you can really make a ray as thick as your wrist," he boomed. "Problem is, it might be a bit heavier, but you could hold it with two hands, or we could put in a metal support to go under your forearm. That would stop your wrist from bending down. What do you think?"

Mark couldn't imagine what he was talking about, but half an hour later when a robot brought in the gun and he held it, he saw what a good idea it was.

Dumple Doo explained, "The metal support presses under your forearm, and also presses into your ulna bone, so we've put a bit of sponge plastic there."

"Ulna?" asked Mark, puzzled.

"You've got two bones in your forearm," Dumple Doo boomed patiently. "The one underneath is called the ulna, and the other, that's like a continuation of your thumb, as it were, is the radius."

Mark felt his arm, and said doubtfully, "It feels like just bone to me."

"Silly," said Ethelinda. "Then you couldn't turn your hand and wrist from side to side. The bones have to be able to turn over and under each other."

Hettie Hobo said, "Isn't it tragic, so backward. That planet, Earth!"

Ethelinda said, "Let's go back to the canoe, and give them the glass one."

Dumple Doo said, "Don't you want one too, Ethelinda?"

"What's my father going to say!" she cried.

"Suppose we don't tell him."

"I can't hide my thoughts from him. He knows everything in my mind."

Clackety Hobo said, "That's one advantage Earthlings have. They don't know what each other is thinking. This business of talking by sounds in the air has something good to be said for it. Of course, it's what they do on Hgeby Xtamn planet. too."

"Jivey Tam?" said Mark, surprised.

"No!" cried Ethelinda, exasperated. "Hgeby Xtamn!"

"I'm sorry," said Mark contritely. "Jivey Tam."

Dumple Doo roared, "'Hgeby Tam!' No, no! Hgeby Xtamn!"

Ethelinda said, "It doesn't matter. Jivey Tam, then."

Mark asked, "Where's Jivey Tam?"

"It's where we're going next. It's only about 10 light years away."

Mark hefted the gun, swinging around and pointing at the walls.

"Carefully, carefully," said Clackety Hobo, extremely nervous. "Where you're pointing now, there are only about ten metal walls between us and the vacuum of space."

They had given him a holster, which hung across his chest. He put the gun into it. "What is a vacuum?"

"Empty of any air. There's no air in space."

"Like there's no air on the moon," said Mark. "I remember that."

* * *

In the canoe, they dived down through the red light to the surface of Bingo Bango Bongo.

They landed, and Mark went outside first, his gun ready. Not one devil.

Ethelinda went into the cave, while Mark covered her. He followed, and again, Ethelinda led him through the passageways.

Lynette appeared and said crossly, "Where have you been? People told me you had left."

"We went up to our ship, to build something for your Artificers to copy, to kill devils with. It's a gift from Mark, and this should change your lives."

Lynette stared at her.

"I think Mark has found a way to make a new life for you all, not only in this cave, but in the other caves far away. You'll be able to go on journeys for days, to climb safely far up on the highest cliffs."

"What are the *Artificers*?" asked Mark.

Lynette understood his thought, and sent the message to his mind, "People who make things."

She sent them both another message.

"Follow me."

A long, long walk brought them to an immense hall, lined with white, sculpted glass, and lit with white light, the brightest Mark had seen here underground.

Centaurs were working at hundreds of benches along the walls, making a lot of noise. In the distance, they could hear a deep hum.

"You hear that noise?" said Mark.

"They're the electricity generators. They're about 20 times as tall as you are."

Lynette brought the Chief Artificer, who greeted them warmly.

Ethelinda gave the glass laser to Mark, who handed it over. She said, "This is an invention of Mark's, for the people of Bingo Bango Bongo."

Mark said, "The robots made it, up on the spaceship. You can take it to pieces and see how it's made, then make as many as like."

"What's it for?" the Chief Artificer asked, the question in Mark's brain.

Mark said, "It's extremely dangerous. You must never touch the trigger unless you see a devil. Then you look along the sights to aim it at the devil, and pull the trigger. It works much better than a spear, and over far longer distances than a spear can."

He looked down the far end of the hall. It was about five hundred yards.

"Does this cave end in a glass wall with rock behind it? Is there anything else down there?"

"Just the glass covering the rock."

He made a movement with his arm for everyone to get well back, and took the gun back.

He lifted the gun, aimed it, and fired. A dark coloured beam, very thick, crossed the cavern and they heard a terrible crash and felt a shock wave.

Everyone hurried down to look. The glass had melted and a deep hole had burnt into the rock, much farther than Mark could reach into. There was a funny smell, that made him cough.

"It works with electricity. The robot has showed Ethelinda how to recharge it when its power is low."

Mark felt the ideas flowing between the other two, and he tried to understand what she was explaining, but he didn't follow it very well.

"That's clear," said the Chief Artificer. Then Mark's mind was overcome with all the noise of excited thoughts from everyone there. They all crowded around, their thoughts making a storm.

The Chief Artificer said, "I must take you to the Patriarch of the Cave," and he and Lynette escorted them out.

"What's a Patriarch?" asked Mark worriedly.

"It means the Father, the Prime Minister, the King, the President…"

Mark looked at his watch. It was the middle of the afternoon. He had escaped all his morning classes and now the kids would be in the afternoon classes. He was getting out of them too. He hoped he wouldn't get into trouble because he wasn't learning anything.

Lynette went ahead, her haunches moving importantly, swishing her tail.

At last, they came to a dark blue, arched door, and Lynette pushed a button. Chimes sounded inside, and an old, grey-haired centaur opened up and peered at them. Lynette explained, and the old centaur motioned them to come in.

Inside, Mark saw a wide chamber with a low roof, in dark blue and purple glass, with a blue light.

An old, grey-haired centaur stood in the center, wearing a purple robe.

The Chief Artificer hurried forward, and they talked for a couple of minutes. Mark could hear the thoughts indistinctly, and the Chief Artificer showed the laser gun to the Patriarch, who did not touch it.

Mark heard the Patriarch sending out thoughts, and another door opened. Ten centaurs wearing golden robes came in, and stood in a semicircle behind the Patriarch.

The Chief Artificer held up the laser gun, and Mark could hear the thoughts going out as he told them about it.

The Patriarch finally 'spoke', his thoughts going straight into Mark's mind.

"Our children have welcomed you as one of us. You have killed Devils, You fought to save Naomi, as she called herself for your sake. Now you bring us this weapon.

"You are one of us, in truth. I say it. You are one of us. The Council says it."

The centaurs in the semicircle nodded. "Whenever you need refuge, this is your home. Whenever you wayfare through deep space, and are weary, or in trouble, bring your ship here, because this is your home for always. You are one of us, with every honour. Your ship can always land here and you will be home."

Mark had a lump in his throat. He didn't know what to say. He felt so happy.

"Go, Mark Clough," said the Patriarch. "Go with our gratitude, honored friend and Bongean,"

Lynette led him out of the Chamber. Ethelinda and the Chief Artificer followed.

They went to the children's hall, with the swimming pool. Mark was dazed, and a good swim was what he needed.

When he came out of the water, Ethelinda said, "I think we should leave. That of Naomi has upset and frightened you. You can come back here in future years, but now it is better to go, till you get better."

"I can never come back here," said Mark sadly. "When I'm back at school in Milton Mudwallop, this will be a place so many millions of miles away in the darkness of space… I'll never go anywhere except on my bike."

"Don't you worry about *that*," said Ethelinda briskly. "We won't leave you stuck at your Mudwallop school. Try and put your mind on what I'm saying. You have to say goodbye, and we've got to go up to the ship. We'll go to Jivey Tam, and that'll give you something else to think about. You'll be always coming back here."

"Yeah," said Mark. "On my bike, between the stars."

* * *

In the canoe, Mark asked, "Can we make a video of these cliffs? I'd like to talk to my mum tonight, and show her these rocks, and maybe what the planet looks like from higher up."

Clackety Hobo said, "That's easy."

"Clackety Clack," said Mark. "You're a real friend."

"Clackety CLACK!" the robot cried. "I love that. I can sing a song:

> Clackety Clack a clacking went,
> Clacking Clackety clacked away..."

"That's very *very* good," said Ethelinda.

To Mark it sounded like a sort of screeching you hear when something has gone badly wrong with an engine.

Clackety Hobo said, "But we can't transmit the video and talk to your mum till we're in hyperspace."

"What's hyperspace?" Mark asked.

"It's the dimension where we found you. The other dimension."

In the other dimension, Mark sat in front of the screen, and called, "Mummy, mummy. I'm here."

No answer.

"Can you whistle?" Mark asked the robot.

Hettie Hobo gave a whistle that lifted him out of his chair.

He saw his mother.

"Mark! Mark! Are you all right? I've been beside myself all day."

"Mummy, I've been on world all day, on Bingo Bango Bongo. Do you want to see some pictures?"

Clackety Hobo projected his video of the huge slabs of rock.

"Oh, my God!" Jane Clough gasped. "That place is unbelievable. It's all steep rock, thousands and thousands of feet high. You didn't try to climb any of it?"

"No, mum. We were in a cave."

"In a cave! What were you doing there?"

"We were with the Bongeons."

"Cavemen! Alien cavemen! My little boy has been all day with cavemen and aliens. Oh, my God, Mark, are you all right?"

"It was wonderful."

"And are you eating all right?"

"We've got a wonderful cook on board. You don't know how well she cooks stuff."

Mark turned to Clackety Hobo. "Bring in Scrumptious Mumkish and show her."

When his mum saw Scrumptious Mumkish, she screamed.

"Is that a washing machine or a fridge?" She had her hand at her mouth.

"My name is Scrumptious Mumkish, and I'm a world-class Blue Chef," said the robot with great dignity.

"A Blue Chef?" repeated Jane, stupidly.

"A Blue Ribbon cook," said Scrumptious Mumkish "A cook – a chef. I'm now going to give him lamb chops done in bread crumbs, with carrots, green beans, peas and mashed potatoes. After that, peaches and cherries, and some ice cream."

Jane was too stunned to speak.

"The policeman came today, to see whether you were just sick, or somebody had attacked you. I had rung the school, to say you were sick. So I had to tell the policeman you had gone to your aunt's at Windy Claybottom, because I couldn't look after you properly while I was away at work. Mark, you've lost a whole day's classes. If you don't do your lessons, you'll never learn anything."

She stopped, her teeth at her knuckle.

"Mark, you haven't been kidnapped or anything?"

"No, I am all right, and I'll soon be back."

"You know, this can't go on. Just running around space and doing nothing all day. Don't you feel bored?"

"It's awfully boring, mum," he assured her. "I love you, and I miss you, and I'll be home in a few days."

Clackety Hobo cut the transmission, and the screen went blank.

When Mark turned around, Scrumptious Mumkish had set the table.

An hour and a half after eating, Hettie led him firmly to the learning room. "What do you want to learn?" she asked him.

"What are the stars like inside, now I know about galaxies and things?"

He put on the metal cap, and learned about brown, dwarf stars, that were too small to become real, bright stars, and all their electrons crowded into the inner circles around their atoms; and about red giants, like he had seen at Bingo Bango Bongo, where they were in the last stages of burning themselves up; and neutron stars, which were from suns more than three times as big as his sun at home, suns which had exploded and collapsed down to ten kilometres across. They were so dense that their atoms of protons and neutrons had changed to neutrons, because the electrons had been pushed into the protons to make them neutrons too – and a pinhead would weigh hundreds of thousands of tons. He learned about black holes, where stars ten times to thousands of times bigger than his own sun had collapsed to about four miles across, and were so dense that light could never get out. They made a gravity well so deep, you needed mathematics to work out how deep it was really was.

When the lesson was finished, Mark found Ethelinda standing behind him.

"I don't know any mathematics," he told her.

She gently stroked his arm, then leant over to give him a really sissy kiss.

He got up, and feeling a real sissy, pressed his cheek against hers.

"Do you love me, Mark?" she asked.

"You're my best friend in the whole world," he said. "Well," he corrected himself, "The whole universe. I love you just as much as my own mum. When I have to go back to Milton Mudwallop, I'll not only have to go back to school. I won't have you any more, and I think I'll die. School's awful but being without you – I don't know how I'll... I'll," and he gave a sob. "I won't be able to go on... breathing!" he cried.

She put her arms around him.

"I'll give you something so you'll always be able to speak to me. I'll put a small satellite over your house."

Clackety Hobo bustled in. "Come with me," he commanded. "More martial arts training."

They went to the big hall, where Mark practised Aikido, Judo, Ju Jitsu, Karate, Taekwondo and Kung Fu with the rubber robot. At the end of an hour, he was covered in sweat.

Ethelinda walked with him to the shower, and sat there while he showered.

"It's not fair," Mark said. "So many boys are bullied, but they can't learn the martial arts. It takes a couple of years to get to the first stages, and costs money. Most boys can't afford it. The schools should teach it, but they don't."

"And teach the bullies too!"

"Everyone knows who the bullies are," said Mark scornfully. "Don't let them into the classes."

"Earth isn't like the other planets," said Ethelinda gently. "It does everything wrong. You can't blame yourself. You kill and hurt because you're born that way. But not every earthling is the same. There are good ones too."

Mark towelled himself. He didn't feel shy anymore, being undressed in front of her. Out in deep space, it didn't seem to matter much.

"And you think I'm one of the good ones?" he asked hopefully.

"I know *you* are."

He got into his pyjamas, cleaned his teeth, and tottered to the bedroom. He was so tired suddenly he could hardly walk.

* * *

Hettie Hobo let him sleep in till five o'clock in the morning. He woke up, starving.

Scrumptious Mumkish gave him two fried eggs, three slices of bacon, a sausage, and pieces of toast with strawberry jam. She gave him a glass of orange juice, and he felt *much* better.

The robots and Ethelinda stood there, watching him, but said nothing.

He went and cleaned his teeth, and came back, full of good cheer.

Ethelinda cleared her throat. Then Clackety Hobo cleared his throat, that sounded like a rusty saw. Then Hettie Hobo cleared her throat. They all looked at him.

Mark felt a spasm of fright.

"What is it?"

Ethelinda said, "We got into hyperspace above Jivey Tam about two hours ago."

They all looked at him.

"Yes," said Mark hurriedly. "I understand. Then what happened?"

"We got an S.O.S. message."

"S.O.S.?"

"Mayday. Asking for help urgently."

"From Jivey Tam? Do they know how to get into this dimension, this other dimension we're in?"

"No," said Ethelinda. "It was from an uncle of mine. He's called Ltyulkga, and he called from the planet Bvunmbvdva."

"He's called Julga, and called from the planet Poompbah?"

"Exactly," boomed Dumple Doo.

"What's wrong? I don't get it."

"He was taking off from a nearby planet with a load of ore, and he had to go to another planet, passing near Bvunmbvdva, see? He got a partial engine melt-down, and fell into Bvunmbvdva's gravity well."

Hettie Hobo said miserably, "Bvunmbvdva's three times as big as the Earth."

Ethelinda said, "So the gravity well's three times deeper."

"Obviously," said Mark, feeling clever. "He crashed?"

"He made a soft landing. But he can't get up out of the well again."

"We can go down in the canoe," said Mark excitedly.

"But then the *canoe* has to get back up and out of the well," said Clackety Hobo, in a tone of voice loaded with meaning.

"It doesn't have enough power?" asked Mark in dismay.

"It does," said Clackety Hobo. "It can just carry up Ltyulkga... and you."

There was a sigh around the cabin, and they looked at him.

"I don't know how to fly the canoe. Clackety Clack, can you teach me?"

"Yes, I can," cried Clackety Hobo, eagerly. "But when you get down there, you can't breathe the air. You'll have to wear a special suit and helmet."

"Can you make me one?"

"It's being made this very minute. But there's more. Ltyulkga can't get out of his ship. You'll have to take a metal cutting torch to free him. The ship suffered structural damage on impact."

"The ship must be five miles long. Where is the door?"

"We'll show you. The planet is covered in crystal. The gravity is so strong, you won't be able to stand up, with your suit and the cutting equipment. You'll have to lie flat and slide along, and crystals could cut your suit. So, we'll give you an aluminium sheet to slide along. You must land *right* alongside the door."

Mark felt a clutch of fear in his tummy.

"You don't have to go," said Ethelinda. "It's an awful risk. I can't go because I weigh too much, but even if I didn't, my father would never allow me. Do you want to speak to your mother?"

Mark took a deep breath. He had to show them he wasn't scared, when he was *very* scared.

"We earthlings enjoy risks," he declared, and then wished he could take the words back.

"First, I'm going to teach you to use the cutting torch," said Clackety Clack.

* * *

In another hall, Mark didn't do very well with the cutting torch. He said, "I'll use my laser gun."

Clackety Hobo said, "Your gun is too strong. You're cutting into a small cargo bay, that's airless. If you cut through an inner wall, the air will get out. You have to get into the cargo bay, cross it, open an airlock door, and put a protective suit inside, then close the door again."

Mark said, "Julga will fill it with air so he can go in and put the suit on?"

Clackety Hobo said, "It's the only airlock Ltyulkga can reach that's still working. There are several other airlocks working, but the ship is about five miles across; he can't open the dozens of the doors he needs to reach those far away ones."

Mark took that in. "Tell him not to worry. That Mark Clough, the Earthling, is coming." He hoped that saying that would make him feel better, but it didn't. He was scared just the same.

"I'm going to teach you to use the cutting tool with the metal cap on your head," said Clackety Hobo.

With the cap on, Mark knew exactly what to do and his hands obeyed him as though he's been doing it all his life. Then he took the cap off, and found he could still do it perfectly.

Clackety Hobo led him to the canoe, and sat Mark inside and showed him all the controls and screens.

"I'll never remember all this," exclaimed Mark. At least now he had an excuse for not going down.

Clackety Hobo put the metal cap on his head, and suddenly the hangar disappeared. Outside, he saw empty space, and he *knew* what to do. He understood all the controls and all the screens. He dived down to a planet, 500 miles below, and struck enormous winds, that threw the canoe this way and that. The on-board computer responded, but Mark knew exactly how to help it.

Suddenly, he was in the hangar again. Clackety Hobo was holding the cap, but Mark still remembered everything.

"Come and put on your space suit," said the robot.

When Mark was dressed, Clackety Hobo explained all the controls on his chest, and the purge valve on his shoulder.

"This purge valve is if you get too much air in your suit, and it begins to blow up like a balloon. You open the purge valve and let some air out."

"What is *purge?*"

"Purge is getting rid of something you don't want."

The robot screwed on his helmet.

Mark asked, "Are we still over Jivey Tam? We can set course now for Poompbah."

"We *are* over Poompbah. We reached Jivey Tam two hours ago, when you were asleep. Then we got the message, and flew here."

"What dimension are we in?"

"We've left hyperspace and we're in our own universe. We're in orbit over Poombah, 500 miles up."

He pushed Mark into the canoe, and Mark strapped himself in.

Clackety Clack left the airlock, and when the green light showed, the door opened, and Mark drove the canoe into the hangar. The airlock door closed behind him, and far off, on the other side of the hangar Mark saw the immense door open to black, empty space.

He accelerated forward, skimmed over the hangar floor, and was in the black emptiness, with the spaceship hanging still, behind him. The sun was much smaller than the Sun at Milton Mudwallop, but the planet below glittered as though made of shiny glass. Mark put the nose down, and raced towards the planet.

Close to the surface, he flattened his dive, and then the computer guided him. He was flying over glittery glass. And then he saw the huge black spaceship. He saw where the doorway had to be, and the computer guided the canoe to the spot, and stopped, hovering about five yards away. Mark took the controls, and edged the canoe closer and closer, till there was about two feet of gap. The curving hull rose far above him for a couple of miles.

He felt as though he weighed a ton. He struggled out of his seat and fell on the floor, then wriggled over to the air lock. He couldn't use the hatch he'd used all the other times.

He got into the airlock, and found the cutting machine on wheels. After emptying the airlock, he opened the outside hatch, and pushed the aluminium across.

Below him, the ground was all sharp, glittering crystals, with sparks racing through them, long snakes of sparks hundreds of yards long. There wasn't much sunlight; it was like a summer evening in England.

He wriggled to the doorway, and cut at it with a sharp green flame.

Halfway through, a voice said in his mind, "Welcome to Bvunmbvdva – but you call it Poompbah, don't you?"

Mark froze where he was, then looked slowly over his shoulder in terror.

He saw a great ball of shining white-blue gas, about 20 feet across. In the middle hung something like the brain-like pictures he had seen of brains. But this was a *big* brain, about twice as big as a whole human head.

The ball of shining gas rolled very close. Would it give him an electric shock? Mark took a very deep breath and asked in a quavering voice, "Are you, a Poompbahist?"

"A Poompbahoomph, but a *Poompbahist* will do. Where in the galaxy do you come from?"

"I'm an earthling from the Solar System."

"Earth…? Earth…? Earth? Ah, yes! We've got that in our data banks. Your star is 'the Sun'. But how did you ever get off world? I remember now. You spend all your time killing each other, and have no spaceships."

"How can you know about us?" gasped Mark.

"We have two satellites out near Pluto. Every 24 hours, one switches off and the other switches on. The one that has been working for 24 hours goes into hyperspace and transmits to a satellite in hyperspace beside us. That one materialises in orbit above us and downloads into our data banks."

"You've got data banks! Out in the open? Made of crystal?"

"Half a million years ago there was a deep chasm in the Earth, near here."

"What is a *chasm*?"

"A deep hole, going deep into the Earth. The bottom had super-hot thermal springs, heated from boiling rock inside the planet. Our ancestors built a crystal building seven miles long and two hundred feet high, covering the chasm. They used the thermal springs to make electricity, and underground, there are forty stories with data banks."

"How could they do that if you don't have arms and legs?"

"We had bodies for about eleven million years. Half a million years ago, we had progressed so far, we took our brains out of our heads and put them in a charged field, as you see. Well, we had to change our brains to do that, and that took 100,000 years to make our new brain – the one you see now."

"And how do you roll around?"

"Magnetic induction."

"Of course," said Mark, who did not understand at all.

"Our data bases are filled with the wisdom of the universe."

"How can you know about the universe from down here on the surface of this planet?"

"We sent out thousands of robot spaceships 500,000 years ago, and they still send us new knowledge. Listen, why don't you come to our big building and you can see it?"

The Poompbahist extended a pocket of gas.

"Open your purge valve."

It caught Mark's air in the pocket.

"We know about the air you breathe from our data banks, but we'll check it with this bit of air. We can fill a big room with your air, and you can take off your suit."

"But your gravity is killing me. I can't get up off the ground."

"We'll make artificial gravity for you in the building."

"I can't come yet," Mark explained. "I've got to rescue a Choo Chooean from inside this ship and take him up."

"I *thought* this ship was Choo Chooean. Has it crashed?"

"Sort of. An engine half melted."

Mark was exhausted. Just lying there, thinking all these thoughts without being able to talk in the proper way, the tremendous weight making breathing hard…

He turned back to the cutter, and cut open the door.

Half-dead, he dragged himself and the suit across the cargo floor, which was dirty from some rock or mineral. He punched the button and the airlock door opened. He got the suit inside, and closed the door, and dragged himself back to the canoe. He could hardly get into the seat.

The Poompbahist asked him, "You'll come down again?"

"Yes. But first I'll have to come down to this spaceship, because it's giving a signal that guides me."

"I'll he waiting here, and I'll guide you."

Julga slithered out of the door with amazing speed. \He saw the Poompbahist and stopped dead.

"What is it?" His thought exploded in Mark's mind.

"He's a friend of mine," Mark thought back.

"I thought this planet was uninhabited. Are you sure he's not dangerous?"

"I thought you Choo Chooeans were cleverer," thought the Poompbahist.

Julga moved his head very cautiously. "I'm very sorry," he said. "I didn't mean to offend you. What is your name?"

"Xküoghy," the Poompbahist said.

"Chuck," said Mark. "This is Julga."

"Welcome to my world," said Chuck coldly.

"Xküoghy, it is an honor," said Ltyulkga.

"Chuck, I must take Julga straight up. Everyone's very worried."

"I'll wait for you here, Mark," said Xküoghy.

They rose slowly, fighting their way out of the deep, deep gravity well, but higher up, they felt lighter, though not much.

Inside the spaceship, everyone was wild with joy.

Julga said, "I never thought I would see an earthling in deep space. And that I would owe my life to him. Mark, all that is mine, it is yours. You are one of my family. You are another son to me."

Mark cast about in his mind what to say.

Julga had taken off his helmet, and his big, serpent's head was grizzled. He smiled, as he read Mark's mind.

"You don't have to say anything to me."

Mark said, "I have to go down again."

There was a stunned silence.

"I've made a friend down there, and he's going to show me where he lives."

"But the planet is uninhabited!" cried Ethelinda. "No one lives there!"

"It's true," said her uncle, Ltyulkga. "I saw him, and his name is Xküoghy. He's waiting for Mark, beside my ship. Mark has to follow down my beacon. My beacon's still broadcasting and will guide him to Xküoghy."

"That's very dangerous," boomed Dumple Doo. "We don't know anything about these aliens."

Hettie Hobo wept. "The only dangerous people we know about are earthlings, but that doesn't mean there aren't others."

Clackety Hobo said, "Nobody knows anything about them."

"I'm going," insisted Mark.

Ethelinda wept, "Now I've found you, I can't bear to lose you."

These earthlings aren't afraid of anything," said Clackety Hobo, gloomily.

"Think about your School Blue Medal," said Mark.

"No, I can't use someone else's, work. But," she said, "I know from your TV that you have summer holidays. If you come to school on Choo Choo for two or three months –"

"School! No! No! Oh, no! Never!"

"– two or three months, you can put in for a Blue Medal with your report, and you'll win it."

A long, thoughtful silence followed.

"School in my holidays! Never! Never!"

Hettie Hobo said heatedly, "And you'll let him risk his very life for a Blue Medal. You've all gone mad."

Dumple Doo boomed, "I cannot approve. I *cannot.*"

Mark said, "Honestly, I'm not scared. I need more fuel."

Ethelinda said, "Let him go. What do you say, uncle?"

Xküoghy was most polite. "Yes, let him go."

Ethelinda said, "Clackety Hobo, fuel up the canoe."

Clackety Hobo made a noise like twoscore of saucepans, pots and pans falling off a high shelf onto a floor of stone flags.

Mark said, "What is magnetic induction? The Poompbahists move like that."

"Oh, dear," said Julga. "What is he doing off world?"

Hettie Hobo said, "Don't worry, he's awfully ignorant, but we're looking after him."

Ethelinda said, patiently, "Suppose you take a short piece of solid copper tube – what we call a cylinder. You magnetise it, you wind copper wire around it, and then you spin the copper cylinder inside very fast – you get an electric current in the wire."

"How do you magnetise the cylinder?"

"By rubbing it with another magnet."

"And where did the first magnet come from?"

"From a bit of magnetic stone or rock. A lot of planets have them."

"Why?"

"Because they've got iron cores, hundreds or thousands of miles across, in their centres. As the planets spin, these cores set up electrical currents and magnetise some of the rocks."

"Ah, I see," said Mark slowly, hoping he did.

Ethelinda said, "So you get gigantic copper cylinders and you spin them, with wires wound around them, the wires fill with electricity, and you take that electricity to cities.

"And then you take it to each house," said Mark, eagerly.

"Exactly," said Ethelinda. "Then you plug in an electric shaver."

She stopped. "You don't shave. Why is that?"

"I'm too young."

"Ah," said Ethelinda, Julga and Hettie Hobo all together.

Ethelinda said, "In your electric shaver, you've got another copper cylinder with wire around it. So when electricity flows into the wire, then the cylinder spins, and you can shave. This time, it works the other way around."

Mark nodded.

"Now, suppose you stretched the wire out flat, and ran electricity through it… the copper cylinder would roll along the wire instead of just spinning around in one place."

Mark said, "I saw lines of sparks in the crystals, down on the planet. So, that must be electricity. And the balls of gas that the Poompbahists have around them must be magnetic."

"Or the other way around," said Julga. "Maybe magnetism makes sparks in those crystals. They could be a sort of crystal no one has ever heard of."

Mark strapped himself into the cockpit. The canoe moved through the airlock and across the hangar into the cold darkness of space.

Free of the ship, he gazed at millions of stars, and wondered where Earth lay. They would be getting ready to go to school… no, they would have begun long ago. He couldn't see his watch under his space suit.

He put the nose down and went into a power dive to the planet five hundred miles below. He poured on speed, then felt the canoe braking, forcing him back into his seat.

The computer said tinnily, "You are taxing the structural integrity of the unit."

"What is structural integrity?" asked Mark.

The computer didn't answer.

But after a long silence, it said, "STOP FOOLING AROUND!"

Mark went red inside his helmet. Who had programmed the computer to say *that*?

Then later still, the computer said, "*Structure* means the whole canoe and everything it's made of. *Integrity* means it's in one piece and everything is where it should be."

"Thanks," said Mark, very surprised.

"My pleasure," said the computer.

Perhaps the computer wasn't programmed, but had radioed back, to ask what to say.

The beacon on Julga's ship guided him to planet surface, and he drew up near Chuck.

Chuck rolled along a line of sparks inside the crystals, and Mark followed. The sparks came to an end, but Chuck still had enough go in him to roll over empty ground to another line and he rolled along that. He stayed

61

away from some lines of sparks, and Mark supposed they were flowing in the wrong direction.

Mark followed all his zigzags, and then saw an amazing building in the half-light – all of glowing glass, about 20 stories high, that stretched for miles.

Chuck rolled in through an open door, and Mark flew the canoe in after him.

They came to an inside door, and Mark heard Chuck saying in his mind, "Stop here, and get out. Follow me when the door opens. It's an airlock our robots have made for you."

They both went in, and the door closed behind them.

Mark could feel that the air had emptied out, because his suit ballooned in the vacuum. Then earthling air came in.

The door opened in front of them, and they went into a high-ceilinged room, about 500 yards long.

"You can breathe the air in here," Mark heard Chuck tell him in his mind.

Mark took off his helmet gratefully – and yes! He could breathe.

Then he saw about 50 spheres roll towards him.

His mind became a jumble with all their thoughts. "An earthling!" "An earthling here!" "An alien life form on Poompbah after millions of years!" "There was another alien on the ship that crashed, but the earthling, took him up." "Isn't he *ugly*!" "Isn't he small!" "I couldn't believe what Ltyulkga was saying when he told us, but it's true!"

Then Chuck said to him, "Old Hoary is coming."

Mark sent him the thought – "What is hoary?"

"Hoary means covered with white or grey hairs, something or someone ancient."

"Grey HAIRS!" exclaimed Mark. "You have no hair."

"It's a way of saying he's very ancient and wise."

"How ancient? How long do you live?"

"Our brains were separated from our bodies about half a million years ago. After some hundreds of years, we discovered how to make our brains immortal. Most of us are almost half a million years old."

A ball rolled towards him that was blinding white.

"Who are you?"

"Mark Clough?"

"You are an earthling? Earthlings now are in space?"

"I'm by myself," said Mark, getting more frightened.

"You are of a race that is different to all others. Come."

Mark followed him.

"Why are you quaking?"

"What is quaking?"

"Shaking. Shaking at the knees."

"Because they told me you are 500,000 years old and very wise."

"How old are you?"

"Ten years."

"TEN! And you are off world! How long do you humans live?"

Mark stuttered, "In my country, about 70 or 80 years, I think."

"The old ones are there, and you so young, you're here. Stop! Look!"

Mark saw a TV screen; it was the BBC World News, with an announcer at a table.

Mark heard all the voices in his brain. "Aren't they all UGLY!"

The screen showed an African soldier in green camouflage uniform, firing a machine gun. Then it showed dead African guerrillas lying on the ground. The scene switched to Russia, and showed tanks firing, rockets launched, explosions, and dead men being loaded on to lorries. The camera filmed a street of destroyed buildings, and old women, with a few bundles, shuffling along, despair in their faces. Then it showed a helicopter over a jungle, firing, rockets, which exploded in great sheets of flame. The burning, wreck of a car followed, with bodies in the street.

"How many people have you killed?" demanded Old Hoary.

"No one," said Mark hoarsely.

"Because you're too young."

"Because there are good earthlings and bad ones."

"And you are good? And already out in space at ten years?"

Old Hoary addressed the crowd around them, "This is perhaps a young god."

He turned to Mark. "Are you a young god?"

Mark shook his head, and Old Hoary said, "Do you understand the Mystery of Life?"

"We are aware in the Present, Happenings flow into the Present and then vanish forever, because only the Present is real."

A stunned silence filled the hall.

"And why the Present?" asked Old Hoary.

"Please tell me."

Thoughts exploded in the hall.

"He is a young god who is a Seeker, who searches and wants to know!"

"He is not a proud young god!"

Old Hoary said, "We just call it the Present. It is where Eternity touches this universe of crazy, dancing atoms, that make up galaxies, or a single crystal, but none of it is real – it all vanishes."

Mark said nervously, "Of course, after things pass, we *remember* them, and teachers tell us about history and that stuff, for us to learn."

"But that's not the same as when you *live* in the Present," said Old Hoary. "We live only in the Present because we are eternal Spirit also. The eternal in us meets the eternal only in the Present."

Old Hoary searched Mark's mind.

"Do you agree that if you're very hungry, it is one thing to eat a big, hot plate of roast beef and baked potatoes?"

Mark suddenly realised with horror that he hadn't eaten anything since breakfast. He was hungry.

"It's one thing to eat roast beef in the Present, but another to see photos of roast beef and potatoes cooked in the past."

"How true!" cried Mark with passion.

The thoughts came from all around him again.

"What passion for the truth!" "With what passion he responds!" "What a strange earthling is this."

"Pictures of baked potatoes from the past are not the same as the awareness of baked potatoes on a table in front of you in the Present," Mark repeated. It was one of the longest sentences he had ever made, but he *knew* exactly what he meant, and he knew it was *true*.

"What do you have to eat?" he asked, hoping against hope it would be something he could eat too.

"We get our energy from electricity."

Mark's spirits fell.

Old Hoary asked, "Are you comfortable with this level of gravity?"

Mark suddenly realised he was standing instead of crawling along the floor, but that without his lunch, his knees were weak.

"It's just right, but could I sit down?"

Old Hoary led him to one of scores of glass chairs along the wall, that were about 20 feet wide, and had projecting walls on each side.

"This is where we think," said Chuck. "When we sit here, electrical currents connect us with the data banks underground. This is how we spend the time."

"Is that all you do all day long?" asked Mark, astonished.

Old Hoary said, "We have robot ships out in thousands of galaxies. They look for planets with advanced life, and send down floating robots to listen to their thoughts and if they speak by making sounds in the air, to listen to that too. But they don't send it back to us in this universe."

"You send it back in hyperspace, I suppose."

There was total, frozen silence.

"Earthlings know about the other dimension?" whispered Old Hoary.

"No, they don't. I'm the only one who does."

Again he heard all the thoughts, like a storm. "He *is* a young god from the earth!"

"And the people on the distant planets, don't they attack the floating robots, and want to know where they come from?"

"Of course not! Why should they? Sometimes they ask the robots about ourselves, and we send them everything they want to know. We couldn't do that on earth. Earthlings would attack and destroy the robots."

"Do you have robots on Choo Choo?"

"Of course."

"And do they know on Choo Choo where they come from?"

"No, they don't. They're not interested. There are other floating robots there too, from other advanced planets.

"That's only in this tiny corner of the galaxy. But the Milky Way is a big galaxy, and we know lots of other planets. Then there are thousands of other galaxies where we have robot ships. Our robots are building ships all day and all night, and have been doing so for half a million years, and then launching them into hyperspace."

"You must have a lot of data bases."

"They go down half a mile into the ground, and are several miles long. Each computer is a crystal square, and we use photons. I suppose there must be millions of them."

"What are photons?"

"PHOTONS! You don't know what a photon is? It's a massless particle that carries light. Everything you see is because of photons hitting your eyeball."

"Ah," said Mark. "If it had mass it could not reach the speed of light."

He heard all the whispers. "He *does* know." "It must be another word on earth." "They *do* say *photons*, that *is* the word."

"You know everything about us," said Mark. "Do you even know what happens when the photon hits the eyeball?"

"It knocks electrons out of their orbit, so that they go along the optic nerve, making an electrical current to the brain."

Mark thought he understood, more or less.

He said, "That's quite right. You know everything. Do you know maths too?"

"Of course."

"I don't. I wish I could."

"We can teach you. We can connect your head up with our computer banks and you can learn anything in minutes."

"Would you do that?"

"A young god! So humble. A Searcher, a Seeker." He heard the voices.

"Just make yourself comfortable."

A robot rolled forward, and placed a cap over his head.

65

Mark was amazed as the maths swirled into his brain. He thought, "I'll never remember this afterwards," but after the cap came off, he could remember everything – prime numbers, fractals, four dimensional geometry, chaos, quantum logic, calculus, statistics, complex analysis...

Then he thought with despair, "This will not be good for anything back in Milton Mudwallop and at school there, or for making money with and helping mum."

Old Hoary asked him, "What else do you want to know?"

"What happens outside, when you're rolling along and a wind comes? Doesn't it carry you away for miles and miles?"

"We don't have any wind."

"No wind! I... I don't..."

"You sound perplexed."

"What is perplexed?"

"Puzzled. Worried."

Mark agreed he was perplexed.

"On your Earth, your atmosphere is a very good insulator –"

"What is *atmosphere* and what is *insula*... ah, um?"

"Atmosphere is the blanket of air or gas surrounding a planet, and in the case of earthlings, you breathe it. Insulation is something that stops cold, heat, electricity or dangerous radiation from passing. Usually something you can't see or hear or smell. Your air on Earth is a wonderful insulation, and when wool catches it up, the wool seems warm. That means it can get very hot in one part while it is cool or cold in another. Then the air pressure changes, because the pressure depends on how hot or cold it is. So your air blows from cold to hot, or your hot air rises.

"Now our air conducts heat perfectly, so it's always the same everywhere, and doesn't blow around. Well, we don't have an atmosphere of air but of gas, and lots of planets are like that.

"Our planet turns awfully slowly. Yours turns every 24 hours, which is fast, so you get the Coriolis effect. At the widest part of your planet, the equator, it moves much faster, and up in England, where it isn't so wide, it turns more slowly, so in the northern half, air and water and so on turn to the right, and in the southern part, they turn to the left. You look at the way water curls when it's running out of your washbasin. Then you go to Australia or South Africa, and you'll see it runs out the other way. This effect helps your winds blow."

"You've got to think about everything when you go to another planet?"

"You have the advantage over us. You've been to two planets, and we've never left ours."

Mark thought, actually I've been to three.

"You are the only earthling who has been to two planets, and the only earthling who knows about hyperspace."

Chuck asked, "What was that about your mum?"

"My mum is usually unhappy, and nothing I can do makes her happy. She has to work hard and look after the house, and she doesn't make much money. She works with computers, but it's nothing very complicated."

"A lot of people can do it?"

"I suppose so."

"Ah, the law of supply and demand."

"What's that?"

"When there's plenty of something, a good supply, people don't pay so much for it, they don't demand it as much. Suppose I put a plate of 20 cream puffs in front of you..."

Mark's mouth watered so much, he had to swallow and swallow.

"You eat the first four cream puffs —"

Mark felt dizzy.

"But when you eat the next four, you don't like them so much."

"Oh," said Mark. "I'm not sure about that."

"Then when we give you the *next* four, you don't want them. Your demand has ended because of too much supply."

"Well," muttered Mark, and felt a big knot in his tummy.

Old Hoary said, "You bring your mother here and we'll teach her things about computers, she'll know more about them than anybody else in all your solar system."

Mark said, "When we arrive, I don't think she would get out of the canoe. She's never seen all the ground covered with glass. I would do anything in the world for her, but there's nothing I can do."

Mark heard the whisper run around the company — he heard the whisper in his head.

"A Righteous Alien!" "A Righteous Alien."

Old Hoary said, "You, Mark Clough, are hereby declared to be a Righteous Alien, and are welcome forever on Poompbah. On Bvunmbvdva you are welcome forever."

Mark thought miserably, "I'd have to bring about ten tons of food, and it probably wouldn't keep."

"Whenever you want to separate your brain from your mortal body which will decay and die, come here and we will make you like one of us."

Chuck sent out the thought to them all — "The Old Treasure."

Old Hoary suddenly shone even more brightly.

"Before we became immortal —"

"What is immortal?"

"You never die. Before we became immortal, we had bodies – well, our race had bodies, and we had two sorts of people, like you have women and men on Earth. Our women covered themselves in jewels, and although those bodies disappeared 500,000 years ago, we still have the jewels. Come with me. Put on your space suit."

* * *

When Mark had screwed on his helmet, and turned on his air supply, they went through a wide door, and along glass passages, till they came to a lift. He got in it with Old Hoary.

The lift went down several floors. On each floor, through the glass walls, he saw thousands of glass balls, with light dancing inside – the computers. Through the glass floor, he saw that the lift shaft went down more than 2,000 feet, all lit up.

When the lift stopped several floors down, they walked along a passage with big glass chests, that were filled with diamonds, sapphires, emeralds, rubies – every sort of jewels.

Old Hoary said, "On Earth, diamonds are more valuable than the others. Fill your pockets with diamonds, but don't pick very big ones, or they'll ask your mum where she got them from."

Mark felt around his suit, and found it had four pockets, like Ethelinda's dress. But it was hard to scoop up the diamonds with his gloves and get them into the pockets.

Finally, his pockets were full of diamonds.

* * *

Back in the big. hall, he unscrewed his helmet, and said, "I must go. I must eat. I feel very weak. But hear what I say – I love you all. I have been so happy, I don't want to go, but I must eat."

He wondered what it was like to starve to death. *When* would he starve to death – in the next hour, an hour and half?

He heard the whisperings in his mind – "Feel his weakness." "He's getting very weak." "Is this dangerous?" "He must get in his space ship."

Old Hoary said, "Give the order to store the air in this hall for when he comes back again."

Old Hoary and Chuck led him through the airlock, into the canoe's airlock. He said farewell to them, weeping.

The canoe glided out into the open, the gravity crushed him into his seat.

He didn't enjoy the ride up to orbit, .he was so hungry. He told the computer, "Tell them I need to eat something. Tell them to warn Scrumptious Mumkish that I want to eat something before I even take off my suit."

On the space ship, Ethelinda and the robots crowded around as Mark unscrewed his helmet and took off his gloves. He unzipped the sleeve and saw his watch. It was 7 pm. Scrumptious Mumkish served him a vegetable salad with fish fingers, then a stuffed turkey with baked apples, baked pineapples and baked potatoes. Then she gave him a golden syrup pudding. He drank and drank glasses of fruit juice.

They helped him take off his suit. He showered, and cleaned his teeth. After he put on his pyjamas, they wouldn't let him go to bed, but plugged him into Dumple Doo, who took from his brain everything he had seen and heard.

He complained, "I need to go to bed," and Ethelinda said, "You'll make history in Choo Choo with all of this, and you'll get a Blue Medal."

Mark hardly heard her. When Dumple Doo finished, he was asleep, and Hettie Hobo carried him to his bed in her arms.

* * *

He didn't wake up till six o'clock.

Scrumptious Mumkish gave him a breakfast which Mark believed was scrambled egg mixed with tomato, bacon, toast, butter and apricot jam. He drank what he thought was a pint of milk, and felt so full, he could hardly move.

At seven o'clock, they took him to the screen, and called his mum.

He could see her getting out of bed, and when she heard his voice, she rushed to the mirror.

"How are you mum?"

"The police have gone to your aunt's, and found you weren't there. They wanted to know why I had lied, and I told them you had run away and I didn't know where you were. They were very suspicious when they found your bike, and they're looking for you."

"Mum, you're going to be rich. I've got a lot of diamonds for you." He held up a big bowl filled up with diamonds.

She caught her breath.

"Have you pinched them? Are they stolen?"

"No, they gave them to me."

"Mark, you must never take anything from strangers. WHERE DID YOU GET THEM?"

"I got them on a planet called Poompbah. They are a gift, not for me but for you."

"Nonsense! I don't know a soul on Poompbah. Who was it? Where is this place?"

"The computer took a video. Look, Mum!"

His mother gazed unbelieving at the surface of Poompbah.

"What happened? There's broken glass everywhere."

"They're crystals, not glass."

"What's that big ball of gas? It's come close to you! It could blow up! Mark, you must promise me you'll stay away from gas!"

She gasped.

"You're wearing a suit and a helmet! Who gave you that?"

"They made it for me on the spaceship. They've made me a suede belt to put the diamonds in. Look!"

He filled one pocket of the belt after another with diamonds.

"I'll have to pay taxes on those diamonds and explain where they came from."

Ethelinda stood before the screen.

"We'll go to Bermuda, and sell them there, and bank the money. You can fly to Bermuda when you want more money."

"You'll never get what the diamonds are worth. It's terrible when someone from the public tries to sell diamonds to these people."

Ethelinda gave a very strange smile.

"We'll make sure what they do and the price they pay us," she promised. "We'll look after that. You bring the money into England little by little, only when you need it."

Then she said, "Mrs. Clough, when Mark has his summer holidays, would you care to come with him to my planet, and we can teach you a lot about computers."

"Nonsense," said his mum. "How am I going to breathe the air? And alien computers are no good here."

"We can teach you how to build computers and patent your ideas – computers that no one has seen on your planet."

Jane Clough softened, and then giggled.

"I'm just a silly woman, and not clever or anything."

Hettie Hobo said from the back, "She'll be clever by the time we finish with her," in a hard voice, and Dumple Doo shushed her.

His mum said, "Have you had breakfast?"

Mark told her what he had eaten.

"Have you cleaned your teeth?"

"Yes."

"When are you coming back? What will you tell the police?"

"He'll tell the police he lost his memory," said Ethelinda. "He'll be back soon."

"Where are taking him now?"

"To my planet to meet my mum and dad."

"How far away is that?"

"It's not far. I think it's about 70,000 million km but I'm not sure. I get all mixed up with your numbers on Earth. It might be 30 million million km. Oh, dear."

"And then is he coming home?"

"My holidays aren't over yet so we'll be going to a couple more planets, and then I have to go back to school."

"Don't you think you're being very selfish, young lady? How old are you, anyway?"

"I'm eleven. A few days more don't matter, anyway, for Mark."

"You're eleven, and your daddy's given you a spaceship about one mile across."

"It's just an old rattletrap of a cargo ship and it's five miles across."

The screen went dead.

Dumple Doo boomed, "I thought it better to interrupt at this point. I don't know what else she was going to say."

They came into hyperspace outside Choo Choo at about 9 pm.

Ethelinda said, "We'll let Mark have a sleep, before we jump back into the normal universe. Is that all right uncle?"

Julga said, "That's all right. I could do with a bit of snooze myself."

Next morning, after breakfast, the humming made Mark sick to his stomach, as they broke out from the other dimension into the ordinary universe.

On the screen, Mark saw a dark planet, with buildings almost a mile high, ablaze with lights.

"It's still nighttime here," he said.

"Our planet is always dark," said Ethelinda. "Our sun is so far away, it gives us no light or heat."

"How can anything grow?"

"It's all rock, and it's got no atmosphere."

She switched on the infrared, and Mark saw a savage, unending jumble of dark rock.

"There's no air to breathe!"

"Hundreds of thousands of years ago, we lived on a planet something like Earth, with an atmosphere like yours. But we saw that a swarm of asteroids was coming, about one and a half million of them. We couldn't stop them, not that many. Half of them were hundreds of kilometres across so that the energy to blow them to pieces, or to make them change direction would have been colossal. We command energies unheard of on your Earth – but not *that* sort of energy. We had about five years warning."

She stopped, and then sobbed. "Oh, Mark, it must have been terrible for them."

She took Mark's hand, and held on to it tightly.

"So, we had to find a planet with about almost exactly our gravity, and which no one was living on, and no earthquakes, because we build very high buildings. Choo Choo was the closest, and the best. As there is no air, there's no wind, and that's good for our tall buildings. We put a million robots on world, and they built the city."

"What are the buildings made of – they must be a mile high?"

"An alloy of metallic hydrogen. It's much, much lighter than aluminium, and stronger than steel. We trade liquid and metallic hydrogen all over the galaxy, plus minerals from Choo Choo that you don't find anywhere else."

"But… but where does the hydrogen come from?"

72

"We sweep it up in space, and compress it in tanks to bring it back to Choo Choo. Our planet is covered in frozen seas, and we use the water to get oxygen, and that leaves us with some hydrogen too."

"Water! Water!"

"Water's made of hydrogen and oxygen atoms. You separate them with electricity."

In the hangar, they got into a very big canoe Mark had not seen. It had a seat for him. It raced out of the hangar, and dived. They slowed.

On the screen, Mark saw that they were inching into a towering, ten-sided building, about ten miles each side. He saw hundreds of big canoes had docked at it.

A docking port came closer and closer, and they stopped.

Dumple Doo boomed, "Docking accomplished."

Ethelinda said, "Follow me."

Mark felt scared to death.

"Just a moment," he gasped. "Is there a bathroom on board for me?"

"There is," said Ethelinda. "Because there is no bathroom for you on Choo Choo – well, yet."

When he came out, uncle Ltyulkga went first, and Mark followed Ethelinda.

They walked a long way along the docking port, then found themselves inside the building, in a brightly lit corridor with yellow walls. They got in a lift and Mark saw strangely written figures whizzing on a screen as they went down at high speed.

At the bottom, they got in a small open car, that raced along more golden corridors, and stopped at another lift. Mark thought they had come miles and miles.

Mark said, "Uncle Julga, is this another building?"

Ltyulkga answered inside his head, "That's right, my boy. Now you're going to meet all the family. All the uncles and cousins, and Ethelinda's parents."

"You don't have any brothers or sisters?" Mark asked her.

"I don't, but we don't have very big families."

"How many people live on this planet?"

"About three million, plus another three million robots."

Mark suddenly remembered Poompbah. "How long do you live for?"

"About 200,000 years ago, everyone stopped dying. There were about one and half million of us. We don't have many babies, but now we're up to three million. I'm the youngest person on the planet."

The lift rose, the numbers blurring on the panel, and stopped.

They went into another passageway that ended in a fantastically decorated dark glass door in a high arch.

Inside, Mark saw an immense room, with rich colours twisting and curving in slow movements over all the walls – golds, reds, greens, purples, blues – every shade of colour, changing every few seconds.

The ceiling shone brilliantly, and the great hall was full of serpents, with big round heads.

Mark's mind was deafened with all the thoughts he could hear but couldn't understand. They were excited, crowding around uncle Julga, stretching out their arms and hands.

Then two approached Ethelinda, and Mark's mind filled with their tenderness. Ethelinda changed their appearance in Mark's mind, and he saw an older man with white hair and grey mutton-chop whiskers. Beside her, he saw an older lady in a big bonnet and wearing glasses, with a motherly expression on her face.

In his mind, Mark heard the fatherly figure say, "And this is the alien who saved Jugla, and is going to win a Blue Medal, telling us about the mysterious Poompbahists."

He suddenly straightened in horror, and cried, "IT'S AN EARTHLING!"

Silence fell, and everyone moved to crowd around Mark.

"HOW COULD YOU LET HIM ON YOUR SHIP! ETHELINDA, HE COULD HAVE MURDERED YOU WHILE YOU SLEPT! WAS HE ARMED? AND NOW HE'S HERE ON XIUCHEU!"

"Oh, my beloved father, he is my best friend. He's not armed."

Trajáncheu searched Mark's mind.

"BUT HE IS ARMED! HE'S GOT A LASER GUN. IT'S ON THE SHIP!"

Mark heard a mental gasp run through the crowd of relatives.

Then he saw Ethelinda sending swift pictures of Bingo Bango Bongo, and the Devils grabbing Naomi. "Ah, indeed," said her father.

"My darling Trajáncheu, he is a *good* earthling, and he saved your brother, my uncle Ltyulkga."

Her father thought about it, and her mother said, "What he has done is wonderful, dear."

Her mother cried, "Look what Ethelinda has done. She's made herself look like an earthling!"

Then she gasped. "Look at ourselves!"

In the face with the grey mutton-chop whiskers, the eyes popped. Then the face laughed.

Ethelinda's mother laughed too, and said, "Look what a face you have when you laugh."

"Damned cheek, damned cheek," said her father. "Ethelinda, you've got no respect."

Mark could hear the whole room laughing as they looked at the Earthling bodies and faces of the three. He heard their thoughts – "What a circus" "They could start a circus" "What a comedy act they could do."

Her father had a dark, button-up suit, with a stiff white collar and a grey tie; and her mother wore a voluminous light blue dress with a purple bodice.

Her mother said to Mark, "I'm Biulbiul. Welcome to Xiucheu. How do you like it here?"

Mark said, "Boo Boo, I'm Mark. And I like Choo Choo very much."

Biulbiul said, "This is my husband, Trajáncheu."

Mark said, "Grouch'n'chew, how do you do?"

Grouch'n'chew grumbled, "I thought you earthlings couldn't fly in space. What are you doing, here?"

Ethelinda explained in very quick images.

"Now are you mollified, father?"

"What is mollify?" asked Mark.

"To calm down, to make you happy when you weren't before."

"You earthlings are killers, without remedy. Screaming babies among shell bursts, dead and mutilated everywhere, blazing houses… what country are you from?"

"England."

"What a government! What Foreign Secretaries! What shame! Tell me, when will the rest of you come out into space?"

Mark said meekly, "I'm only ten years old. I don't know anything about that."

"The people from Pumpkin will give you a hot reception, they'll play so many tricks with your brains…"

Mark said, "Grouch'n'chew, I'm sure it'll be a long time before that happens."

"And now you'll go back and tell them about hyperspace."

"No I won't," said Mark sturdily. "Besides no one would listen to me. Everyone listens to themselves."

"If earthlings find out about the other dimensions, they'll start looking. While they don't know, they won't go looking."

"That's a very clever thought," Boo Boo soothed him.

"And do you go to school, earthling?"

"Yes, sir."

"Some education I'll bet you get." He stroked his whiskers. "Tell me, what's an electron?"

"Please sir, they orbit protons and neutrons in the nucleus of an atom."

"Can electrons be pushed out of their outer orbits into their inner orbits, permanently?"

"Please sir, in a brown dwarf star, and in a neutron star, they get pushed into the protons making the protons into neutrons."

"Harumph!" said Grouch'n'chew. "I can see why my daughter has deigned to accept you as her friend."

"Please, what is deigned, sir?"

"Condescend. A superior Choo Chooean allows herself to make friends with a simple earthling. But," he cried to everyone, "Suppose they find hyperspace!"

"They're too violent to study things properly," another uncle assured him.

"And their brains aren't very good," said another relative.

Boo Boo hugged Mark to her ample bosom. "Don't you listen to one word they're saying. I think you're very clever, and I know why Ethelinda loves you so much."

Grouch'n'chew suddenly exclaimed, "Where does this nonsense of Ethelinda come from?"

Ethelinda said, "It means *noble snake* in English."

There was a guffaw from everyone in the room, and Mark heard in his mind, "Oh, I say, that's a good one! What a good one! That's really clever!"

Uncle Ltyulkga said, "Now, everyone listen to me. Mark saved my life, at great risk to himself. He came down to the bottom of a very deep gravity well – VERY DEEP. He didn't hesitate. It could easily have cost him his life. Then he risked his life to go down again to bring, us back incredible information on the Poompbahists, who have made him one of themselves and opened their planet to him. Dumple Doo used the metal cap to find out everything Mark knew, and while Mark slept, I reviewed it all from Dumple Doo's data base. What he has done is equal to any of our greatest explorers, because the information is quite extraordinary, in my opinion. Quite extraordinary. If he asks the Poompbahists on our behalf for access to their data bases, life will never be the same on Xiucheu."

"Harumph!" said Grouch'n'chew.

Ltyulkga said, "I know of nobody – *nobody* – in our galaxy anything like the Poompbahists. It's an important discovery."

"Can we trade with them?" asked Boo Boo

"I don't think we have anything at all that they need. What they have are unbelievable memory banks, and I'm sure if Mark asked them, they might let us read them."

A snake, almost half as tall as everyone else, pushed forward to Mark, and everyone stood back.

"This is our Patriarch," Ethelinda whispered.

"Mark, what you have done impresses me very much. Whether we worry about the Poompbah memory banks is neither here nor there for the moment. You are welcome to Xiucheu. You have saved one of us from certain death. I now pronounce you a citizen of this planet. As you are being educated on Earth, I now make it known that our schools are open to you. You may come here when you wish, and you most certainly will stand for the Blue Medal."

There was a silence of disbelief, then everyone said "Oooh" at once.

They all crowded around him, crying, "Welcome, welcome."

The Patriarch said, "We all know that Earthlings are dangerous, but it is clear that Mark is a Virtuous Earthling, that he is a Virtuous Alien, and so I do declare him to be from this day onward."

Mark didn't quite understand everything but he felt shy, a bit silly and embarrassed with everyone looking at him. He wanted to explain that he wasn't very clever, but was scared to open his mouth... well, to form the thoughts in his head so they could read them.

Ethelinda said, "On Earth, he finishes school in a couple of months, for the summer holidays."

The Patriarch said, "Put a satellite over his house, so we can know when his school closes. We will come and pick him up."

He looked keenly at Mark.

"And what are you going to do when you grow up?"

"Don't know, sir, "said Mark truthfully.

"But you must think about it?"

"When you're ten years old, you don't think much about that. Sometimes I'd like to be a plane pilot... well, a spaceship pilot."

"Good boy, that!" said Julga heartily.

"But I'd like to do something, that would keep me near Ethelinda," he added shyly.

Ethelinda bobbed her golden locks.

She said, "We don't have much time for our holidays. I think we should leave. "

Another tall snake pushed forward.

"Mark," he said, "My name is Hgiulbu."

"Joombo," said Mark. "Hello."

Hgiulbu said, "Ethelinda, we need a few more minutes of your time. Mark, do you know anything, about UFOs on Earth?"

"What are they?" Mark was puzzled.

"Flying saucers."

"Oh, them," said Mark. "I'm only ten years old. I don't know anything about that. They've never come to Milton Mudwallop, and our teachers tell us they're not true."

Hgiulbu said grimly, "Oh, they're true enough. But we don't know where they come from."

"Pumpkin," suggested Mark.

"Pumpkinoneans deny absolutely that they have anything to do with it. Whoever they are, they have put planes in danger on your planet about 100 times, and sometimes killed the pilot."

"Impossible," said Mark scornfully. "KILLED!"

"They killed young Frederick Valentich on October 21, 1978. He was only 20. They killed him south of Melbourne, in Australia."

"Joombo, that's awful! I can't believe it."

"It's the most famous case on your planet since the disappearance of Amelia Earhart on July 3, 1937."

"Another Flying Saucer!"

"No, she wanted to fly from Australia to America across the Pacific. She probably ran out of petrol. She may have crashed on a Pacific island they've found – they're not sure. After Amelia Earhart, the Flying Saucer killing Federick Valentich over Bass Strait is the next most famous story on your planet."

"Where is Bass Strait?"

"It's between Australia and Tasmania. Fred had to fly from a point on the coast of Victoria, along the Great Ocean Road, to King Island, between Australia and Tasmania in Bass Strait, 48 miles away."

"What happened?

"He had rented a single-engine, propeller light plane, called a Cessna, model 182L, at Moorabbin airfield in Melbourne and took off at 6.19 pm. The sun was going to set at 6.48 pm. His flight plan said he would fly at 4,500 feet height, and he left the coast of Australia at about 7 pm. There was still light in the sky, and people on the Great Ocean Road saw him turn away to Bass Strait."

Everyone was nodding.

Mark said, "You all know about this?"

"Of course," said the Patriarch. "This is some rogue planet that is sending out Flying Saucers, and we don't know who it is. They might know in their memory banks on Poompbah. We really know only the trading planets, although Ethelinda goes to some planets where we don't, but those planets don't have space capacity."

"What is space capacity?" asked Mark.

"They've haven't got to the point of knowing how to build space ships."

"And what happened to Fred, Joombo?"

Hgiulbu said, "We've got the Australian Government transcript of the radio conversation between Fred and Melbourne airfield. The Cessna was called 'Delta Sierra Juliet', or DSJ."

Another snake hurried forward with a sheet of paper, and Joombo gave it to Mark to read. The paper was official, so it did not give local time, but General Australian Time… 7 pm local changed to 9 pm, GMT.

Official Voice Transcript Between Flight Service (FS) and the Cessna Aircraft (DSJ)

Time (GMT)	From	To	Text
9:06	SJ	FS	Melbourne, this is Delta Sierra Juliet. Is there any known traffic below five thousand?
9:06	FS	DSJ	Delta Sierra Juliet – No known traffic.
9:06	DSJ	FS	Delta Sierra Juliet. I am – seems (to) be a large aircraft below 5,000.
9:06	FS	DSJ	Delta Sierra Juliet – What type of aircraft is it?
9:06	DSJ	FS	Delta Sierra Juliet – I cannot affirm. It is four bright… it seems to me like landing lights.
9:07	FS	DSJ	Delta Sierra Juliet. [This statement affirms to the pilot that the person on the ground heard his transmission.]
9:07	DSJ	FS	Melbourne, this (is) Delta Sierra Juliet. The aircraft has just passed over me at least a thousand feet above.
9:07	FS	DSJ	Delta Sierra Juliet – Roger – and it, it is a large aircraft – confirm?
9:07	DSJ	FS	Er, unknown due to the speed it's travelling… is there any air-force aircraft in the vicinity?
9:07	FS	DSJ	Delta Sierra Juliet. No known aircraft in the vicinity.
9:08	DSJ	FS	Melbourne… it's approaching now from due east towards me.
9:08	FS	DSJ	Delta Sierra Juliet.
9:08	DSJ	FS	//open microphone for two seconds//

9:08	DSJ	FS	Delta Sierra Juliet. It seems to me that he's playing some sort of game. – He's flying over me two, three times at a time at speeds I could not identify.
9:09	FS	DSJ	Delta Sierra Juliet – Roger. What is your actual level?
9:09	DSJ	FS	My level is four and a half thousand, four five zero zero.
9:09	FS	DSJ	Delta Sierra Juliet… And confirm – you cannot identify the aircraft.
9:09	DSJ	FS	Affirmative.
9:09	FS	DSJ	Delta Sierra Juliet – Roger… standby.
9:09	DSJ	FS	Melbourne – Delta Sierra Juliet. It's not an aircraft… it is //open microphone for two seconds//
9:09	FS	DSJ	Delta Sierra Juliet – Melbourne. Can you describe the…er, aircraft?
9:09	DSJ	FS	Delta Sierra Juliet… as it's flying past it's a long shape //open microphone for three seconds// (cannot) identify more than that. It has such speed //open microphone for three seconds// It is before me right now Melbourne.
9:10	FS	DSJ	Delta Sierra Juliet – Roger. And how large would the – er… object be?
9:10	DSJ	FS	Delta Sierra Juliet – Melbourne. It seems like it's (stationary). [It has been determined that this word should be "chasing me" based on special filtering.] What I'm doing right now is orbiting, and the thing is just orbiting on top of me also… It's got a green light, and sort of metallic (like). It's all shiny (on) the outside.
9:10	FS	DSJ	Delta Sierra Juliet.
9:10	DSJ	FS	Delta Sierra Juliet //open microphone for 5 seconds// [measured as 3 seconds] It's just vanished.
9:10	FS	DSJ	Delta Sierra Juliet.
9:11	DSJ	FS	Melbourne would you know what kind of aircraft I've got? It is (a type) military aircraft?
9:11	FS	DSJ	Delta Sierra Juliet. Confirm the – er… aircraft just

vanished.

9:11	DSJ	FS	Say again.
9:11	FS	DSJ	Delta Sierra Juliet. Is the aircraft still with you?
9:11	DSJ	FS	Delta Sierra Juliet… It's ah… Nor //*open microphone for two seconds*// (now) approaching from the southwest.
9:11	FS	DSJ	Delta Sierra Juliet.
9:11	DSJ	FS	Delta Sierra Juliet – The engine is, is rough idling. – I've got it set at twenty three – twenty four… and the thing is – coughing.
9:12	FS	DSJ	Delta Sierra Juliet – Roger. What are your intentions?
9:12	DSJ	FS	My intentions are – ah… to go to King Island – Ah, Melbourne, that strange aircraft is hovering on top of me again //*open microphone for two seconds*// it is hovering and it's not an aircraft.
9:12	FS	DSJ	Delta Sierra Juliet.
9:12	DSJ	FS	Delta Sierra Juliet – Melbourne //*open microphone for 17 seconds*// [A very strange pulsed noise is heard.]
9:12	FS	DSJ	Delta Sierra Juliet, Melbourne.

End of official DoT transcript

Joombo said, "The magnetic field of the Flying Saucer stopped the electricity working on the plane, so the engine stopped. The plane dived and went into the sea. It was never found, and Fred's body never recovered."

"There's nothing anyone can do?"

"If we find out, we'll do plenty," said Joombo harshly "We'll make them stop. You can't go around killing anybody, not even earthlings, even though they' re always killing each other. What might they be doing on other planets apart from Earth?"

Ethelinda stamped her foot. "Please! May we have permission to leave?"

The Patriarch said, "Make your farewells, and depart. Enjoy yourselves."

They travelled through hyperspace all day. Clackety Hobo took Mark to the Hangar, which they filled with air, and strapped two boxes on to him, one on his chest, and the other on his back. When Mark pushed a lever on one side, he flew in the air, and he learned to rise slowly, then quickly, fly forwards, and turn. He had a lot of trouble, but got better. Then Clackety Hobo put the metal cap on his head, and he could fly like a bird. When he took the cap off, Mark found that he now he *could* fly like a bird.

"Clackety Clack," he said, "We're practically weightless in here, but on a planet, down the bottom of a gravity well, will these boxes lift me?"

"Here we have one-fourth the gravity you have on Earth, and the planet we're going to is exactly that. It's a shallow gravity well, compared to Earth, and you'll be able to fly the way you are doing, now."

* * *

When Mark awoke next morning, they told him they were in the ordinary universe, in orbit around Jivey Tam planet, Hgeby Xtamn.

From the canoe, Mark saw a bright green planet, and as they got lower, he saw glints of water. At a thousand metres high, he saw dense tropical forest, inside great craters, like bowls 10 or 15 miles across, and around the rim, cliffs rose steeply to flat, rocky country, miles wide, separating one crater from the other. On most of these flat plateaus he saw enormous rectangles of metal, each about a mile long and half a mile wide, and wondered what they were. They flew over low, rocky mountains, flat on top, and he saw several spaceships parked there, each about seven kilometres across and about one kilometre high.

Then they flew over more craters, and landed near one of the metal rectangles, which he saw was open at the sides; metal pillars held it up.

Hettie Hobo warned him, "You can fly for about ten miles, and then you must wait for the small pump to fill your tank with compressed air again. The tanks are made of metallic hydrogen alloy, and hold about 1,000 times air pressure. You'll find the air very thin, as though you had climbed Everest, but you'll always have about 60 parts in a hundred of oxygen, so it's really not like climbing Everest at all. You'll never be gasping for air – you'll always have enough oxygen. Now look, I'm putting this little green box on top – it's a voice translator. It'll tell you in English what they're saying, and when you speak, it'll translate your voice into Hgeby Xtamn."

Mark laughed nervously, "I never thought I'd hear myself talking in Jivey Tam."

They stepped straight out of the canoe, without an airlock, and Mark tried jumping into the air. He jumped about six feet high and landed without jarring himself much.

They stood on the tops of the cliffs, and far below them they saw green and yellow so bright, so beautiful, it made his eyes ache. In the distance, he saw flowers of every colour, with big centres and petals that must have been ten feet across.

The green box on his chest squawked, and he heard, "Hello, Ethelinda. This is a surprise. On school holidays?"

Mark swung around to see a bird man, about 11 feet tall, with black, dull, leathery wings that reached from his shoulders down to his feet; and wrapped right around him.

He had long arms, with hands, and a big head that came to a point in front as though it was a beak, but looking at him, amazed, Mark saw all his face was of skin.

"And who is this?" the bird man asked.

"I'm Mark, please, sir," Mark said, *very* nervous.

"My name is Ynkhgl Pgh Poy. I welcome you to Jivey Tam."

"Inkle Pah Pog, I'm very happy to meet you, sir," Mark said with his very best manners. He had a clutch in his tummy. Quickly, he asked Ethelinda, "They aren't telepathic – they can't talk with their minds?"

She said, "They're telepathic with their music. They go into your mind, right into your soul, with their music."

"Where are you from?" asked Inkle Pah Pog. "You are an interesting life form – you are something like ourselves, but much smaller and without wings. You stand up on two legs, and you have two arms with hands. Extraordinary!"

"He's from Earth," said Ethelinda.

"FROM EARTH!" exclaimed the bird man. "I had never heard of Earth in my life, and a few weeks ago, a space ship put down, and listened to our music. We were talking and they told us about Earth. They say it's hell. People *kill* each other. They live by avarice –"

"What is avarice?" asked Mark, unhappily.

"It means you want everything for yourself, you take and don't give. Of course, if they even take other people's lives..."

Ethelinda said, "Most of them are like that, I believe."

"Our visitors told us that the Earthlings didn't have space capability and would not have for a long, long time, that they are not very clever. What is Mark doing here?"

"He is the only one of all his race who is in space," said Ethelinda. "Of course, some of them are cleverer than others, but I don't think they listen to them. They go by what the majority decides, not by what the clever ones tell them. And their leaders are called 'politicians', and they are not clever at all."

Ynkhgl Pgh Poy said, "Mark, you *are* clever, if you are the only one who is in space. How many are there?"

Ethelinda said, "About 6,000 million."

He said to Mark, "You *alone* in 6,000 million! It is our privilege to have you on Jivey Tam."

Mark said, "I'm hungry, and we thought we'd have breakfast with you."

Ethelinda said, "He can eat only the orange-coloured fruit."

The bird man said, "We have fruit here for you, Ethelinda, but no orange fruit. We must fly to get some. A pity Mark can't fly."

Mark said eagerly, "Oh, but I can," and he flew about 20 feet into the air, flew in a small circle, and landed again.

"Wonderful!" said Inkle Pah Pog. "I'll take you."

Ethelinda said sharply, "Please, just one question before you go. Where did these people come from – the ones who knew about the Earth?"

"From about 8,000 light years away. Away somewhere in the galaxy."

"What was the name of their planet?"

"I never asked them. They were telepathic, so we could talk."

"EIGHT THOUSAND LIGHT YEARS!" cried Ethelinda. "It makes no sense. Why should they come here? Were they traders?"

"I don't think so."

"Were their space ships like ours?"

"They weren't. All the planets around here build with metallic hydrogen in alloy, but their ships looked different. I asked them, and they told me they were made of carbide, cobalt and tungsten. They travelled in hyperspace."

Mark was starving. He rose in the air, and the bird man flapped his enormous wings. He looked like a small plane.

"Isn't your body pretty heavy?" asked Mark doubtfully.

"All our bones are almost hollow. We don't weigh much."

Ynkhgl Pgh Poy soared off to the left, down into the crater, and Mark followed. Mark thought he had never liked anything so much in all his life. He'd like to fly in the air for the rest of his life. He felt free!

The bird man came in to land on a big wooden platform in the tree tops, and Mark settled beside him.

All around the platform grew orange fruit, and Mark's tummy rumbled.

"You can eat it all, skin and everything." Mark picked a fruit and bit into it. It tasted better than anything he had eaten ever. It was so many tastes at once, he could never say what it was about it.

He ate six pieces, and no longer suffered from any hunger whatsoever. He felt bursting with energy.

Mark said, "You like the treetops and the cliff tops. Is it safe to go down to the ground?"

"Not very safe at all. When we came here a million years ago, we brought lobsters with us, because we're very fond of them. But they have to feed on plants, and they've evolved into an enormous form, about 15 feet long, and a body thicker than ours."

"But you can still eat them?"

"They taste better than before, but they're extremely dangerous. Do you want some for lunch?"

Mark had left his laser gun up on the spaceship.

"How do we hunt them?" he asked worriedly.

"We don't. I call some robots from the ship." He spoke into a wrist watch.

"Let's fly around and find one. My wrist watch is a beacon for the robots."

They flew down into clearings between the trees, and wound in and out among the tree trunks, at about a height of thirty feet.

"The lobsters are about 15 feet long, but their pincers are another six feet," Inkle Pah Pog warned.

The trees ended, and they flew over marsh and bog, and then saw a score of them. As they hovered overhead, the lobsters reared high up, their pincers clicking at them.

Suddenly, five shining metal balls appeared; the first one chose a lobster, and fired an explosive at its head to kill it. The five balls swooped, and extended claws, which lifted the lobster into the air, and bore it away to the cliff tops. Mark and the bird man flew after them, but couldn't keep up. When they arrived, the robots had cut it into ten parts, and took off with the other parts, leaving one behind.

They landed. Ethelinda cried, "Oh, goody! I love lobster!"

About twelve more bird men came up, said hello to Mark and Ethelinda, then went under the metal roof, and picked up musical instruments.

Inkle Pah Pog sat down with them, and Mark felt wretched. Music! He wanted to fly some more.

The music stole over him, and possessed him. He had never heard anything like it. He closed his eyes, and went into a trance, following each note.

Then he opened his eyes. The music had stopped. He looked at his watch – *four* hours had passed.

Mark had never felt like this. Everything he wanted didn't matter. All his worries didn't matter. What everyone else wanted – let them have it. What everyone else thought about him didn't matter a fig. What everyone wanted to do better than anyone else, he couldn't care less.

He felt he loved himself, that he was all right. He loved everyone else and didn't care what they did.

Ethelinda came over and he threw his arms around her, and pressed his face against her golden hair. She made him so happy, he couldn't bear it.

Her thought came into his mind – "I feel exactly the same as you."

He saw the bird men get up, and take an enormous mirror, which focused the sun's rays onto the piece of lobster. It cooked slowly, with a delicious smell.

Inkle Pah Pog asked Mark, "Do you like it here?"

"I really love it. But it's all so strange. Where do you live?"

"Under this metal awning. In the middle, we're so far from the edges, the rain can't reach us, and we're out of the sun."

"How long is the day here?"

"There's no night. We have two stars."

"And you sleep in daylight?"

"A million years ago, it wasn't so easy, but now we've evolved."

"What is this *evolved?*"

"It means to change over a long period of time into something else, usually something better."

"And what makes you change?"

"Our genes. They're tiny little cells in our body that tell all the cells in our bodies what to do. They keep changing into something different, so they tell the body to grow in new ways."

Mark asked the question he was asking everywhere. "How long do you live for?"

"We had learned how not to die before we came to this planet. We have already lived about a million years."

"Just on this planet! But what do you do?"

"We don't do anything. We listen to music that we play, and then we enter bliss."

"What is bliss?"

"Total, thrilling happiness. Didn't you feel that when the music seized you?"

Mark had to confess that it was true. He could spend thousands and thousands of years just floating in that music.

"The spaceship that came here a few weeks ago – they told us that on Earth you are about to live forever. In perhaps another 70 years – before your year 2100 comes. What do you think about that?"

Mark was so astounded that he didn't know what to say. Finally, he said, "Our teachers haven't taught us anything about that."

"Life on your planet seems to be hell. Were you happy?"

Mark shook his head.

"If earthlings are going to live for hundreds of years, then the greedy people, the killers are going to live in long hells, and the people who love, who give, will live in hundreds of years of happiness. The space travellers told us that you have a book called the Bible, and the Bible tells how thousands of years ago some people lived more than 900 years. Soon, you will be living thousands of years, but on one of the worst planets."

"I suppose I'll die when I'm about 70 or 80," said Mark.

"Because you don't know what your scientists are doing doesn't mean it's not going to happen," the bird man said impatiently.

Mark was bewildered. To change the subject, he asked another question that was bothering him badly.

"Why did you come here 1,000,000 years ago?"

"Now, that's a long story. We lived about 15 light years from here, and we knew that a star about 20 light years away was going nova one day – about 35 light years from here."

"Nova?"

"Blow itself to smithereens, and send out a shock wave that would, destroy everything for about 20 light years around. If the shock wave didn't destroy us, it would push thousands of big rocks – asteroids – ahead of it to smash into our world."

Mark said, "If it was fast enough and big enough, a rock could have mass that would be terrible."

"Ah, you earthlings know some things, I see. When it did finally happen, and we had left, robot satellites photographed it all. The first asteroid measured 2,000 km across and travelled at 300 km a second. It tore the entire surface of one hemisphere right off our planet."

"What is a hemisphere?"

"One half of a planet."

Ethelinda said, "On earth, you've got the Western Hemisphere, which is all north and south America. The southern hemisphere is the bottom half of your world below the Equator and the northern is the top half."

"Complicated," muttered Mark.

The bird man went on, "Then 14 more asteroids of about 1,000 km across hit our planet at the same speed of about 300 km a second and produced great cracks and sent huge chunks flying out into space. By the time the asteroid shower finished, there wasn't much planet left."

Mark said excitedly, "The people on Choo Choo said the same thing happened. They had to get out and find Choo Choo."

Inkle Pah Pog asked, "And what about Earth?"

"They don't teach us anything about that at school," said Mark. "I'm sure everything must be okay."

Ethelinda hurried over to the canoe, opened wide the door, turned up the loudspeaker, and said, "Dumple Doo, what do you have on asteroids and the earth?"

Dumple Doo's voice boomed across the open ground, and spoke in the Jivey Tam language.

Mark ran over, and said, "I don't understand."

Dumple Doo told him, "Switch up your translator box to maximum power. It can't hear me properly."

Ethelinda came over and fiddled with the dials.

Dumple Doo said, "The earth is in incredible danger, but as earthlings have poor brains, they don't take any notice. Some distance from the earth we find the asteroid belt, with rocks between 100 km and 1,025 km. The earthlings have given names to some of the big ones. About 90 in every 100 are in the Main Belt, completely surrounding the earth, many are nudged out to follow maverick courses –"

"What is maverick?"

"Maverick is a wild, untamed horse – you don't know what it's going to do. These mavericks plunge among the planets, threatening them with appalling impacts."

"What is an impact?"

"To hit with a big bang."

"Now then, there're a whole lot more asteroids in the Apollo-Amor Belt, which crosses the tracks of the Earth and Mars. These weigh between 150 and 15,000 million tons. These might be the ones which have hit the earth in the past, with catastrophic destruction. In March, 1983, one of these came dangerously close. One of these will hit again – it's not if, but when."

"Would it wipe out the earthlings?"

"It might kill two-thirds, or one-half of them – or all of them. It would probably destroy civilisation and they'd have to begin all over again, as herdsmen and farmers."

The bird man said to Mark, "Just when you got to live forever, it looks as though you're not going to make old bones."

Ethelinda asked, "Do they have atomic rockets up in space to protect themselves?"

Dumple Doo said very slowly, "Nothing. Nothing! Their politicians are the ones who lead them, and they're not nearly clever enough. Besides, these two asteroid belts aren't the only danger. The Oort Belt of comets envelops the whole Solar System like a huge shroud –"

"What is shroud?"

"Shroud is a big cloth to wrap a dead man in."

"…a huge shroud way out beyond Pluto. This Cloud could hold 6,000,000 million comets, whose total mass equals that of five 'earths'. Strong shake-ups in the Cloud launch wild cat comets into the inner Solar System, where many have plunged down upon earth in the past, and will go on doing so. To give you an idea, the Crater Meteor in Arizona, in America, measures 854 m across and 174 m deep. The rock that did it was 150 m across no more, and weighed 10 million tons. In 1896, an aerolite of about one pound in weight – 200 grams to be exact – crashed into Madrid in Spain with a thunderous explosion, and enormous flash, and the blast broke hundreds of windows. That was about the weight of a beef steak… but its mass – !"

"Have there been big impacts on earth in the past?" Ethelinda asked him.

Mark tried to remember the classes in maths they gave him on Poompbah. He was never terribly good at mental arithmetic, but he said, "That aerolite in Madrid must have hit with a mass of about 10 tons."

Dumple Doo said, "An asteroid some 600 m across slammed into the Pacific Ocean, 700 miles west of Tierra de Fuego, 2.3 million years ago –"

"Where is Tierra de Fuego?"

"At the very bottom tip of South America. They reckon it tossed 300 million tons of debris into the atmosphere."

"What is debris?"

"All the bits and pieces after you smash everything up. The result was ice covered a lot of the earth."

"Six hundred metres," marvelled Mark.

"An asteroid killed off the dinosaurs which ruled the earth, and let mammals come in, leading to humans. That asteroid was probably 10 km across, and travelled at 60 km a second. It could have landed in Yucatán in Mexico, or else in the Indian Ocean, where it may have caused 7,500 square kilometres of Africa's east coast to slide into the sea."

Dumple Doo went on, "Let me see. Some 210 million years ago, a gigantic asteroid slammed into Canada near Quebec, leaving a crater 60 miles wide, and probably killed off most of the reptiles, opening the door to the superior dinosaurs.

"The first early mammals to follow the dinosaurs, 65 million years ago, were cumbersome and ugly. Terrible asteroid impacts 40 million years ago probably wiped them out, and let more streamlined, handsome animals to come forth, to lead to the modern world.

"Mass extinction seem to happen every 26 to 32 million years. Some scientists say that an invisible Brown Dwarf star strays close to the Oort Cloud with its trillions of comets, and disrupts the Cloud to send comets to bombard the earth."

Dumple Doo stopped, then said, "The Dwarf has its appointment with the earth now, so the next mass extinction will be the human race."

"What is mass extinction?"

"Everyone gets killed."

The bird man asked, "What was the greatest extinction ever on Earth?"

"That was some 240 million years ago, when 95% of all life in the sea disappeared. That means we have had just time to travel right around our galaxy, so the Earth will be ripe for another mass extinction – this time of man and mammals."

"And can the astronomers on earth see them coming?"

"No, they see them leaving."

"What happens when an asteroid hits?" wondered Mark.

Dumple Doo said, "Well, blast would hit a whole hemisphere at least, supposing the asteroid rock was 10 km across and travelled at 100,000 km an hour. Say, 2,000 km away from impact, the wind would blow at 2,500 km an hour and the temperature would be five times that of boiling water. At 5,000 km away, the wind would still crush you, at 400 km an hour, and the temperature would kill you in an instant. At 10,000 km away, the wind would still blow at 100 km an hour, and in the tropics, the temperature would kill you. The air would be full of all sorts of very deadly chemicals. And tidal waves up to two km high would race across the continents at 1,000 km an hour, slowing down as they got inland."

Mark turned white as a sheet, and trembled all over.

He pulled himself together. After all, he was an earthling, and had to show some dignity.

"Inkle Pah Pog," he stuttered, "When you knew your planet was lost, what did you do?"

"We thought we had thousands of years before the star went nova, and then suddenly, it was only 500 years away. We knew about this planet, Jivey Tam. It was all red desert, with a little of carbon dioxide in its atmosphere. Full of dust, and dust storms. We had sent robot probes, and we knew the rock was porous."

"What is porous?"

"Absorbs water easily, like a sponge, or like paper. The nearest star to ours had a big cloud of comets around it – like your Oort Cloud around your Solar System. So we sent ships there, and they nudged hundreds of comets out of the Cloud, and sent them to Jivey Tam."

"How did you do that?"

"The Cloud was turning, very fast, and all the comets in it. You explode a big bomb near a comet, and the blast pushes it in a new direction. When the comets – they were miles across, and made of ice – got close to Jivey Tam, we cut them up with rays, and the smaller pieces crashed onto the surface here, making craters. In the terrific heat, the ice melted, and in a few months the whole planet was covered in water about 30 feet deep. After a couple of years, that water had all gone underground, sucked into the rocks. A lot of caverns lie down there, and they filled up. Then more comets arrived, we cut those up too, and they crashed into Jivey Tam. They were sucked up too. The third lot gave this planet shallow seas, and lots of marshes. The atmosphere was full of steam. Robot ships sowed millions and millions of seeds, and the trees breathed oxygen into the air."

"Oxygen!"

Ethelinda said, "On earth, during the day your plants breathe out oxygen. At night they breathe out carbon dioxide. But you earthlings are cutting down all your forests, so maybe one day you won't have any oxygen any more."

Mark paled.

Inkle Pah Pog said, "We put big fusion plants at the edge of the seas, and they cracked the water with electricity, breaking it into oxygen and hydrogen."

"What's fusion?"

"Like your hydrogen bombs on Earth. You join two hydrogen atoms to make one atom of helium. A lot of energy escapes, and you use it to make electricity."

"And water's made out of hydrogen and oxygen!" cried Mark.

"One atom of hydrogen and two atoms of oxygen," boomed Dumple Doo.

Inkle Pah Pog said, "We had about 3,000,000 people, so we built space ships about seven km across, and about one km high, with 250 decks, and loaded everyone on board."

"With all the people on earth, we could never do that," worried Mark.

"Six thousand million earthlings," said the bird man, "Well, on one floor we had people, and on the next hydroponics."

"What are hydroponics?"

"You close in the whole deck, and put in a lot of water, with very humid air – wet air – and strong lights, and you grow plants with chemicals for food. We don't have hyperspace capability, so it took us almost a hundred years to fly across the 15 light years. By then, the planet had been getting oxygen for 400 years, and we could breathe the air."

"These space ships I saw on the ground are ONE MILLION years old?"

"They are full of robots, who make plastic to keep covering them with. The robots manufacture injections we have to take to keep us young. They manufacture small robot ships which are out to a distance of about 20 light years away looking for asteroids, or runaway planets."

"I thought all planets circle some star."

"*Almost* all. Some go running through space till they hit something, or fall into a gravity well."

"And haven't you *ever* left this planet?"

"Why should we? When you reach transcendence, this universe with its change and its crazy dances of atoms and galaxies doesn't count any more. We reach transcendence in our music."

"What is transcendence?"

"A high spiritual state, when your spirit no longer sees this universe."

"You see hyperspace?"

"No, not hyperspace either. We don't know how to get into hyperspace. We see perfect awareness."

"Awareness in the Now?"

The bird man stared at him in amazement.

"That's right," he said.

After a pause, he said, "This planet is warm and has food. We are no longer worried about physical things. We don't feel the passing of time, and change. We only are aware of the Present. It's as though a million years have never happened."

Mark was very hungry, and he saw the lobster was ready. He saw a bird man flying towards them, carrying a sack.

Inkle Pah Pog said, "He went to get you more of the orange fruit. You can eat it with your lobster."

They sat on the grass, and Mark ate hungrily.

Another bird man asked him, "And on Earth, what do you do all day?"

"I go to school – and ride my bike – and talk to my mum…"

He looked at his watch. It was two o'clock.

"Everybody's in class now," he said. "We have teachers, who teach us stuff. Right now, they're all in school, in Milton Mudwallop."

"Trillions and trillions of miles away," he added, suddenly realising there was no way he could get to school today or tomorrow.

He lay back in the sun, feeling warm and sleepy. After a while, he sat up, and looked at the far cliffs, around the crater. Miles away, opposite them, he saw another big metal rectangle, like the one behind him.

"Can I fly around a bit?"

"Off you go."

He flew across a corner of the crater, then swooped down to the tree tops, saw a wooden platform, and landed on it. He took off again, and flew on to the cliffs. He stopped on top of them, and walked back towards the metal rectangle, a couple of miles away. The ground was stony, and he didn't have proper shoes. After fifteen minutes, he took off again and flew back.

Standing beside Ethelinda and the bird man, he said, "There aren't any insects."

"We didn't want to bring any with us. But we changed the genes of the flowers, so they're ten or 20 feet across. You need insects to pollinate the flowers, but now they're so wide, the breeze carries the pollen and they capture it. The petals have tiny cilia."

"What?"

"Tiny little hairs or whips, that respond when they feel a chemical in the pollen, and the hairs push the pollen down the petals to the stigmas in the middle –"

"Stigmas?"

"The part of a plant that receives the pollen, so the plant can make new seeds for the wind to blow away to take root in the ground."

"I like that idea much more than insects," said Mark. "I don't like insects at all."

"The space travellers who came here said that earthlings had hair on their faces – on their chins and under their noses."

To Mark's horror, Ethelinda suddenly grew a blonde beard with a dark moustache.

"No!" he cried. "Ethelinda!" and he looked away.

"Look at me," laughed Ethelinda, but he wouldn't.

"Look at me," she insisted, giggling. "It's all right now." He looked, and the beard and moustache had gone.

The other bird men had gone to get their musical instruments. Inkle Pah Pog smiled slightly, and joined the others.

With the music, Mark's eyes closed by themselves. He felt intensely, burningly *alive*. He always knew he was alive, but he never took any notice. Suddenly, awareness filled him like a light. Then he felt everyone loved him, and he loved everyone else. He felt as though he would explode with so much energy and life. He felt he could do *anything*, that he wasn't afraid to try what he wanted. He felt he could do everything right, and would never listen to anyone who tried to stop him by frightening him when there was nothing to be frightened about. He heard sounds he had never believed he would hear, and saw colours he had never imagined. He wanted it to last forever, but it stopped, and he opened his eyes. He looked at his watch, and saw that, again, *four* hours had passed.

He sat there, and thought of his mum, and how much he loved her, and how happy he sometimes made her.

He went over to the canoe, and said, "Can I talk to mum from here?"

Clackety Hobo carried a box out and put it on the ground. He plugged a screen into the top.

The bird men crowded around, and Ethelinda stood beside him. He held her hand.

His mum appeared on the screen, and stared and stared.

"What a beautiful place," she breathed. "Look at all that green – and those flowers! They're enormous! When does it get dark? It's gone eight o'clock."

"It never gets dark. This planet has got two suns."

"Who are those men? What are those cloaks?"

"Mum, they're wings. I can fly, look. And see how they can fly."

The bird man took off, and Mark followed, while Clackety Hobo tracked them with the camera.

When he came back, he saw that his mum was having a fit. Ethelinda put a block on her mind.

At first, she couldn't speak, and then she said, "Police are searching for you everywhere. What will you tell them?"

Ethelinda told her, "He'll say he lost his memory – that he had an attack of amnesia. We'll soon be back."

Clackety Clack cut off the transmission, and Mark breathed a sigh of relief. He didn't know *what* to say to his mother, or *how* to say it. He didn't seem to able to say or do anything that made her happy.

Back in the space ship, they transited to hyperspace. Mark had a shower, had something to eat, cleaned his teeth, and fell asleep as soon as he fell on his bed.

Next morning, when he woke up, they told him they were back in the ordinary universe, in orbit above the planet Gunkhae Khelwunkhae.

Mark stumbled over the words. "Hunky Clunky."

The robots and Ethelinda laughed and laughed. He tried again, but he could manage only Hunky Clunky.

Dumple Doo was so excited his voice rose several notes and no longer boomed.

"I've got a reading! I have a reading! About three million miles away. Perfectly round. One mile across. It's an artefact. A perfect sphere!"

Mark gasped, "What's an artefact, and what's a sphere?"

"An artefact is not natural. It's something someone has built. A sphere is a ball, a globe."

Ethelinda snapped in annoyance, "What is its speed and direction?"

"It's just hanging there."

"What?"

"It's in no orbit around a gravity well. It's in empty space, just sitting there."

"But that's impossible," cried Ethelinda. She stamped her foot.

Mark asked timidly, "What's in orbit?"

"Your earth is in orbit around your Sun – it takes one year to do one orbit and come back to where it was a year ago. Your earth circles around your Sun…" She was talking to herself, and not thinking about the earth at all.

They made the sickening jump back into hyperspace.

Hettie Hobo explained to Mark, "We've been some hours in ordinary space, in orbit around Gunkhae Khelwunkhae, but it's taken all that time for our beams to bounce off the other ship, and then come back to us. That's not normal. It was absorbing our beams, and at last, decided to let them bounce back to us so we'd know it was there."

Their ship drove forward for a couple of minutes, then made the disagreeable crossing back to ordinary space.

Their screens showed a gigantic black ship, perfectly round, hanging right alongside them.

No lights, no movement, no radiation of any form.

"It seems to be inert," said Dumple Doo.

Ethelinda said, "Inert means without life or movement or activity."

They climbed into the canoe, and drifted right alongside, then rose slowly, looking at the hull, yard by yard.

"There's a door," cried Mark.

A rectangle was marked out on the hull, about two yards high and three yards wide. Alongside, they saw a small outline, sunk into the hull.

"I'll go out on a tether," said Clackety Clack.

"What's a tether?" Mark wanted to know.

"A rope tying him to the canoe."

"Can I go?" begged Mark. "I'll put on my space suit. Please, please, let me go."

"It's dangerous," said Ethelinda and Clackety Hobo together.

"It's not so dangerous," said Hettie Hobo. "He's on holiday like you. Let him enjoy himself."

It took 20 minutes to suit Mark up. He had to go out through the airlock.

But when he pushed himself away from the canoe and floated towards the gigantic hull, he saw deep, black space all around him – and underneath him. Nothing stood underneath him but millions of miles of nothingness. He began a scream, but choked it. His tummy tied up in a stabbing knot. Millions of miles of blackness around him.

A light struck out from the canoe, bathing the door and the hull around it.

He banged hard against the hull, knocking the breath out of him. He had kicked off too hard – his legs were much stronger than his arms.

He was back in space, floating away from the hull. He opened a jet on his back, which pushed him gently back to the hull. He put his hand into the recess beside the door and his fingers caught there. He pulled, and the plate opened, showing two knobs. He pressed the first knob, still hanging on tightly to the plate, so he wouldn't drift off again.

Nothing happened.

Maybe that was the knob for *closing* the door. He pressed the other knob, and the door slowly opened. He pulled himself inside, and found a bar to hang on to.

The walls were bright glass, brightly lit. It was a big hall, and on the other side he saw six knobs, arranged like this:

1 2
3 4
5 6

He kicked gently against the doorway, and floated over the knobs, where he grabbed another bar in the wall beside them.

He pressed the first knob.

Nothing happened.

"Must be to open the door," he said out loud, in his helmet. "The door's already open."

He pressed number two, and the door closed behind him.

He pressed the third knob.

Nothing happened.

He looked at the pressure gauge on his wrist, but the needle didn't move.

He pressed number four, and the needle on his pressure gauge rose. It went up to one and half atmospheres – one and half times the pressure of the air on the surface of the Earth, the pressure at, say, Milton Mudwallop, which suddenly seemed to him to be a very long way away.

He took a plastic bottle from his pocket, unscrewed the cap, waved it around to fill it with the air or gas in the hall, and screwed the lid back on.

He pressed button number five, and nothing happened, so he pressed number six.

The inside door swung open, showing a long passageway, in bright yellow, leading to distant doors on each side, and to a door at the end.

No one was in the passage.

He tried pressing the fifth knob, and the door closed. He tried the third knob, and saw the needle fall on his pressure gauge, and stop at zero.

He pressed the first knob, and the outside door opened, and Clackety Hobo hovered there.

Mark said, "Clackety Clack, the two outside knobs, the one on the left closes the door, the one on the right opens it. Inside, they're six knobs – can you film them?"

While Clackety Hobo filmed, and sent it back to the canoe, Mark said, "On the left, the top and bottom ones open the outside and inside doors. On the right, they close them. The middle knobs are to empty and fill the chamber with air. Here's a bottle of it."

Clackety Hobo took the bottle, and put it into his side. After half an minute, he said, "Methane gas. Mark, I don't suppose it would hurt your skin, but you stay in your suit. You can't breathe it. Ethelinda, it won't hurt your skin, but you'll have to wear a helmet on your head."

They waited three or four minutes till they saw Ethelinda and Hettie Hobo exit the airlock of the canoe.

They drifted into the chamber, and caught the bars in the walls.

Clackety Clack closed the outside door and pressed the pressure knob.

Mark said, "I read once that if an earthling goes into a vacuum in space, his body would explode."

"Precisely," said Hettie Hobo, "But Ethelinda has an incredibly strong skin which has been genetically changed to resist open space. She has special muscles underneath."

They left the airlock and went down the passageway.

"Will we take the door at the end?" suggested Mark. "Go first to the centre of the space ship?"

"All right," said Ethelinda. "Why not?"

Mark pressed the right hand knob beside the door, and it opened into a big room with what looked like computer banks.

No one was there.

It was about 50 yards across. Clackety Clack stuck a big piece of red plastic beside the door they had just come through.

On the far side, they went though another door and Clackety Clack marked it with more plastic.

Before them stretched a passage about 80 metres long, with about 20 doors on each side.

They went into five of them, and they were the same. A large cabin with a sort of bunk against the far wall, made of shiny metal, the top curving gently downwards to make a rounded trough.

Beside each one, the wall held a panel with about a dozen buttons.

Ethelinda said, "They could be sleeping bunks, and the buttons could be to bring food, or put on TV, or have a shower…"

Mark moved over to press one of the buttons.

"DON'T!" cried Ethelinda. "DON'T EVER TOUCH ANYTHING! What could be something of simple routine for them, could kill us!"

Mark, blushing, backed out of the cabin into the passage.

Beyond the door at the end of the passage, they found themselves in a control room, about 100 yards across.

Four curved banks carried buttons and screens. Screens and panels filled the walls. In front of the control banks, a huge screen hung against the wall in front.

"This is huge," whispered Ethelinda. "So many controls. I don't understand."

"Where is everyone?" asked Mark.

Hettie Hobo said, "This could be a million years old. They could have all died, and their bodies turned to gas."

"So close to Hunky Chunky," Mark scoffed. "Someone would have seen it."

"It didn't have to be right here all that time."

Mark said, "Perhaps they're invisible to us, and are watching us now."

"If their bodies aren't material," Ethelinda said, "How can they push the buttons? If they don't have hands and fingers, how can they build this ship?"

"Their ancestors could have had hands and fingers, but they evolved into another form that's invisible. The robots would do the building, and would build other robots."

A thoughtful silence followed.

Mark was walking along the control banks. He put his finger over a small square – he didn't dare touch.

Instantly, coloured lights hung in the empty space behind him.

Clackety Hobo cried, "Look, there's Hunky Chunky!"

"I told you not to touch anything!" shouted Ethelinda. "Mark, darling, can't you realize…"

"I didn't touch anything, I promise," said Mark.

He moved his hand, and the lights disappeared; new lights, tens of thousands of them, filled a much bigger space.

"It's our galaxy," reported Clackety Hobo.

"This is getting awesome," said Ethelinda.

"What is awe?"

"Wonder. Amazed, religious wonder," she told him, absently.

He moved his hand and lights appeared across half of the control room, suspended in the methane gas.

Clackety Hobo whispered, "They're galaxies. But galaxies across to the edge of the universe!"

One light winked.

"That's a galaxy 10,000 million light years from here," the robot gasped.

Mark said, "In hyperspace, they'd take a million years to get here."

"We only travel at one fifth the speed we could. They'd need 200,000 years if they flew at the speed we can do when we're flat out."

Mark moved his fingers a little more, and all the lights in the cloud changed around.

"Is this another universe?" exclaimed Clackety Hobo. "I've never seen anything like this…"

Then he cried, "It's the universe seen from *their* galaxy. They're at one end, we're at the other. It's the universe as we could never see it!"

Mark asked, "Is it a view that's 200,000 years old, or as they'd see it today?"

Clackety Hobo said, "I'm going to radio Dumple Doo, from the airlock."

The robot shot out of the control room, down the passageways through the open doors, and into the air lock. He let out the gas, opened the outside hatch, and radioed up to Dumple Doo.

Dumple Doo answered in two minutes, and Clackety Hobo came barrelling back.

"This view of the universe is recent," he announced. "This ship has crossed most of the universe in about a year or more."

"They are so far ahead of us," Ethelinda breathed, "I can't take it in. If we are ahead of the earth, these people are even further ahead of us."

She thought carefully.

"Hettie Hobo," she said, "Go to the airlock, and radio Dumple Doo. Tell him to go back into hyperspace, and send an urgent message to Choo Choo, for them to send a couple of ships here, to take this ship apart, and find how it works. When you come back, Clackety Clack will leave a train of particles for you to follow so you can join us again."

"I'm *not* Clackety Clack!"

Mark laughed, and said, "I'm sorry, honestly, it was a nickname because I like you so much."

"You have mollified me," said Clackety Hobo.

"What is mollify?"

"Calm him down, stop him being annoyed."

Then Ethelinda added, "Tell Dumple Doo to come straight back into this universe, and park where he is now."

Hettie Hobo raced off, and the three went through a door on the far side of the control room, and through more rooms, crowded with screens and what looked like control computers.

After the fourth doorway, they came to a central space, behind glass, almost a kilometre across that went down and down – right down to the bottom of the ship as best they could see.

"This must be the engine," said Ethelinda. "It opens in the bottom of the sphere, when the exhaust comes out."

The glass walls were covered in metal tubes and piping, and all sorts of pieces of engines.

Clackety Hobo said, "Perhaps it's a fusion engine, or perhaps it works on anti-matter. It's like nothing I have ever seen."

He filmed.

"I'm taking X-rays of the molecular structure."

"What is molecular?"

"You take something like iron. It's all made of the same atoms – iron atoms. But different atoms join together, and that makes a molecule. Two oxygen atoms join one of hydrogen, and when you have billions of them together, you have a basin full of water. Sometimes you get a dozen, or a score, or hundreds of atoms of different sorts joining up to make a large molecule. When you get billions of those molecules together, you get wood, or a twig, or the quill of a feather, a muscle or a nerve. Mostly everything you see is made of molecules, not just simple atoms. Paper, bricks, crockery, clothes, skin, bones…"

They drifted upwards, and reached a ceiling, where the engine ended. They found a hatch, opened it, and rose up through the opening into a large hall, with a curved wall. They found a door in the curved wall, and looked in.

Ethelinda said, "This is the cavity unit for going into the hyperspace we use. It's almost the same as we've got on board our own ship."

They floated upwards again, found another hatch in the ceiling about 150 feet above them, and went through it, leaving it open.

Again, another large hall, with a curved wall, as before. They opened a door in the curved wall and stared.

Clackety Hobo said, "This is for going into another dimension, but it's not the dimension we go into. I've never seen anything like this."

"It's awesome," whispered Ethelinda.

Hettie Hobo joined them. She had been using her jets, to move fast.

She cried, "That's for another dimension, but not the dimension we use! This ship is incredible. Did you see that engine? That glassed-in tunnel!"

"WHERE ARE THE CREW?" cried Mark, frightened.

"They must be dead."

"And suppose they've got secret cabins. Doors that you can't see, they fit into the walls so perfectly!"

"They wouldn't do that," said Hettie Hobo. "They'd want to talk to us. They want to know all about us, and about this part of the universe. They'd never let us on board their ship to wander all over the place."

"We haven't touched anything."

"We touched the control for the map."

"And suppose it wasn't me at all. They projected it, and I thought it was my fingers doing it."

Ethelinda smiled tenderly. "You earthlings have such funny ways of thinking. There's no one here. They've left, or they're dead. It makes sense because THEY'RE NOT HERE TALKING TO US."

Mark settled into an unhappy silence, not convinced.

"And when your Choo Chooean ships send robots on board, to cut up everything –"

"No, we won't have to do that. They'll find out how to work it, and put it into hyperspace, and fly it back to Choo Choo, to study it there."

They flew up to the ceiling, went through another hatch, and found a third curved wall – and a third chamber to take them into a *third* dimension.

They found two more chambers, making five chambers to transit into *five* different dimensions.

Ethelinda stamped her foot.

"What are these other dimensions? What are they for? *Four* more dimensions we don't know about! I want to know! I think I'll go crazy! Who are these people?"

Mark said, "Now Clackety Clack has finished, let's go back and leave."

His unease affected them.

"Yes, we can leave," said Clackety Hobo.

They opened the outside hatch of the air lock, and Mark saw with dismay that the tethers were floating in space.

"How do we get back?"

Clackety Hobo gave a chuckle that sounded like knives and forks falling on the floor.

"I tied a big magnet to the end of mine. Now I send out electromagnetic waves and –"

The tether whipped across and slammed into Clackety Hobo. He tied it to a bar.

They all clipped on to the tether and floated across to the canoe's airlock.

They took the canoe to the spaceship, that hovered about 300 miles away. The time was 11 am on Mark's watch.

Next morning, their spaceship felt a bang, that shook it.

"The spaceships from Choo Choo have arrived. Before you materialise in this universe, you send out beams from the other dimension, to make sure nothing is in the way. Well, we're in the way, and if they had come through without looking, they would've crashed right into us."

Mark sat down, still shaking, and watched the screens. Two Choo Chooean spaceships suddenly popped into sight, about a mile away.

He saw the face of Grouch'n'chew, Ethelinda's father, on the screen.

"I'm so proud of you both," he said. "You're going to get the best Blue Medals ever seen for all these discoveries. The news of your Medals – we'll send it a thousand light years. Clackety Hobo's films are amazing. Our best scientists are working on them. Now we'll send 15 robots on board, to find out how to fly it back to Choo Choo. Perhaps it never had a crew. It's a robot ship, what do you think?"

Mark said, "We saw cabins, with bunks, like shallow metal troughs."

"The crew died, and turned to gas. Perhaps a million years ago," said Ethelinda.

"I think they're still there," insisted Mark, stubbornly. "They were hiding and watching us on videos,"

"They could be invisible," said Trajáncheu.

"How could they work the ship?" Mark argued. "The unbelievable thing was there were no robots, like. Know what I mean? The robots had hidden too; we didn't see a single one, and that's well, sort of suspicious. *Very* suspicious."

"Ah, you earthlings!"

"You saw there were five chambers for five different dimensions?"

"Indeed," said Grouch'n'chew.

"They might come from another dimension, not from this universe. We saw that galaxy winking on the other side of the universe in the map floating in the air. Suppose that was just to tell us where the next map of the universe was taken from – we saw the universe back to front in that next floating map, like. Suppose they broke into our universe at that galaxy. Why should they have this enormous engine? It's no good having big engines in this universe – it doesn't matter how fast you try to go, you can't get much faster than one-third, or one-quarter the speed of light. You need hundreds of years just to get anywhere close, and that's if you don't hit an asteroid that's really big – sort of too big to atomise. One of those other five dimensions could have planets and galaxies, but not have mass and the speed of light like we have here."

"Remarkable! Remarkable!" said Grouch'n'chew. "That's all been taped, and will go towards your Blue Medal. Everyone here is listening, and I see the others like your ideas. You could be right. But we all agree that Ethelinda is right when she says she believes no one is on board. She would have sensed their presence with her telepathy."

"Unless they set up mental blocks."

"Aren't you stubborn, Mark."

"What's stubborn?"

"Won't give up. Keeps on saying the same thing."

They sat, watching the screens.

One spaceship unloaded six robots, which floated with their tethers across to the mystery sphere.

The robots disappeared through the airlock.

Thirty minutes later, the air lock hatch on the black sphere opened, and the six robots drifted out, without their tethers.

The Choo Chooean space ship launched six more robots, with tethers, who captured the six robots adrift, and drew them back into the space ship.

Ethelinda's father appeared on the screen.

"Our robots have been deactivated. Not harmed, but deactivated. Their videos have been erased."

"What's deactivated?"

"Put to sleep. Made to stop working."

"And *erased?*"

"Their films have been wiped clean. There's nothing on them."

The black sphere vanished. They stared at the empty space.

"Well, that's it," said Ethelinda's father. "We've got Clackety Hobo's films and X-rays, and in a few months, we should find out a lot."

He stopped. "Just a minute."

"We left another space ship in hyperspace, right opposite where we are now. It reports that the black ship materialised within a mile of it. Then it must have seen our ship, and it instantly dematerialised. It went into a third dimension somewhere."

On the screen, he shook his head.

"Aren't they unsociable. Not friendly at all."

"But not unfriendly," said Ethelinda.

"Indeed! Indeed! Well, what are you and Mark going to do now?"

"We'll go back to orbiting Hunky Clunky. It's just a couple of million miles away —"

"Of course," said her father. "I see it over there."

"Then we'll take the canoe down. I'm almost at the end of my holidays."

Grouch'n'chew said, "Mark, I won't see you now till your school course ends, but that's not far off. A ship will bring you to Choo Choo, and you'll see what a ceremony we'll have when you two get your Blue Medals."

The screen went blank.

They exited to the other dimension, and saw the other three ships appear suddenly, close to them.

The three ships sped away through the gloriously coloured clouds, while Ethelinda ordered them to orbit around Hunky Clunky.

Mark's watch showed 1 pm. He was not at school, not learning anything.

Ethelinda said, "We'll eat, and go down in an hour."

As they ate, Hettie Hobo came with thin cotton clothes for Mark. She gave him a tube.

"This is sunscreen for your face. The sun is powerful. Outside, you'll have to wear this hat to protect your head. Inside, button it to the shoulder of your shirt, like this. Put the sunscreen on the back of your hands too. Wear your laser gun."

"My gun!"

Ethelinda said, "The Hunks live in caves, but there are pterodactyls nearly 40 feet across. The Hunks have to come out of their caves twice a day, because their bodies can't live without the sunlight. They have to stay outside for one hour twice a day. Their caves are at the foot of high rocky mountains and pterodactyls nest in caves a couple of thousand feet up in the mountains. They like nothing better than a juicy Hunk to eat. When they go outside, we go out with them, because we're their guests."

Mark gulped, but could hardly swallow, because he didn't have any spit in his mouth.

"What are pterodactyls?"

"They're very like the flying monsters you once had on earth, in the days of your dinosaurs. Their wings are forty feet across, and made of dark, strong skin. They don't have feathers. Their beaks are eight feet long, and have big, vicious teeth. They have claws, each claw a foot long, and very sharp."

"I don't remember any dinosaurs on earth," argued Mark, but he knew it was hopeless.

"They died 65 million years ago, when an asteroid hit you."

"Oh, that! Now I remember. You told me."

"The dinosaurs reigned about 200 million years on earth, and nothing else could evolve while they were there. They were terrifying, and unbeatable. They lived on the ground, but the pterodactyls reigned in the air. Some were small, others were big, and towards the end, some began to grow feathers. When all the other dinosaurs died, the feathered pterodactyls evolved to become your modern birds. The crocodile survived too, but that wasn't a dinosaur, that was a reptile. First there were reptiles, and they evolved into the dinosaurs."

"So this pterodactyl is a sort of dinosaur on Hunky Clunky?"

"No, silly!" said Hettie Hobo. "This is another planet altogether. They are two monsters which have evolved in the same way on different planets, without having anything to do with each other."

Mark said nervously, "So the pterodactyls have to eat Hunks or die of hunger?"

"No, there's a fat animal, like a mole without any fur, that lives about 50 feet underground. Down that deep, there's water, and plants grow there, that the animals reach with their burrows. But they need the sunlight every day, or they die, so the pterodactyls eat them. They're about a foot long, so they don't make much of meal. Besides, Hunks have minerals and things that the little animals don't have. The pterodactyls like to feed Hunks to their baby pterodactyls. Their bodies are much richer… like yours, for instance," she added, thoughtfully.

Mark's heart was beating very fast.

"Now, the sun's blinding and the air is full of dust. These are sunglasses, and this is a filter to put over your nose to breathe through. Hang them around your neck, and put them on when you step out of the canoe, or go out of a cave."

Mark looked out the window of the canoe, and saw a whitish-greyish planet with a chain of mountains running for hundreds of miles.

They landed, and when Mark stepped outside, the temperature was about 50°. He had never been so hot in his life. Around him stretched whitish desert, the light so blinding his eyes ached.

He pulled up his sunglasses, grasped his laser gun, and searched the sky.

He saw three bird-like shapes circling far above, with long, wide wings that came to a sharp point, and a long thin beak. They looked black.

"Quick!" said Ethelinda. "Inside".

He saw a cave entrance, and they hurried inside.

It was much cooler, out of the merciless sun. The rocks on the walls and ceiling had been left ragged, and as they went in further, it got darker.

They turned a corner, and Mark saw electric lighting, from tubes in the ceiling.

They walked a couple of hundred yards further, and Mark found relief as the walls grew damp, and dripped drops of water.

They squeezed through an opening, and found themselves in a great cavern, lit with electricity. The jagged roof rose about a hundred feet above them, and it was about 300 feet across. He saw creatures with round bodies, about five feet across, with four legs, and a body rising in the middle with four arms. The head sat on a thin, scrawny neck, and must have been three feet wide. The skin was leathery, yellowish; the eyes were large, in the front, above a big mouth.

"No nose?" whispered Mark.

"They don't need to breathe," said Ethelinda; and in his head, Mark 'heard' excited greetings.

"Ethelinda! Welcome! Who is this?"

He could hear their voices perfectly.

"I'm an Earthling," he said.

He heard their thoughts – "It makes a funny noise."

He heard Ethelinda's thought, "This is Mark. He is from Earth."

They crowded around him. "Where is Earth?"

Mark sent the thought to them, "It's another planet, very far away."

"We have never seen an earthling. We have never even heard of your planet. Ethelinda, did you know about it?"

"Well, er–" said Ethelinda. "I did actually. I never mentioned it, because there are so many planets."

"Have you just mastered space capability? Will a lot of you be coming now?"

"We haven't", Mark admitted.

"Then how has he got here, Ethelinda?"

"He's very special," she told them.

"So, he came on *your* ship?"

"That's right."

One Hunky stood before him, and he felt its affectionate thoughts.

"Don't you ever fall over? Why have you got only two legs? Where are the others?"

He felt it exploring his mind. "I'm young like you", it said.

Suddenly, it changed into a lovely, black-haired girl, about 11 years old, with a dress like Ethelinda's, but with *five* pockets.

"Hello," the girl said. "I'm Naomi".

Ethelinda hissed furiously. "Naomi! Naomi!"

Mark said with pain, "That's not a lucky name."

"I know. I know what happened to Naomi on Bingo Bango Bongo, but now you've got a gun, and you'll look after me."

"How do you know?" gasped Mark.

"It's all there in your mind for anyone to read," snapped Ethelinda. "You're exasperating."

"What is exasperating?" asked Mark timidly.

"Wearing out a person's patience. Annoying."

"It was a terrible thing," said Mark angrily.

Naomi took his arm. "We'll comfort you," she said. "Don't get upset."

Ethelinda hissed again, but six Hunks came in from the far end and hurried towards them.

Ethelinda said, "Zgyedlu Zgooed, greetings. We have come to visit you."

"The Council welcomes you," said Zgyedlu Zgooed. He turned to Mark. "And the Council also welcomes you, most strange one."

Mark said, "Tickle Tuck, I thank you. This is a very hot planet, but here inside, it's cool. I'm very pleased to be in here. Where does your electricity come from?"

"We have thousands of windmills – big metal propellers – the wind never stops. Can you understand what I mean?"

"On my planet we have electricity, and we have propellers."

Tickle Tuck paused. "But you don't have space capability. Nevertheless, Ethelinda has brought you here. You are the only one of your kind in space."

"Do you have space capability?"

"We don't need it. We live a life of spirit… we no longer wish to go anywhere.

"You live in the Present?"

"Ah, you have wisdom. Where else can one live? The rest is change and unreal. No, I must explain. We have two brains…"

Mark couldn't help thinking to himself, "Are they both the same size?", but the Leader caught his thought, easily, and said, "…both of the same size. One is for every day. With this brain, *we* are in charge – well, one is never really in charge of anything. *We* are the ones who control our thoughts and worries. The other brain is for Dreaming. With that brain, we have fantastic Dreams, and things happen *to us*. We can't control what happens."

"You dream awake – when you're awake?"

"Yes. But when you're *awake*, you command your thoughts, more or less. So, we aren't really awake, because we have to put up with what happens to us in the Dreams."

"But do you go to sleep at night?"

"There's no real night inside the caves. Outside, our day and night take 41 hours. How long is it on your planet?"

"Twenty-four hours. Do you dream when you sleep?"

"Goodness, no! We'd get no rest! Do you dream?"

"Very much, but when we sleep."

"When you *sleep*! How strange. You must wake up feeling tired?"

"No, we wake up full of energy again. But sometimes we have bad dreams, called nightmares, and they can wake us up in the middle of the night."

"That's extraordinarily interesting. I didn't think anyone else ever Dreamt. Ethelinda doesn't dream — and her robots don't dream. So that's why she brought you to us."

"Why?" echoed Mark, alarmed.

"You can join in our dreams. We join our minds together when we dream, and the one having the best dream — well, we follow that dream, and our own dreams stop, or fit into the main dream. Ethelinda has joined our dreams, but she doesn't really enjoy them, or understand them. But every time she comes here, she tries. That right, Ethelinda, my dearest dear?"

"They are very strange for me," Ethelinda said, "I must confess."

"What is confess?"

"Admit to something that you've done and you don't really want anyone to know."

The Leader said, "You don't need to worry, my dearest Ethelinda, because we understand you are not used to it."

The thought ran through Mark's head on its own. "What do they eat?"

But Zgyedlu Zgooed caught it instantly.

"Inside the cave, we have plants and mushrooms. Naomi, please take Mark and show him. Ethelinda, would you stay and tell us about the rest of space — what the other planets are doing?"

Naomi took Mark's hand, and Ethelinda hissed.

She led Mark to the far end of the cavern, and with other Hunks following them, led him through a winding passageway to another immense cavern.

A wide swimming pool stood in the middle, and all around stood small trees of a yellowish-white wood, with dark brown fruit the size of a big melon. Mark went to one, and. lifted it. It was *very* heavy. He felt the branch, and it was as hard as metal. The plant had no leaves.

"That fruit has a sort of meat inside," Naomi told him. "We have several caverns growing these trees."

"How many people live here?"

"About 500."

"Are there other caves?"

"Lots and lots, but we can't reach them, because of the pterodactyls."

"And when you go out into the sun, do you all go at once?"

"About 50 of us go at once. We take turns."

"Have you always lived in the caves?"

"About two million years ago, the climate changed, and water disappeared from outside. It got very hot, too hot to live out in the open."

The thought hurried across his mind without his realising it: "I wonder how long these people live for."

But Naomi heard him, and said, "We take injections. We have a laboratory, all of glass, where no one is allowed in except ten people. We never really die, I was born about ten years ago, and I'm the youngest here. Before me, no one had been born for some thousands of years."

"Can we have a swim?"

He saw several Hunks in the water.

"It's ordinary water, is it? It won't hurt me?"

"Put your finger in."

He put it in, and nothing happened. He touched the tip of his tongue, and it was ordinary water.

Throwing off his clothes, he dived in, and swam around. Naomi threw off her human clothes, and swam with him. Mark saw a human girl. They splashed around with the other Hunks, and Mark thought of the blistering glare outside.

A Hunk came to the edge of the pool, and called to Naomi.

Naomi said, "Let's get out and put on our clothes. We're invited to a dream."

She didn't take him back the way they came, but through other caverns with thousands of mushrooms growing on shelves cut into the rock.

She offered some to him, but he was frightened they could poison him.

"It's safe," said Naomi. "One of the Council asked Ethelinda, and she said they had tested them in your spaceship for your body. They have been carrying our mushrooms for many years."

Mark was hungry, and he ate. They were delicious and left him satisfied.

They came to a chamber with smooth walls, with Hunks crouched around the walls. Naomi told Mark to sit and close his eyes.

He was suddenly in green fields, and running with several other people. They were humans. They came to a city made of golden glass columns and streets of gold. They walked through it, and Mark gaped at high towers, glassy arches – it was so beautiful he never wanted to leave. But a big man pulled him along, to black cliffs outside, and they climbed up the rocks, then flew till they were thousands of feet in the air, following sloped, tortured rock that was black, grey and red. At the top, they walked across snow, in a freezing wind, on and on. Mark sobbed with the cold, gasping for breath. At the far edge, the rocks dropped straight down, and the others flew out into space. The big man pushed Mark, but he couldn't fly, and he screamed. He thought, "I need a parachute", and the big man pushed one into his hands. He didn't know how many seconds were left as he struggled with straps. He got it on, and pulled the ripcord.

Below, he saw a black, raging sea, and a wooden galleon, with bare masts. The others flew to it, and Mark landed with a heavy bump on the pitching deck. A wave washed him against the bulwarks, and he hung on for his life. The wind drove the ship against the cliffs, where it struck with a crash of breaking timbers. He was in the water, and drowning… drowning… he couldn't breathe!

He found himself inside a cave, with Naomi shaking him. The cave was dry – the sea couldn't get in.

"Get up," begged Naomi. "Get up."

Mark gasped for air, his heart pounding, weeping in terror.

"Where are we?" he whispered.

"Hunky Clunky."

He didn't know whether it was an island or a country.

"Wake up! Wake up!" said Naomi, shaking him.

He didn't know where he was, but he realised with horror that he wasn't on earth.

He stood, swaying, and saw the other Hunks, crouched around the walls, their eyes closed.

Then he remembered everything.

"What a dream!" said Naomi. "Snow, ships, green fields! I wish you would stay with us. We could have dreams we have never imagined. A *sea* of water. *Stormy* water."

"How long will they go on dreaming for?"

"About eight hours, but without you leading them. Some people are going out to sunbathe, so we can go too. I'd like to stay in the dream, but you'll feel better outside."

She led him through caverns and tunnels, and his heart slowed down and returned to normal. His cotton clothes were drenched in sweat, but they dried quickly on his body.

They came to a hall near the entrance, and about four score Hunks were collecting metal rods, each 10 feet tall.

Mark pulled up his sunglasses, and the filter over his nose, and followed them through a narrow crack in the rock out into the desert.

The heat hit him like a blow, rolling over him and making him sway. Through the sunglasses, the light still pounded on his eyes.

They moved away from the mountain side, and sat in a circle, pushing the poles into the ground.

The red poles had a metal box near the bottom, and a thick sheath that went into the earth. The green ones stood alongside, and went bare into the desert floor,

Naomi said, "You see this box? It's an electric condenser, and is charged to 100,000 volts, but it can't discharge because the pole has a sheath that insulates it from the ground. But if a pterodactyl attacks, it hits the two poles at once and makes a bridge between them. The 100,000 volts flow through the monster, electrocuting it, and across to the green pole where it flows down into the ground."

"What's a condenser?"

"You take something like –" and she searched his mind, "like your aluminium foil back on your Earth. You lay it on insulating cloth, and then roll the two up. When you pour electric current into it, it collects there, and builds up a deadly electrical charge."

"So pterodactyls never attack."

"The young ones without experience do sometimes, but when they see the dead ones, they learn."

Mark felt dizzy in the heat. He concentrated on breathing, and wondered how the Hunks could stand it. A hat and long-sleeved cotton clothes shielded but they sat there with their bare thick skin soaking up the light. He looked longingly at the canoe, parked just outside the fence of tall rods, when a huge dark shadow swept over him. He instinctively gripped his laser gun, as the pterodactyl, flying very low, turned and circled them, then slowly glided up the rocky mountain side. The thought came into his mind, without his thinking it, that his gun must carry a condenser too, to give his gun electricity.

Another great shadow swept towards them, but this time he didn't stiffen or worry.

The pterodactyl dived at them with a loud crash. It clutched a rock in its claws, that knocked down four of the tall rods in an explosion of electrical sparks, that killed a Hunk. Another pterodactyl flying right behind grabbed Naomi in its great claws, and as she screamed, lifted her as though she were a feather and carried her up the mountain.

Mark fired at the pterodactyl with the rock and almost cut it in two. As it fell, he switched his aim to the other, and saw he would kill Naomi.

112

He jumped to his feet, screaming with rage and terror, and ran through the gap in the rods to the canoe. He slammed open the door, pulled it closed behind him, jumped into the seat, pushed the buttons to start it and cried to the computer, "Follow that bird! Catch it!"

Hettie Hobo gasped.

"What are you doing?"

"I'll teach you to mix with an earthling! I'll teach you!" he was yelling at the top of his voice.

Hettie Hobo said, "Please be careful! Do you know what you're doing?"

"It's not going to happen again! Everyone thinks they can do as they like with me! Now they're going to see what an earthling is! Computer, how high are we?"

The computer replied in an unexcited voice, "2,200 feet, 2,300... 2,400... 2,500... 2,600... we are closing, we are now 200 feet away... 170 feet and closing. Altitude is 2,800 feet."

The pterodactyl darted into a big cave, about half a mile wide, with a rocky shelf under a big overhang that went in for about 100 feet.

The computer laid the canoe alongside the rock platform, and Mark jumped out. Hettie Hobo closed the door behind him.

Mark pulled his laser gun out of the holster, pushed off the safety, and sprinted across the rock to what looked like a shadowed recess.

He ran into the recess and saw it narrowed, but there was still plenty of light. A pterodactyl danced towards him with a comical jumping step, and Mark blew off its head. Three more came at him in comical, dancing steps, and he cut holes through the bodies.

"Come on!" he shouted. "Come on! Here I am! Come and get me!"

He saw the light disappear from behind him, and he whirled. He fired straight into the body of a diving monster that crashed into the rock.

He ran inside, and saw Naomi in a nest of big sticks of a yellowish-white colour – the plant he had seen before. She had picked up a stick and was fighting a baby pterodactyl, about ten feet long, that lunged at her with a wicked beak.

His laser bit into the small pterodactyl, with bits flying everywhere, and Naomi scrambled out the nest and ran to him.

"Keep behind me," he yelled. He swung his laser this way and that, then saw a crowd of pterodactyls prancing out of the deep darkness at the back of the cave.

He hit the first – and another – and another – and another. The rest retreated, and he fired at the roof, bringing down an avalanche of rock, trapping them inside.

They ran to the canoe and got in.

Naomi said, "I wasn't *really* scared. I could read your thoughts and I knew you were coming. Well, I was a little bit scared – well, pretty scared…"

In the far distance, he saw pterodactyls flying in and out of the mountainside.

"Computer, fly over to those birds."

When they got close, he shot two from the open window of the canoe. The canoe drifted up to the edge of the cave and he fired at the roof, bringing down a landslide of rocks.

Then his gun went dead. He looked at it in dismay.

"Give it to me," said Hettie Hobo. She plugged it in. "Computer, please recharge this."

Hettie Hobo said, "You should have recharged while you were flying to this second cave. Let's go back, because everyone will want to know that Naomi is safe."

Mark was trembling all over, and then began hiccupping, and couldn't stop for two or three minutes.

He saw pterodactyls swaggering out of another cave on the far side of where they had been sitting in the sun.

"Computer!" he cried, "Over to that cave!"

"Do you think you really…?" Clackety Hobo said.

The computer said, "The gun is recharged." Hettie Hobo unplugged it and handed it to him.

The canoe eased up to the edge of the cave and Mark jumped off.

Six pterodactyls came high-stepping out, and he shot them. Then he shot deep into the cave, at the roof, which collapsed.

A pterodactyl came down in a slashing dive and a claw caught Mark across the face, and ripped across his neck and chest. He fired, and it rolled over in the air, and fell.

Mark tottered back to the canoe, blood coursing down his face and front, fell into his seat, and collapsed.

Hettie Hobo said, "Computer, close the door, and go back to Naomi's cave."

Mark didn't remember much. Naomi had her arms around him and didn't stop talking, but he couldn't understand properly what she was saying.

He passed out.

When he came to, he was in the spaceship. A robot he had never seen was fussing.

Ethelinda said, "This robot is called Doc, and he has sewn you up. You're all right, but you're going to have a big red mark for some weeks. We're taking you back home."

"I don't want to go," he said weakly.

"You have to go back to school, and so do I. We'll come and get you when your summer holidays start."

She put her arms around him, and gave him a soppy kiss.

"At least I know that when I'm with you I'm going to be safe. Or did you do that only because it was Naomi? What if it had been me?"

"I would have tried to pull the whole mountain down," he joked, but he didn't feel like joking.

Apparently it was a good joke, because Ethelinda was all over him with hugs and kisses, and Doc pulled her off.

"He's got to rest, and I want him to go back to sleep."

* * *

He woke up at 5 am, and struggled to his feet. He felt all right, but weak and hungry. The weal on his face, neck and chest itched, and in the bathroom mirror, he saw an angry red but perfectly healed skin.

When he tottered out into the hall, they were all over him.

Ethelinda said, "Did Doc tell you to get up?"

"No," said Mark, unsure of himself.

Doc rolled in, and said in his deep voice, "I want him to get up. He needs food, and some movement of his limbs and body to encourage the circulation of his blood."

Ethelinda said, "Vboungh Vbaushtda, you have done a fantastic job. Mark, how long does it take you on earth to heal a deep cut?"

"It takes weeks." Mark struggled to get his tongue around Vboungh Vbaushtda. "Bone Buster, I thank you. The skin is dead smooth."

Bone Buster said, "I'm sorry about the redness. It will go. There's always the problem of how you earthlings are made."

"Doc, you can be proud," said Hettie Hobo.

"I thank you, Hettie Hobo," said Vboungh Vbaushtda, and rolled out of the room.

Scrumptious Mumkish rolled in and set the table.

She gave Mark a breakfast of two fried eggs with bacon and sausages, four slices of toast with peach jam, and two glasses of milk with cocoa.

Mark devoured it all, and felt *much* better. He sat in a reclining chair that Clackety Hobo had built for him, and said, "Clackety Clack, we had to have given laser guns to the Hunks and shown them how to make them."

"You were unconscious and had to be carried straight up the ship, to Bone Buster. But that is a clever, well-thought-out idea which I'll implement as soon as we go back."

"What is implement?"

"Put into practice – to do something."

"I think that should be impulmanted as soon as possible."

"*Implemented*," said Ethelinda.

"If we give them some, they can't make new ones – they don't know about metals and all that stuff."

Clackety Hobo said, "Deep inside their caves, they mine many metals. That's how they built their propeller windmills. Tunnels to one side, near the entrance, lead to caves with cracks in the roof that lead outside. They work their electric foundries there, and the gases escape through the cracks."

Mark took that in, contented after his big breakfast, and waiting for strength to come back to him.

He said, "Ethelinda, that spooky black spaceship. They must have been hiding behind secret doors all the time."

"Half of the spaceship – much more than half – was taken up with their engines. What we saw of the rest was nothing. If we had gone on exploring, we would have come to a door that wouldn't open. They might have been in the part with their hydroponics. On some planets, crews spend their time among the hydroponics because of the greenery. It's like enjoying a park with all its plants. We didn't see any hydroponics, and they take up a lot of space."

"Do you have hydroponics on board here?"

"Acres and acres. Of course! But we Choo Chooans don't worry much about greenery and scenery."

"Is that why your planet is so dark and rocky, without any air?"

"We had to look for a planet that no one else was living on, and that had the same gravity well as our own. This one was the closest. We could have gone further, and found a planet with a sun and greenery, but what for? We live and work inside our buildings. All the inside walls never stop changing colour – *all* the colours. We need to see changing colours all the time."

Mark remembered the flowing, swirling, mixed-up colours on the walls of the building he was in at Choo Choo.

"You don't have those colours on the spaceship."

"I'm on holiday. This is an adventure. I want to make everything strange. Look!"

She pressed a switch, and walls sprang alive with writhing purples and greens, orange and golds, browns and reds and pinks. She switched them off.

"That makes it just like home. Here, on the ship, we could have built your bedroom, bathroom, dining-room just like your home in Milton Mudwallop. Would you like that?"

"Oh, no!" he cried.

The ship shuddered and shook, and Mark felt queasy to his stomach. They were coming out from hyperspace.

He activated the screen, and far below saw his own planet. With its blue and white, there was no mistake about it. They were bringing him back.

Hettie Hobo said, "Get your belt of diamonds and put them on."

She handed him a small suitcase.

"This is full of small leather pouches that tie at the neck. You'll need to put the diamonds in them when you go to the jewellers' shops."

"Hettie Hobo, Clackety Clack, I'm going to miss you. Honestly, I'm going to miss you so much! And Dumple Doo – I'm going to be weeks without talking to you."

All the robots began talking at once. "What about us? We're going to miss *you*! We'll be thinking and talking about you all the time!"

Mark was crying when he got into the canoe.

"And what about my mum? When I walk through the door all of a sudden –"

"She's expecting you. We told her quarter-past-seven. "

They raced down to the Earth's atmosphere, and dived through it.

"When the space shuttle and space-craft enter the atmosphere to return, they get white-hot. The canoe doesn't."

"We're safe inside a force field."

"Why don't they use a force field on Earth for their re-entries?"

"You've got to be clever to do that. But we'll teach you how to do it next summer."

"Then maybe I can teach them?"

"They'd have to be awfully clever to listen to you. Ten years old! They won't listen to you. What makes earthlings different to the rest of space is that they think they know everything when they really don't know anything."

The canoe hovered over the back garden of his house.

"You're sure the neighbors can't see anything?"

"They all have a mind block on them."

They descended a long flight of stairs to the lawn. The earth was wet, and everything smelt funny – the smells of grass, cooking, factory smoke, car exhausts. It made him cough.

He went through the back door with Ethelinda. His mother was sitting at the kitchen table. She saw him, not believing her eyes, then scrambled to her feet and flew at him, smothering him in a tight hug. She was laughing and crying and he couldn't understand a single word.

She took a deep breath, put her hands on his shoulders and stepped back.

"You're back home. Goodness me. The police are all out searching the moors. The neighbours have been in. Where have you been, and what happened to your face?"

"I've been in deep space."

"Ethelinda, dear. I recognise you. Was all that wardrobe mirror real? Or have I gone crazy?"

"It was real, Mrs. Clough."

"And his face? Did some alien attack him?" her voice caught.

"A monster bird, like a dinosaur bird, grabbed a girl in its claws, and Mark killed it."

"Oh, my God!" she whispered. "You could be dead."

Ethelinda said, "It's the bird that's dead, not Mark. You can be very proud of him. They are talking about him over hundreds of light years away and more. On planet after planet, he's welcome to return, and has been given honors."

"Mark? Don't talk about him like that. He'll get a swelled head, and then nobody will be able to do anything with him. He'll be fit for nothing if you prattle on like that."

"Yes, ma'm," said Ethelinda

"Are you staying, or going back – wherever? Up into the sky, I suppose. Is all of this really true?"

"Yes, ma'm. Please come outside a moment."

Ethelinda held open the back door and Jane stepped out into the garden. She gasped when she saw the huge canoe hovering overhead, the shiny hull, the windows and massive exhaust nozzles.

"Oh, Mark," she cried, frightened. "You were on that!"

"I know how to fly it, mum," he told her, and she clutched the door post.

Then she exclaimed, "What will the neighbours say?"

"They can't see it," said Ethelinda. "They have a mental block."

They went back inside, and Mark took off his belt of diamonds.

"I've brought you a present, mum," and he emptied the pouches on the table.

"But," stuttered his mother. "That's worth a fortune. Where can we sell them? We'll have to explain how we got them! And think of the taxes!"

She ran her fingers through the gems.

Ethelinda said, "We'll take you down to London now on our ship, and land in Hyde Park –"

"In front of everybody! Do you know what will happen?"

"Nobody will see us. Mental blocks. We'll go to the best London jewellers and sell them."

"The jewellers will want know who I am and where I got them —"

"Mental blocks," smiled Ethelinda sweetly.

"And the taxes!" groaned Jane.

"We'll take the money straight to the Channel Islands and put it in a Bank there."

"But that's breaking the law! I won't break the law."

"What law?" peered Ethelinda. "Laws made by your politicians and leaders. If you knew what rude things we say about your leaders on other planets — better left unsaid."

"I have to pay taxes on all my earnings," said Jane.

"But you didn't get these in England."

"I have to pay taxes on anything I earn anywhere —"

"You didn't earn these, Mrs. Clough. They're a gift."

"I have to pay taxes on gifts too."

"What robbers! But," said Ethelinda cunningly, "these don't come from earth. Are there any laws about earnings in space?"

Jane said thoughtfully, "If you're getting a salary flying on an earth spaceship, you pay taxes. But this spaceship doesn't belong to the earth. No, I don't suppose there's any law — yet — covering this case."

"Good," said Ethelinda, pleased. "Let's get in our ship."

"I'm frightened," said his mum. "I've never been in one of these. Mark isn't going to drive, is he?"

Mark scowled.

"Of course he isn't," said Ethelinda. "Let's switch out the lights. Do you have some sort of identification for the Bank in the Channel Islands?"

"My driving license. Some bills I've received for the gas and electricity and for the phone."

She bustled around, collecting everything and putting it all in her handbag.

Mark filled the leather bags with diamonds, and tied the necks with careful knots.

His mum climbed up the stairs, her legs shaking, and recoiled when Clackety Hobo spoke to her in English. She collected herself and said, "I saw you in the mirror."

Clackety Hobo said, "Kindly sit here, and fasten your seat belt," and she replied, "Certainly, my good man."

They flew low and fast over the English countryside, swept in over London, and settled in Hyde Park. People walked right alongside, without seeing them.

119

Ethelinda searched the surrounding districts with her mind, and said, "The jewellers aren't open yet," so they walked around the London streets, and went into a tea shop, and had tea with cakes.

Jane worried, "Those jewellers are going to give us terrible prices," but Ethelinda smiled and promised, "Their hearts will fill with generosity."

They went from one jeweller's to another, while Mark filled the suitcase with banknotes. When they sold the last bags, they walked back to the canoe, which rose swiftly, and flew to the Channel Islands.

Mark counted the money and it came to £850,000.

"That's a lot of money!" exclaimed his mother.

Ethelinda said, "Instead of paying taxes, you can pay for private health insurance and not go to the government hospitals and doctors. You can have your own private room, and private doctors. You'll save the government money, and get special treatment."

"Is that fair?" she worried.

"Is what's yours, yours or theirs?" demanded Ethelinda. "Was it fair for Mark to go tens of light years to get them?"

His mother was struck dumb.

In Jersey, they landed at a park, and walked into a bank. Jane asked to open an account in her name and that of her son, and showed her driving license and bills. The clerk was about to ask for personal references from someone else, but couldn't remember what he had to say. He wrote down that his mother-in-law recommended them.

Mark unloaded armfuls of banknotes, which the clerk counted – Mark's mother saw – without surprise, gave them their account number and receipts, and bade them a good day.

They went back to the canoe, and flew to Milton Mudwallop.

Ethelinda said, "You must never take money from this bank account from inside England. Always go to the Channel Islands, bring back the money in your purse, and keep it at home while you are spending it. Never put it into your bank account in Milton Mudwallop, because if the taxman sees it…!"

"I understand," said Jane bravely.

She was carrying £3,000 in her handbag.

"It's terrible enough as it is, having to live on earth," said Ethelinda.

Jane was indignant. "There's nowhere better anywhere than England!"

"I bet that's what the Yanks say in America," said Mark.

"Stop quarrelling," commanded Hettie Hobo.

They landed in the back garden at Milton Mudwallop, Mark weeping unashamedly.

Ethelinda said sternly, "Now you have to talk to the police. Remember, you don't remember anything."

Ethelinda broke into sobs, pushed Mark away, and said, "Take this watch. It's better not to wear it but keep it at home. When you need to send a message, press this button, and a robot ship will land in your garden. The ship's about three feet across, and like a ball. You just talk to it. Bye!"

She rushed up the steps, the hatch closed, and the canoe rose swiftly out of sight.

His mum sighed, and said, "I'm going to phone the police. You don't remember anything, right? You just walked in here?"

Mark nodded dumbly, went up to his room, put away the watch, and after going to the bathroom, came downstairs and sat at the kitchen table.

A police car pulled up outside, and two policemen came in.

"This is him?" one asked his mother.

His mother nodded.

"So where've you been?" he asked Mark.

"I don't know. I found myself in the street outside, and came into the house."

"What happened to your face?"

"I don't know."

"I think we should all go to the hospital and let a doctor have a look at him."

* * *

At the hospital, the doctor said, "You've been missing for over a week, and this happened to your face and chest in that time. It's closed completely. It looks as though it happened five or six weeks ago, so I don't understand. You don't remember anything?"

"That's right."

"He shows no signs of malnourishment or hypothermia."

Mark asked, "What is malnourishment and hypothermia?"

"Not getting enough to eat, and being very cold because of being exposed in the open air," said his mum, while the doctor scowled at being interrupted.

"I'll write a report now, and give it to you," the doctor said to the policeman. "He has all his faculties."

"What are faculties?"

"You can think and see and hear, and so on," said his mum.

The doctor said, "He may have lost his memory, but he's pretty cheeky. All those questions."

"Bone Buster," muttered Mark.

"What was that?" asked the policeman, but Mark fell into silence.

The policeman asked, "Can he go to school?"

"Perfectly fit, perfectly fit," said the doctor.

"Ma'm, if you wish, I'll drive you home, and then ring the school. How does he travel to school?"

"On his bike."

"That might be best, then, because he'll need his bike to get back home again."

The policeman said, to the doctor, "I'll come back for a copy of your report. Now I'll take them home."

The doctor looked nervous and annoyed. He squinted at Mark, and said abruptly, "Do that. I don't understand this, but all I can do is write the report."

* * *

After ringing the school, Mark got on his bike, and with his cut lunch and a pound note in his pocket, rode to school.

He got there at a quarter-to-one.

After putting away his bike, he went to the headmaster's study.

The headmaster studied him, and said, "Sit down."

He puffed on his pipe.

"What happened to your face?"

"I don't remember anything."

"The doctor says it's all right, mm. Does this have anything to do with that attack the boys made on you?"

"No, sir."

"You've been away more than a week. You don't remember a thing? You had to stay somewhere."

"Yes, sir."

"You haven't gone hungry, I see. Very funny business. You just vanished, leaving your bike at home."

"Yes, sir."

"It's lunch time. I see you have your lunch with you. You can go to the canteen."

As he walked into the canteen, a silence fell. He bumped into the Club and the Hatchet, who turned around and ran in terror to the other end of the room.

Everyone watched this in amazement. Mark saw Naomi at the far end of the room start up in astonishment when she saw him.

Six boys got up and surrounded him.

122

"Where've you been? What's that line painted on your face? You suddenly got so tough you're scaring the Club and Hatchet. What've you got in your lunch today? Hand it over."

One boy shoved him and he fell back against another, who pushed him forward.

Mark tossed his lunch on to a table. He was a blur of arms and legs.

He hit the boy in front in the face, knocking over a table. He kicked the next boy in the knee, who doubled up. As he whirled, he hit the next boy on the nose, which sprayed blood everywhere.

With another kick in the stomach, the next boy doubled up, and he grabbed the next boy by an elbow and shoulder and threw him over a table to crash into the next table.

He went into a crouch as he faced the last boy, and as he advanced, the boy fled.

Everyone stood well away.

Naomi reached, him, embraced him and wept.

"We didn't know whether you were dead," she cried.

"I'm all right," he said. "I just lost my memory. I've got a pound. Can I buy you something?"

"Oh, Mark," she said. "Can I have an orange drink?"

A teacher pushed through the door, and looked at the shambles.

"So you lost your memory?" he said. "They couldn't wait to pick on you. You seem to have sorted it out. Remarkable loss of memory, remarkable."

Mark and Naomi sat at a table, while she asked him lots of questions he couldn't answer.

* * *

The first afternoon class was mathematics.

The teacher said, "As Clough has been absent some days, today we'll do revision."

First he gave them multiplication:

a) 5×7	c) 3×8	e) 9×6	g) 3×8
b) 6×4	d) 7×4	f) 1×5	h) 6×6

Mark felt weary. He got 35, 24, 24, 29, 54, 5, 24 and 36. He got 7×4 wrong.

Then he had to find the different ways to get 36.

He thought, "2×18, 3×12, 6×6" and gave those answers. Half the class had missed 4×9, and Mark with them.

The teacher asked, "How can you measure distance?"

A girl said, "Using your feet?"

A boy said, "Measuring your steps."

Another boy said, "Using a tape measure."

A girl said, "Using grams and kilos, to buy potatoes and stuff like that."

The teacher asked, "And what about you, Clough?"

Mark said, "You can use light years," and the class tittered.

He said, "But it all depends. You go at one quarter the speed of light, you can measure the time it will take you to get to a star system 50 light years away. But on earth your measurement will be 200 years, but on your starship, only a few years will pass."

The teacher stared at him, and the class roared with laughter.

One boy shouted, "He's lost more than his memory," and Mark blushed.

Mark said doggedly, "Your measurements always depend, like. You're sitting in a car when it's stopped, and your rest mass is say seven stone – or, say, 50 kilos. When the car does 60 miles an hour, your mass goes up to a couple of tons. You sometimes have to measure two things at once – like rest mass multiplied by speed."

The class roared again. One girl cried, "Mark weighs two tons."

Some boys chanted, "Two-ton Mark, two-ton Mark."

"Silence!" said the teacher. He looked at Mark. "Some amnesia," he said.

Mark said, "When you go at a quarter the speed of light, your mass gets so colossal everything slows down, and that's why 200 years pass on earth, but only a few years on your ship."

The teacher asked, "And what would be the mass of a ship?"

Mark said, "I suppose more than an asteroid or a smaller planet weighs? That's why you live so slow. But you can't go much faster than a quarter the speed of light, because you'd be dragging along a fuel tank about the size of… an asteroid, or the size of the moon? I don't know."

"So you think more slowly when a car goes at 60 miles an hour?" smiled the teacher.

"Sixty miles an hour is nothing," grinned Mark. "I'm talking about 75,000 kilometres a second."

"Indeed, indeed," said the teacher. "What amnesia does," he said thoughtfully.

Then he said, "Next lesson. I have £16 and I want to buy some presents. Here are the costs of some of the things I like."

1	£1
2	£1.60
3	£2
4	£3
5	£6
6	£6.40
7	£7.60
8	£9.60
9	£12.50
10	£16

"Now, what combinations of presents can I buy so that I spend all my £16 and have nothing left over?"

Mark wrote down, "Presents n°s 10, or n°s 6 and 8, or n°s 3 and 6 and 7."

Next, the teacher asked them to draw a right angle, an obtuse angle and an acute angle.

Then he told them to draw an equilateral triangle, an isosceles triangle and an acute angled triangle.

He asked them, "Where can we find triangles in the world around us?"

Mark said at last, "Milton Mudwallop forms a triangle with the villages of Murky Hoot and Slurpy Muckle."

"Very good. What else?"

A boy said, "Three flies on a ceiling can form a triangle," and the class laughed.

Mark said, "Three planets or three stars can form a triangle, although they're not on the same plane."

A boy shouted, "You mean they're not on the same Boeing or the same Airbus?" and the class laughed.

"Planets in the Solar System are practically on the same plane," he persisted.

The class laughed at him, and the teacher said, "Explain to the class what you mean by plane."

"Those three posters on the wall are on the same plane and form a triangle, because the wall is flat. On my desk, these two books and my ball point are on the same plane because the desk is flat."

The teacher looked at him queerly, then looked at the class, "Is that quite clear?"

The children chorused, "Yes."

Mark got through the rest of the class as best he could.

That evening, at home, he went out into the garden and looked up at the sky. Clouds blew away and he could see some stars.

Where were *his* planets? They would be thinking of him and he was thinking of them. But where did they lie? They might be opposite the other side of the world, somewhere under his feet.

He went back inside and sat at the table, waiting for his mum to finish cooking the meal.

Tomorrow morning, he'd have to get up again and go back to school. Another day of school.

But nobody would bully him any more.

He sighed, put his elbows on the table and rested his chin in his hands.

BOOK TWO

Mark felt down in the dumps as he wheeled his bike out of the rack at school, and walked it out of the Milton Mudwallop school yard. At least, he didn't have to worry his head about bullies. Every since he had knocked six kids into a heap with his martial arts, no one raised a finger. They were a bit scared of him, and no one talked to him in all these weeks since Ethelinda had brought him back to Earth from space.

Naomi hurried alongside him, and rode with him for half a mile before he had to turn off and leave her.

"What are you thinking about?" she asked him, uneasy.

Mark didn't think it sissy any more to spend all his free time at school with Naomi and her friends… after travelling more than 50 light years in deep space with Ethelinda and visiting incredibly distant planets with her. Of course, girls were inquisitive, and always trying to find out what was going on in your head. If Naomi even guessed about the space ship…

"I'm tired," he said. "I'm really fed up with school."

"What would you really like to do?"

Naomi was nine, while Ethelinda, back at school on her planet, Xiucheu – Choo Choo (because Ethelinda was a Choo Chooean) – Ethelinda was eleven.

What would he really like to do! He couldn't tell Naomi that! Climb up 500 miles from the surface of the Earth and cross over into hyperspace…

"Go for a ride on the moor, I s'pose," he muttered.

"Oh, how I wish I could come with you," Naomi almost wept. "I live so far away. Do you suppose one night your mum would let me stay the night at your place?" she said timidly.

Now Mark felt really badly at that. He cast around in his mind for an excuse, and feeling ashamed of himself, said, "You don't know what Mum's like." But he still felt really badly.

"I see," said Naomi, miserably.

The truth was Mum had changed out of sight, since he came back from space with all those diamonds from the planet Bvunmbvdva. The Poompbahists were about the best friends he had, giving him all those diamonds to make Mum happy. Now Mum had almost £850,000, hidden in a bank on the Channel Islands away from the taxman, she was much happier than before. She finally decided *not* to buy a car, but she bought a lot of new dresses, and went out more at night. She got another job where she worked only in the afternoon. That let her go shopping and look after the house in the morning.

But the thing was, she loved Mark more now than she used to. She was always telling him how proud she was of him and hugging him, and that made Mark feel really loved. She never asked him about deep space, and twice when he talked about it, she hushed him up. He couldn't talk to *anyone* about what had happened, and everyone would think he was crazy if he tried.

Of course, Mum had seen the huge canoe hovering over the house, with its immense, blackened nozzles. She had met Ethelinda and the robots, seen those distant planets in views beamed across space and picked up by the silver box under her wardrobe that put the pictures on her wardrobe mirror.

What long weeks they had been. And now, in a week, school ended, and they would come from Choo Choo for him.

The Choo Chooeans had put a satellite in space, above his house, and sometimes he felt like calling it down and talking to it. It was awful being different. Of all the billions of people on Earth, he was the only one who could go up into space and roam there, thanks to Ethelinda – it was probably just as well no one else *did* know *that*.

Naomi was looking miserable. Mark said, "I like that dress you're wearing. It makes you look really pretty."

Her face shone, and she said, pretending to be cross, "Silly, I've worn this one lots of times!"

He said, "Today, you make it look different. Every day, you get prettier and prettier."

That was pretty soppy, but after all, he had fought pterodactyls to the death on the planet Gunkhae Khlwunkhae, so who was going to call him a sissy?

Naomi gave him a marvellous smile.

130

"Sometimes you can be so nice!" she exclaimed. "But other times you're thinking so much and you seem so far away."

Mark grinned at her. "I suppose I must be thinking of you," and wondered how she would take that.

She didn't think it was silly at all.

She went all red, and said, "Mark Clough, I like you more than anybody else in the world." She stopped, a bit shocked at herself, and looked at him very hard.

"And after my Mum, I like you better than anyone else on this whole planet."

Naomi giggled. "On this whole planet – what a thing to say! I'm going to remember that."

Mark thought, now she'll tell her other girl friends. But Mark was always in their company, and he liked them. Other kids sniggered – but never to his face – but what did he care, after being in deep space. He was going back to deep space and deep space was where he belonged, because deep space didn't scare *him*. He was the only kid in the school who kept company just with girls – and he didn't care.

* * *

He said goodbye to Naomi, and the rain came down. He got home in a downpour, and wheeled his bike into the back garden.

His heart leapt up, leading him giddy. A shiny silver ball about two feet across sat on the grass, and a musical voice came out. "Hello, Mark."

Mark gasped, and couldn't speak. Then his eyes darted this way and that. Had the neighbours seen anything... no! Not in this rain.

"Have you come to tell me it's time? School hasn't finished."

"Put your bike in the shed, and let us proceed into your house."

'Proceed', thought Mark, wheeling his bike into the shed. Had he heard that word?

He closed the shed, dug out the house key from its secret place in his belt, opened the kitchen door and ducked inside, out of the rain. The silver sphere floated in after him.

"It is not yet time for you to come to Choo Choo," said the silver ball. "But I have an important message. You are to find some books. When you have bought them, use your watch to summon me, and I will take the books."

"'Summon' you?" worried Mark.

"Call me for me to come," supplied the sphere. "The books are on Typology."

Mark looked at him, his jaw slack.

131

The sphere explained, "On Earth, you have a theory called evolution. It says that you and all the animals evolved from primitive slime, billions of years ago."

"Slime?" repeated Mark.

"Slime," said the sphere firmly. "Now, many wise men of Choo Choo have argued that this is true. Others say the opposite, that a great intelligence built life. But we don't live on the planet where we first appeared, billions of years ago."

Mark said, "I know. Your planet was destroyed, and you found Choo Choo where nothing lived, so you went there."

"Exactly," said the satellite. "So we can't study rocks that are billions of years old and look at the fossils. But on Earth, you can, and you are looking at fossils from your past."

Mark said, "I don't understand *fossils*."

The robot said, "If something dies, and is buried in mud or clay, over a very long time, minerals in water fill it up with minerals, and it turns into stone. You dig out the stone and you can see it, exactly as it was –"

"I understand," interrupted Mark. "And what is *typology*?"

The robot said, "You take the pig family – you get pigs, and boars and wart hogs, elephants, mastodons. Then you take the cat family – you get cats, and tigers and lions, panthers, leopards, cheetahs. So there has been evolution with the cat and the pig families. Cats have produced sabre-tooth tigers and pigs have produced elephants –"

"What is 'evolution'?"

"Over millions and millions of years, animals change, from a common ancestor. But typology says that there is no common ancestor for a pig and a cat. That searching all over the rocks of this planet, you have found there are millions of fossils, but no one has ever found a common ancestor for a horse and a rat, for a pig and a cat, for a monkey and whale, or for a bird and a kangaroo."

"And Choo Choo wants books from *Earth*!" cried Mark.

"On Xiucheu, they are not living on the planet where they first arose. You Earthlings are. The great Scientific Council wants to meet to argue about this question. Before it could not, because we could not get books from Earth. Now we have you, Mark Clough."

* * *

Mark's Mum got home soon after the silver ball rose swiftly into the air and disappeared, and Mark told her.

"Oh, dear, oh dear!" she said. "You will have to ask your teachers, but we can't do anything to make them suspicious…!"

She walked up and down the kitchen, thinking, then sat at the kitchen table. "*The Great Scientific Council*. Damn them. Tell your teachers you want the books for me, and I want them for some friends."

"What does it matter?" complained Mark.

"Saying we have come up out of slime, I think they've got an awful cheek!" cried his mother. She looked down at herself and ran her hands over her dress. "*They* might have started off as slime, but some amazing intelligence made *me*, and just let anyone ask me!"

"Yes, mummy," said Mark, obediently.

"You ask your teachers, tomorrow. Thank goodness someone's got some sense, even if they do have to live on Choo Choo."

* * *

The Science Master peered suspiciously at Mark. "You want a list of works on Typology?" he asked, not believing his ears. "This has been a most remarkable amnesia you have suffered. You return to school with a tremendous wound, a mastery of the martial arts, you have upset the arithmetic teacher with talk of relativistic phenomena, and you have all the other teachers gossiping."

"Please, sir," said Mark. "What is relativistic and what is phenomena?"

"'Relativistic' means going at the speed of light, or close to it – a phenomena in which you appear to have a surprising and unhealthy interest, and 'phenomena' means happenings, something that has happened."

Mark felt *most* confused, but he straightened his shoulders manfully.

"Yes," he stuttered. "Yes, sir."

"Now we have you asking about Typology? What is your interest, if one may enquire."

"My mum," muttered Mark. "Friends of hers."

"A-ah! Friends here in Milton Mudwallop."

"They live a bit far away."

"A bit far away… mm. And, do you yourself, pray, have any views on Creationism?"

Mark looked at him stunned. "On what?" he blurted.

"'Creationism!' my boy, 'creationism'. That God created us, that we did not evolve out of mud and slime!"

Mark struggled desperately. "'Evolve' means to grow and change over millions of years."

"Indeed it does," snapped the Science Master. "Charles Darwin gave us that theory more than a century ago."

"A century?"

"One hundred years, young Clough. One hundred years!" said the Science Master, very sharply.

"Of course," said Mark. "Like in cricket."

"If the British Press or Television gets the slightest whiff that we've got a pupil talking about creationism they'll be down on us like a ton of bricks, and most of we teachers will probably lose our jobs."

Mark stared at him in amazement.

"Don't look at me like that," expostulated the Master. "*Creationism* is considered to be something like the superstition of primitive native tribes in darkest Africa."

"That God created us? What does it matter?"

"What does it matter?" roared the master. "Look at yourself. At your body. Don't you think it's complicated? Where did it come from?"

"It's just there, please, sir," said Mark.

"Boy, you are a fool and an ass. Do you think it grew over millions of years out of mud and slush and clay?"

"Please, sir, the Bible said that God made us out of clay."

"But God *made* us! But if you say that, our school will be closed down."

"What does it matter?" said Mark, almost tearful. "What does that man, Damwom, matter?"

"Darwin! Darwin! Last century, everyone believed that the earth was about 5,000 years old. Darwin said it was thousands of millions of years old, and that caused such an upset as you can't imagine. Then he said that thousands of millions of years ago, life came forth from muddy muck, and then got more and more complicated. He said that the fossils showed it grew step by step. And that today is the sacred scripture of science. Because science is a Mafia, you see."

"Please, what is a Mafia?"

"It's the biggest criminal group in America and in Russia. You know we have bullies at school."

Mark's mouth hardened. He nodded.

"So, we've got bullies in science. The top scientists, they run the show. If young scientists contradict them, then they don't get jobs, and they don't get printed in the science magazines, which the big bullies control also. So Charles Darwin is *right*, and typology is *wrong*, and creationism is *wrong*. too. Because they say so. Scientists at the top tell us what is *true*."

"So typology is creationism?"

"Heavens, no! But the problem is that ever since Darwin, everyone has been digging up fossils. They *don't* make a continuous chain, as Darwin said they should. You know how a chain is made up of links, or a necklace made of beads. So, you've got all these links or beads, if you like, with all the fossils in the world, but there are no fossils joining them up. Millions of years ago, you got the first horse, about the size of a dog. The horse got bigger and bigger, as evolution tells us, till we get the horse of today – so there we *can* see evolution working. But that first little horse of millions of years ago just popped out of nowhere. There're no fossils to join it up with, say, a dog, or anything else. You've got dogs – they've evolved into wolves, coyotes, hyenas and a thousand different races you see today – but the first dog just popped out of nowhere. There aren't any fossils joining it to something that came before. So Darwin's wrong – but you can't say that, or you lose your job.

"What I want to know is why ten-year-old Master Clough is venturing into such a dangerous place."

"Please, sir, it's friends of my mother."

"Harrumph!"

The Science faster pulled out a sheet of paper, and wrote down the names of three books. He told Mark which bookshop to go to order them, and to tell his mother they should arrive within a week.

* * *

After school, Mark rode his bike to the bookshop, and ordered the books. At the shop, they asked for his mother to phone in first.

Mark rode home confused and resentful. On Choo Choo. they had no right to ask him for something like this. He was just a boy, and kids didn't have to *think*. Perhaps it was better in Milton Mudwallop, going on the moors on his bike. In space, they were always making you think. At school too, and kids weren't supposed to have to think. Kids were no good at thinking. Kids weren't supposed to know anything. On Choo Choo, they told him that as soon as school ended and summer holidays began they'd send a ship to pick him up and take him the 40 light years across to Choo Choo, where they'd teach more stuff. But Mark didn't want to go to school on Choo Choo, not in his summer holidays. He *did* want to get back into space, but he was counting on getting out of going to school on the other planet.

But suppose he couldn't get out of it?

Suppose he *did* end up in school, with Ethelinda?

He'd convince Ethelinda to grab some old cargo ship, whip off into hyperspace, and go and visit other planets and have fun...

135

A week later, mum brought home the books from the bookshop. Mark got out the special watch which Ethelinda had given him, and pressed the button.

That evening, as they were eating, they heard tapping on the glass of the kitchen door, and outside in the darkness Mark saw a dark sphere, about four feet across – bigger than the other one. Mark opened the door, and worried about his mum getting upset, but she didn't turn a hair.

"You've come for the books?" she asked the big ball, politely.

"Thank you, madam," said a musical voice.

Jane Clough went into another room, and came back with the three volumes. A panel opened in the side of the robot, an arm stretched out, and took the books.

"Thank you most kindly, madam," said the musical voice. "I'll just be on my way to deliver these. I wish you a most pleasant meal."

"To think of all those millions of millions of miles," said his mother, wonderingly.

"Nothing to worry about, madam," said the satellite, reassuringly. "At hyper relativistic speeds you get in hyperspace, it's all looked after. Good evening."

The dark sphere floated away from the door, and ascended swiftly.

On the night before his school holidays, Mark had a long talk with his mother, and told her how much he loved her, and how much he would miss her. She didn't want to come with him, but had decided to go to the Caribbean on a cruise ship.

The silver robot had come 24 hours earlier, to tell them that the canoe would be over their house at 8:30 pm.

Mark had packed a small bag, and now they sat in the kitchen, holding hands. Mark got up and gave his mum a big squeeze, then sat down, and then got up and gave her another squeeze, with a lot of kisses.

At 8:28 pm, they heard the tapping on the glass, and they opened the door. Ethelinda came in, laughing and crying and embraced Mark so hard he couldn't breathe. Then Ethelinda embraced his mother, and kissed her, and made his mother cry. Ethelinda cried too, and the two women had a good cry, while Clackety Hobo and Hettie Hobo, the two square robots on wheels looked at them.

Hettie Hobo said wistfully, "Have you missed me?" and Mark cried, "I thought of you all the time! It's been awful. Clackety Clack! I'm so happy to see you!"

Clackety Hobo said, "I've missed you, because no one calls me Clackety Clack except you. Oh, what a happy moment this is! Now we are all together again."

Jane, Mark's mother, said loudly, sniffing, "Thank you, Ethelinda, but no! I can't come with you – I'm too old. I'm used to living on earth. I don't want to go off-world at my age! It's lovely to see you all, but I've arranged my holidays." She sniffed and wept some more. "Ethelinda, I'll never be able to thank you for looking after Mark like this."

The eleven-year-old 'girl' – because in human eyes she appeared as a human girl in a dress – said, "I have to thank you for letting him come, because I've never been so happy in my life since I met Mark."

She stepped back, smiled at Jane, and said, "The Great Council of Science of the planet Xiucheu is awfully pleased at the books you have sent. To express its thanks, it wishes you to accept this gift," and she gave Jane a small silver sphere, about six-inches across. Any time you have a problem with your computers, or you need new solutions to a problem, ask it."

She placed it in Jane's hands. The sphere spoke in a very sweet voice. "Jane Clough, I wish you a very good evening."

Jane was very flustered. "Good evening. What can I call you?"

"As I am silver to look at, would 'Silver' be a name?"

"Not really, " said Jane. "'Silvia'. Would you like 'Silvia'?"

"I would love you to call me *Silvia*," said the little, very clever robot.

137

Inside the canoe, Mark saw his mother standing in the lighted doorway, as the huge craft gently floated upward. Then it drifted forward, and the roof of his house cut her off, and they rose more quickly.

* * *

Higher up, he saw the lights of Milton Mudwallop getting smaller, then saw lights of other villages and towns scattered across England into the distance.

The on-board computer announced, "We have company. Two hundred yards on our starboard. Clackety Hobo and Hettie Hobo rolled across to the windows. Ethelinda adjusted her screen so she could see. Mark, rashly, unbuckled his belts and ran across and stared from the window.

The craft was about 30 yards across, like a silver saucer, with orange lights around the edge. It held station with them as they rose. Another craft came towards them, very fast, like a cigar, about 70 yards long, with lighted portholes along the sides, and crossed to the port side.

Mark ran to the other side, the robots behind him.

The on-board robot said, "Our beams show that the disk has melted metal alloys, extremely hot, whizzing around just inside the outer edge. It creates some sort of field that annuls the dark energy field. It is a technology far beyond the powers of Choo Choo. The craft on our port is using some sort of jet – but of beams of unknown type. A field surrounds it, annulling the dark energy field."

Ethelinda said, "Radio the ship to get ready, that we have unknown company. Keep on our course, straight up to the ship."

"Understood," said the computer. "Ethelinda and Mark, do you want me to do anything else?"

Mark blinked in disbelief, then filled with pride. "Nothing else," he said manfully, and Ethelinda smiled at him.

Mark said, "You told me once about the dark energy field, but now I don't remember."

"Higgs bosons are intrinsic –"

"I remember. You said intrinsic before. What does it mean?"

"Our bodies, our canoe, our space ship are full of Higgs bosons, inside us. If we move very fast, we gain more and more mass – if we are down in a gravity well – because now, near the surface of the Earth, we are close to the bottom of the Earth's gravity well – it means we get heavier. It's like a snow plough – as the plough goes forward, the blade builds up a wall of snow in front. Or suppose a beautiful film star goes out into the street – people recognise her and crowd around, making it harder and harder for her walk forwards. The Higgs bosons pile up the dark energy field in front of us."

138

"Like Julia Roberts?" said Mark.

"Like Julia Roberts," hissed Ethelinda. "So the faster we go, the greater our mass, and we have to burn more and more fuel to move our growing mass. But these ships –"

"They're flying saucers," said Mark.

"*Heavenly galaxies!*" cried Ethelinda. "Of course!"

Mark said, "We've got to tell Joombo, back on Choo Choo!"

Ethelinda said to the on-board computer, "Warn Dumple Doo" – the shipboard computer on the spaceship – "that the moment we're in hyperspace, we've got to warn Hgiulbu that we've found Flying Saucers."

Mark said, "Do you remember how angry he was at them killing that boy, Fred, in his plane just south of Melbourne in Australia? He said they've put about 100 planes in danger, all over the world."

Ethelinda said, "They killed Frederick Valentich, who was 20 years old, in his Cessna, on October 21, 1978, in Bass Strait. His last words to Melbourne Air Control were, 'It's not an aircraft...'" Her face grew so grim she looked about 14-years-old instead of 11.

As they approached their space ship, 500 miles above the Earth, the great hangar gate yawned open and they flew into it. Everyone was scared the Saucers would follow, but they stopped outside.

They waited for the hangar to fill with air, then hurried to the control room.

"Mark!" boomed Dumple Doo. "Welcome on board. We have missed you."

Mark said with deep feeling, "Not half as much as I have missed you, down there in Milton Mudwallop, going to school every day. What do you think of these Flying Saucers? They scare me."

"Where do they come from?" complained Dumple Doo. "Our traders and merchants from Choo Choo have explored every inch of this quadrant of the galaxy for about a thousand light-years in every direction – and more than that, in fact. They come sneaking into earth, capturing people, doing vivisection on them –"

"What is vivisection?" asked Mark.

"Cutting people open while they're still alive to see what you are made of inside. I know *all* about your insides, Mark, because we used beams to look inside you – we didn't have to cut you open."

Mark shivered.

"They take people on to their ships, and when they've finished with them, they hypnotise them, and put them back on earth. Then they've got everything wrong with their minds, and when doctors take off the hypnotic spell, and they remember what happened, and they tell everyone, everyone thinks they're crazy."

Dumple Doo was booming, and getting angrier and angrier.

"For more than 50 years, plane pilots, specialists down on aerodromes, radar operators, and all sorts of people have seen them. They have landed in front of cars on lonely roads, stopping the car engines, and scaring the people to death. But what they do, they keep jumping into hyperspace and then back into this universe. So the rest of you earthlings don't believe they exist, because *nothing* can be there in one moment and then *vanish* – so you earthlings believe. They dart in and out of hyperspace and make the people who say they have seen them look like silly fools."

Ethelinda said in alarm, "Dumple Doo! Mind your circuits! You're getting too hot!"

Dumple Doo exclaimed, "Those craft are moving off!"

Mark cried, "Follow them!"

Dumple Doo warned, "Strap in! They're accelerating."

Although gravity was much weaker up at 500 miles, they were pressed back hard in their seats as their ship sped up.

"Five hundred miles an hour," intoned Dumple Doo. "Seven hundred... one thousand... 1,300 miles an hour... 1,700... 2,000... 2,500... 3,000 miles an hour. Hah! They don't like being chased. They prefer earthlings who don't know anything..."

At 3,000 miles an hour they made a sharp right-angle turn and winked out of sight.

"Into hyperspace!" yelled Ethelinda.

They made the sickening transition.

Among the beautifully coloured clouds of hyperspace they saw... nothing.

"Hah!" chortled Dumple Doo. "My beams are picking up the track of their turbulence. They went that way." He accelerated the ship to the speed of light in a short time and veered off to one side. As they had no mass in hyperspace, they had no limit to their speed, and could turn sharply at millions of miles a second.

They scanned the hyperspace ahead of them, and saw only clouds and colours.

"I still have their turbulence," announced Dumple Doo, happily.

Mark said to Ethelinda, "Back in our universe, they turned at right angles at 3,000 miles and hour. That's impossible, but newspapers say they do that, and everyone laughs."

Ethelinda said, "That's because they are free from the dark energy field. They have no mass. The Higgs bosons inside them meet no resistance. They are free from gravity, too. If you get high enough above the Earth, you are free from gravity too, but you can't make those turns because you still have mass, you still have Higgs bosons and the dark energy field in empty space. You could be floating inside your space ship, but if you turned like that, you'd be smashed to death against the wall."

Mark's watch showed ten o'clock at night back in Milton Mudwallop. He suddenly felt exhausted.

Hettie Hobo clucked anxiously, "Mark, you look terrible. Bedtime."

Mark embraced Ethelinda and gave her a big soppy kiss. He didn't usually give big soppy kisses, but he was so happy to see her again, and he'd rather be with her than with anyone else.

He stumbled to his bedroom, cleaned his teeth in the bathroom they had built on board for him all those months ago, crawled into bed, and fell asleep.

* * *

They woke him up nine hours later and he felt awfully hungry. He had a shower, and then Scrumptious Mumkish rolled in with a breakfast of scrambled eggs, slices of bacon with sausages, and toast with apricot jam.

Mark remembered that they were really giving him a nourishing slush, but Ethelinda planted in his mind that he was eating this delicious breakfast. Ethelinda didn't really talk to him at all. She was telepathic, but she made him believe he heard her voice instead of her thoughts. She also made him believe that she was an Earthling girl of 11 years, in a dress with four pockets, instead of a long, grey snake, half coiled on the floor, thicker than his body, and under her huge head, out of proportion – with large, brilliant, clever eyes, and no nose – she had four arms, and hands with fingers.

His watch showed eight o'clock in the morning.

"How long have we been chasing them?" he asked.

"Almost eleven hours."

At half past one in the afternoon by Mark's watch, Dumple Doo told them, "They have left hyperspace. We have overshot the place. There's no turbulence here. I'm turning back to find the place."

"How many light years have we come?" asked Mark.

"Twenty-four light years," said Dumple Doo.

141

Mark remembered from his journey months ago that Ethelinda used to hold her speed down to 11,000 times the speed of light because her father didn't like her speeding, or going too far away from home.

Dumple Doo projected a holograph into the middle of the control room, showing the Earth and the Sun 24 light years away and Choo Choo another 64 light years away.

One light year was one inch.

Dumple Doo turned the great ship around and searched slowly for where the Unidentified Flying Object had left hyperspace.

Mark asked Dumple Doo, "How could those ships leave turbulence behind them if there is nothing in hyperspace?"

Dumple Doo boomed, "Hyperspace is an intense energy field, especially of light. All the particles are massless, as are the photons which give us light and colour, in your universe as well as in this. As photons have no mass, they are the fastest particles in the ordinary universe – light goes faster than anything else. In your universe, you can't travel faster than the speed of light. But in hyperspace, all the particles travel at the speed they want, because they have no mass. The only other particles in hyperspace that you can find in the ordinary universe are neutrinos – but in your universe, the neutrinos have a tiny, teeny mass, although they can go through the Earth and not know it's there. They could travel through light years of lead and probably not bump into anything. In hyperspace, the neutrinos have no mass at all. Hyperspace is a parallel universe to the one you live in."

"How many parallel universes are there?"

"Probably millions and millions but we only know this one. All the light and beautiful colours in this hyperspace are from the photons, from the light."

"And what separates us from hyperspace?"

"A thin skin, about a millimetre thick."

"And why do I feel sick to my stomach when we go through it?"

"Because we have to make a field that vibrates millions of millions of millions of times a second to get through it."

Mark thought about that. He waggled his forefinger, and reckoned it waggled three times a second.

"It's not possible," he whispered. "That many times a second."

"Indeed it is," said Hettie Hobo. "Don't you worry your little head about *that*."

They crossed into to the ordinary universe, and saw a star.

Ethelinda said, "We've explored this star. How can there be a planet here?"

Clackety Clack said, "This star has five planets, all of them gas giants like Jupiter in the Solar System near Earth. Three of the gas giants are close to the star while in the Solar System where Mark comes from, the three gas giants – Jupiter, Saturn and Neptune – are far away from the Sun, and the Earth, Mars and Venus are close; they're the rocky planets. But this star has no rocky planets. The other two giant planets are far away from the star – and no life is possible at all on those five gas planets. And their gravity wells would be hundreds of times deeper than Earth's or Choo Choo's."

"Then why have these people entered into this system?" cried Ethelinda. "It's crazy!"

Dumple Doo exclaimed, "They left here! I found it."

Ethelinda said, "How far behind us must Hgiulbu be?"

"About 36 hours. Do you want to wait for him? Perhaps he's coming with more Choo Chooeans."

"Are you frightened?" Mark asked her. "Do you think they might be dangerous? Might be like us earthlings?"

Ethelinda pulled herself together. "Now you put it like that, that's impossible. They have space capability, and if they were like earthlings, they would seek out other planets to destroy them, and kill everyone there. But it's clear they aren't interested in any other planet – they are hiding somewhere. They only worry about earth, which is a frightening threat to us all, supposing one day you do get space capability. No, I suppose they're all right. We've left a robot in hyperspace to guide in Hgiulbu."

Mark felt nausea, in his stomach. They hung some millions of miles from a vast green and silver gas planet. Beyond it, they could see as tiny four other great gas planets, two of them orange and two red. And close by, they saw a small rocky moon – a rocky planet – covered in green vegetation and blue seas.

"In the name of all the galaxies!" cried Ethelinda. "Our ships must have orbited the sun over there" – it was distant and not very bright, perhaps as bright as the Sun on Earth on a day of light cloud – "seen these gas giants which could never have life on them, and left. But the planet that was farthest away has a big moon going round it! This moon must have been behind the gas giant when we came to look and we never saw it!"

They climbed into the canoe and dropped the thousand miles to the moon-planet. Six disks rose swiftly, surrounded them, and followed them down.

Then one disc went ahead, and led them to a flat, green plain, with hundreds and hundreds of space ships, some round, some like tubes, others like triangles or balls. At one end they saw tall, white buildings that stretched for miles, and they landed near them.

Dumple Doo told them, "The air is nitrogen, with 28% oxygen, and some carbon dioxide. Almost the same as on Earth, where the oxygen is 23%."

Ethelinda did not need to breathe.

Dumple Doo went on, "The air is 15% thinner than on Earth, so, Mark, you'll be breathing almost the same oxygen as back in Milton Mudwallop. The gravity well is 20% more shallow than on Earth, so you'll be able to jump one-fifth higher than back home," and he gave a bubbly boom, which Mark realised was Dumple Doo trying to laugh at his own joke.

Through the windows, they could see six creatures on two legs walking towards them.

Mark's heart was pounding in his chest, and he kept swallowing, his mouth was so dry.

"Out we go!" he said trying to sound strong. "Let's face these nightmares!" But his voice came out as a croak.

He opened the door, went out first, and waited for Ethelinda at the foot of the steps.

He heard Ethelinda send the thought to the aliens.

"What planet is this?"

The one in front sent back the thought, "Khrooval Measddaa. We are the Khroovals."

Mark said, "The planet is Grubble Narstee, and they are Grubbles."

144

Ethelinda sent telepathically, "I am Ethelinda, from the planet Choo Choo. I am a Chooean."

In the distance, they saw more Grubbles coming.

The six in front of them were between one metre and one and a half metres tall, short and skinny beside Mark and Ethelinda. They had very large heads, bulging at the top and bald, with huge, slanting eyes, like almonds, that stretched right across their heads around to where their ears should have been. When they stepped closer, Mark saw some had short, bristly hair. They had small mouths, with perfectly round lips forming a circle, and they had two openings where their nose should have been.

"What are you doing on this planet?" one of them sent to Ethelinda.

"Xiucheu is a mighty trading planet, with a hundred thousand space ships."

The Grubbles took a step back.

"We know all the planets for a thousand light years away, but we did not know of this planet."

"How did you find us?"

Mark saw they were all wearing the same sort of olive grey skin-tights, that came up to their necks. Their cheeks had no wrinkles, and their faces came down to a long, almost pointed chin .

"We were on-world on the planet Earth, in the Solar System. When we went up in our shuttle, two of your ships followed us, all 500 miles of altitude to our space ship. When we followed your ships with ours, you went into hyperspace, so we followed you."

The Grubble at the back said mentally, "No one was behind us in hyperspace."

Three other Grubbles sent out the thought together, "You have hyperspace capability!"

"We do," said Ethelinda, grimly. "We followed your turbulence in the energy field."

A collective gasp hit the minds of Ethelinda and Mark.

Suddenly one of the Grubbles sent out a thought that exploded like a thunderclap in everyone's mind.

"HE'S AN EARTHLING!"

The Grubbles took a step back.

Apparently, their thoughts could carry hundreds of yards because crowds of Grubbles came running out the buildings towards them. Soon two or three thousand Grubbles surrounded them, staring at Mark.

Ethelinda pretended not to notice, and tried to calm them with a different question.

"We never discovered your planet, because when we came into this system and saw five gas giants, we did not believe anything could live here.

Your planet must have been behind your gas giant. How long does it take your planet to orbit the gas giant?"

"Ten months."

"Then you must be five months in darkness, hidden from your sun."

"No, we are four days in darkness behind the top tip of our gas giant. Then we orbit down the side towards the front, cross over the bottom in front, then go up the other side, still in sunlight."

A figure dressed in red, about one metre and a half tall, came out of the biggest building and walked towards them.

The immense crowd parted.

He stopped in front of them, and Clackety Hobo and Hettie Hobo rolled down the ramp, and stood beside them slightly to the front.

The Grubble dressed in red sent, "I am the Grand Potentate of Khrooval Measddaa. What is this Earthling doing on our world?" Ethelinda put his thought into Mark's mind.

"This Earthling, Mark, is highly honoured on our planet, as he is on other planets. Our Patriarch has pronounced Mark as a citizen of Xiucheu. He has also pronounced Mark as a Virtuous Alien."

The faces of the Grubbles never showed any expression. But now they felt anger from the Grand Potentate.

"You are not welcome on our planet."

"You have entered our planet for years and years," shouted Mark. "You have killed some people. You have captured others and cut them open, or hypnotized them. Your Flying Saucers have interfered with our planes and cars. How dare you!"

Mark was so amazed at his own words that he felt dizzy and was afraid his knees would give way.

Hettie Hobo opened a panel in her side and put out an arm and held him. "Very good, Mark," she said. "But *very* good."

"You Earthlings are evil, all evil," said the Grand Potentate. "We have sent our ships to watch you, because you are a danger, dangerous beasts in this part of the galaxy. When our Grubbles come back from watching you, they urge us to kill you all. Now you are here, I am going to call the Dreadful Council of the Five Thousand, and see if they will vote at last to wipe you from the galaxy. They have never seen an Earthling, they cannot make up their minds, but now we have you, they will be able to decide."

Mark said to Hettie Hobo, "Send a message to Joombo, who must be only 30 hours behind us, to signal to all the Chooean ships in hyperspace to come here as fast as they can."

"There are probably 40,000 ships," protested Hettie Hobo.

"Tell them *all* to come," said Mark.

"Tell them to come!" said Ethelinda, harshly.

146

The Grand Potentate said, "Follow me!"

* * *

They went into a big building, rose up in a lift, and found themselves in four rooms, with a bedroom for an earthling and an earthling bathroom.

Clackety Hobo said, "They have had earthlings here, and they must have killed them."

Scrumptious Mumkish said, "Don't you worry, Mark. You'll be comfortable, and you'll see what a wonderful dinner you are going to have."

Mark was shaking all over, and felt as though he wanted to throw up.

Ethelinda put a mind block on him, and Mark grew calm.

After Mark had eaten and cleaned his teeth, he sat comfortably in a stuffed armchair and said, "Did you see what skinny arms they have. And what long fingers. They have five fingers like us, and they reach down to their knees. How can they build spaceships if they don't have any muscles?"

Hettie Hobo said, "They build them with their brains, not with their muscles. Mark, sometimes I think you'll be the end of me. They probably have robots who do everything."

"Don't you need muscles to build robots?"

"Do you need muscles to build a computer?" answered Ethelinda, impatiently.

"On earth, we built all sorts of machines over hundreds of years, and only now are we making robots and computers."

"But if you're really clever," said Clackety Hobo, "You start off with computers and simple robots, and those robots build big robots, and then the robots do all the work."

"Did they really say they want a meeting to decide to kill everybody on earth?" quavered Mark.

"Yes, they did," said Ethelinda, and put her arms around him.

Mark felt the tears starting in his eyes.

"I wanna go back to earth, now," he said, fighting to keep his voice even. "When I get back, I can pretend none of this has ever happened."

Ethelinda said gently, "But it *is* happening."

Mark said, "No one back on earth knows anything about this, and if I tried to explain it to them, they'd never believe me. Let's contact mummy on the mirror in the wardrobe, and tell her I'm coming. I'll go on the cruise with her."

Ethelinda said, "Mark, they want to kill all you earthlings. You are going to have to speak up."

"I'm just a boy. No one ever listens to me. And I don't know what to say."

"Then you must *think*."

"I'm not used to thinking. Kids on earth don't think – they're not expected to. No one expects them to and no one listens to them when they try to. Here in space, everyone is always *thinking*!"

"Now, now," said Hettie Hobo, "That's why we're in space in the first place, and why you earthlings aren't. It's not as though you're alone. You've summoned tens of thousands of space ships, something never ever seen in space. It's time for you to have a good sleep to be ready for tomorrow."

Ethelinda put a mental block on him, and he suddenly felt impossibly sleepy.

A Grubble came at mid-morning, and led them across several lawns of grass to a towering building with an immense arch of a doorway that reached up about 150 feet. The doors themselves were of dark bronze, intricately carved with twisting designs and figures.

Inside, their guide said, "This is the Hall of The Dreadful Council."

Seats ran around in a semicircle, rising towards the back to a half-invisible roof, it was so high. Their guide told them, "There are 5,000 members of the Council here, waiting for you."

They sat Mark and Ethelinda on a podium, facing the 5,000, and sitting beside them on the podium he saw half a dozen Grubbles dressed in red, light blue and one in gold.

The thoughts impacted powerfully in Mark's brain –

"For centuries we have sent observers to the planet Earth, and for centuries observers have returned in horror and urged us to kill all earthlings, and leave the planet for another race of Life with the Higher Spirit. Today, we have an earthling here before us. Dhê has been 50 years at the Earth. I order him to speak."

Dhê was sitting in the second row. He stood, and broadcast his thoughts.

"Earthlings are poisoning their planet. If we remove them, we can put in Beings of the Higher Spirit. Underground, they have endless supplies of petroleum, a very valuable soup indeed of different chemicals, and which can be used to make hundreds of things. THEY ARE BURNING IT, to make electricity and in their cars – millions and millions of cars."

The gasp in the Hall hit Mark's brain like a punch.

A Grubble in light blue, on the podium, asked, "Why so many cars?"

"Because each human wants to have his own car. To move about, he takes up a space about two metres long – or longer! – and more than a metre wide. They crowd the cities and the roads, so they can often hardly advance."

A thought came from among the 5,000 – "You must be mistaken."

Dhê said, "I am NOT mistaken. It is so."

The Grubble dressed in red asked from the podium, "Why don't they build coaches, buses, trains, to carry a lot of people together?"

"They do build buses, trains and so on. But everyone wants to be alone, in his own car."

"Why?"

Dhê told them, "On earth, thousands of different animals still live, animals which have no language, and small brains. Take hens, as an example. One hen is the number one, and can peck all the others. Number two hen will not dare peck number one, but will peck the rest. Number three hen will not dare peck numbers one and two, but will peck all the hens below her. And so on."

A thought came from the 5,000 – "A sort of pecking order."

"Exactly! But all the animals have it – tame cows, horses the same as wild wolves or lions. And this controls the earthlings. Each tries to be superior to the others. To travel in a train or bus with others means that you are low on the pecking order, near the bottom. You try to show you are higher by having a car, and the cars are all different. Some are magnificent and luxurious, others more simple and practical. It depends how high up you are in the pecking order, and how much money you have. Because the earthlings do not exchange goods directly, they don't swap a television set for a lot of wristwatches. They used round discs of metal and rectangles of strong paper, which they call money. When you make something, you get money, and when you want something, you exchange it for these rectangles of paper. And everyone wants more and more money. Some earthlings have no home but must live under the sky, and more than three-quarters of the world does not eat properly. That is because they have not enough money. But some men have mountains of money, and all they want is to get more money from those who don't have much. Everyone wants to make himself richer and richer, and make those around him poorer and poorer. Anyone who has to give a rectangle of strong paper to another person without getting something back feels pain."

The thoughts stormed around the Hall.

"Death! Death!"

Mark could feel the sweat dripping down his face, although it was not hot. He was shivering too. He whispered to Ethelinda, "Take me back to earth, please." His lips were twisting as he got ready to cry.

The man in gold cried, "What does the earthling say?"

Mark stared at him blankly, and thousands stared at him.

Well, he wasn't going to take this sitting down. He swayed to his feet, but his knees shook, and he thought they would fail him. He tried to speak, but his throat was dry.

He finally stuttered, "I have a bike. It works by my pushing pedals with my legs. It doesn't use petrol. My mum doesn't have a car, because she doesn't like them. She's got enough money to buy one. Most people on earth are too hungry or poor to have a car. And I don't have much money, and I don't care. Lots of people don't care about money. But everyone I know worries about the hungry people in the poor countries, and my country tries to help them and send them money and food. Most of the countries with industry who are richer than the others do all they can to help the poor countries and they're always talking about it, about what else they can do to help."

He straightened up, and pulled himself taller. After all, he was slightly taller than the Grubbles on the podium.

Was the Grubble in gold the Magnificent Potentate, the one who had come out to speak to them yesterday? If it was, yesterday he wore red. The Grubbles worked their spaceships in a way that was so far ahead that not even the Choo Chooeans understood. They were frighteningly clever, and this Grubble dressed in gold must be even more clever.

Mark suddenly became aware of a deep silence that filled all the Hall. He looked and all thousands of eyes were on him. He tried to hold himself stiffly. All he wanted was to be back on his bike.

These aliens were *clever*. Had he been silly? Had he made a fool of himself? School, back in Milton Mudwallop, was nothing like this. And he used to complain about the classroom.

The silence lengthened. Should he sit down? He tried to stay on his feet.

The Grubble in gold said, "Dhê, you may sit. Thank you, but your arguments are not complete. We will meet tomorrow." The Grubble dressed

150

in gold turned, and left the podium, and the other five Grubbles followed him.

Ethelinda said, "We can leave the podium."

"What is 'podium'?" asked Mark.

"Where you're standing now. It means a high platform in a meeting, that everyone faces towards."

They walked out of the building slowly, surrounded by thousands of Grubbles with their bulging heads and almond-shaped, dark, shiny eyes, their long skinny arms, hands and fingers reaching almost to their knees.

Next morning, they decided to go for a walk.

It was pleasantly cool, and the silver and green gas giant filled one quarter of the sky. They saw woods, and walked towards the trees.

Mark said miserably, "I am going to have to sit on the podium again, today."

Ethelinda stopped and put her arms around him.

"You were wonderful," she cried. "I was so proud of you. You're the best friend I've ever had and always will be."

Clackety Hobo made a noise like an old rattle-trap on a road full of potholes.

"Hettie Hobo and myself were so pleased with you we nearly burnt out our circuits! We have never been so proud!"

That made Mark feel *much* better, but he wasn't sure whether they were right.

A Grubble crossed over to them, dressed in olive-grey, and said, "May I accompany you?"

Mark asked, "Are there animals in the woods?"

"Hundreds of thousands of years ago, our ancestors, in their great wisdom, destroyed all the animals and all the insects, except the bees."

"How do the plants make seeds for new plants without any insects?" Ethelinda asked him.

"They make seeds with fine webs that float in the wind, and the wind carries them to new places."

"Why did you keep the bees?"

"We eat a lot of honey."

151

Mark asked, "But you can't eat meat, without animals?"

"We eat fish. Robots fish them from the sea. One half of this planet is sea. We also eat cakes made of many different grains. We have thousands of miles growing grain, which robots look after. We also grow fruit and vegetables."

"But that's like on Earth!" exclaimed Mark.

"It is most curious," said the Grubble. "But you have two legs and two arms like ourselves, and hands and feet. What is truly amazing is that you have five fingers and five toes."

Ethelinda said, "What I don't understand is how either of you stay upright without falling over. Balancing on two legs – it's silly."

Mark saw Ethelinda as an earthling girl in a dress, balancing on two legs, but he knew that was a picture she had planted in his mind.

They walked through woodland paths, among dozens of different sorts of trees, some yellow-green, others dark green, some with pointy leaves, others with huge round leaves. They were trees Mark had never imagined in his life.

"Do you have winter and summer?" he asked.

"No, because we orbit our gas giant 'vertically', so we are always the same distance from the sun, and always tilted 16 degrees. Most of the sea is in the north, where it is tilted away from the sun, and here on the continents, we are tilted towards the sun."

Mark saw a piece of orange fruit, way, way above his ahead. He jumped, and to his astonishment reached it easily.

"You can't eat that," the Grubble warned.

"How could I jump so high?" Mark cried. "I thought the difference in gravity between here and earth was only 15%."

"On your earth, we weigh 15% more than here. But here the gas giant has a tremendous gravity, and it was pulling you up when you jumped. We 're two million miles away, so the effect isn't very big."

Mark asked Clackety Clack, "Why does gravity get less and less as you get further away?"

Clackety Clack said, "Imagine a beach ball with red spots all at the same distance from each other. If you could pump it up with air, so that it got twice as big, the red spots would be twice as far away from each other. It's the same with gravity. As you get away, gravity has to cover twice the space it did before, so it pulls on you by only one half of what it did before."

"Thank you, Clackety Clack," said Mark, and Clackety Hobo rattled with delight.

A Grubble came to collect them and take them to the Hall of the Dreadful Council later than the day before. Mark's watch showed half past five in the afternoon.

Hettie Hobo said, "Look up at the sky!"

They saw what looked like thousands of space ships, hovering, glinting in the sun. Clackety Clack signalled the on-board computer in the canoe, and told it to contact their ship. Dumple Doo spoke to them directly, through the canoe link, and said, "They *are* thousands of space ships. And more keep arriving. They want to know what is happening. I think Clackety Clack – oops! I keep using Mark's name for Clackety Hobo – I think Clackety Hobo should go inside and televise everything to Hettie Hobo who should wait outside and send it to the canoe. The canoe can send it to me, and I'll send it to all the space ships."

Then he added; "Ethelinda, how clever to call up all these spaceships."

Ethelinda said, "It wasn't me, It was Mark!"

"MARK! It was MARK! Nothing like this has ever been seen in the history of space. The space ships are not only from Xlucheu. Thousands of Bhoobhcgemn spaceships picked up our messages in hyperspace, and they've come too."

"Bhoobhcgemn spaceships!" breathed Ethelinda, not believing it.

"Pumpkin spaceships," repeated Mark, not able to believe it either.

"So far, we have 18,000 ships from Choo Choo and 15,000 already from Bhoobhcgemn. They were all out already travelling through hyperspace when they got the messages. So tell Mark he isn't on his own."

Mark felt a choking sensation in his throat.

As they walked across the green sward, Mark thought about Milton Mudwallop. Milton Mudwallop *was* real. But *this*! He looked down at his shoes treading the green grass, and *that* looked real enough. He looked at the Grubble leading them to the huge doorway and wondered whether if he pinched the Grubble very hard, it would vanish. He quickened his step, and Ethelinda's thought whiplashed into his mind – "Don't even think of it!"

Mark slowed down, and went into the Hall, with Clackety Hobo rolling along behind.

They climbed onto the podium. Clackety Hobo lifted himself on with three arms that came out of his box.

The Magnificent Potentate turned to them, his face as always expressionless, and sent an angry thought thudding into their heads.

"What's this robot doing here?"

Ethelinda said, "He'll televise what's happening, and broadcast it up to the thousands of space ships."

"Are you threatening our planet? What are all these space ships?"

"Oh, Magnificent Potentate," said Ethelinda, "As your planet has just been discovered, they have flocked here to see it, and to find out whether you would like to trade. The discovery of a new planet, with Higher Spirits, right in the middle of the rest of us, has caused a sensation – and disbelief. They have come to see with their own eyes, because it seems impossible. Also, for you to judge whether life on another planet be killed – this is unheard of!"

"They know of earth, and what it is like?"

"They know."

The Magnificent Potentate turned to the 5,000 Grubbles, seated on rising benches before him and said, "Let the Dreadful Council begin."

A Grubble stood, and said, "Let all know that I am Fbí, and have been thirty-seven years patrolling the earth. Yesterday, we heard how earthlings have but one thought – to know who is best. Yesterday, one of our company invented a very good phrase – the Pecking Order. I tell you that earthlings have 'sports', and sometimes have 'super sports' called Olympic Games. They spend a fortune of money – money which could feed the hungry – to see whose leg muscles can move the fastest, and calculate the differences to hundreds of a second –"

"Fbí," said the Magnificent Potentate, "This is a Dreadful Council. Your years on earth have spoiled your brain. This is serious business, and no place for nonsense –"

"But it's true," protested Fbí.

Another Grubble stood up and said, "Let it be known that I am Hco, and have patrolled Earth for forty-three years. What Fbí says is true. They see who can swim fastest –"

"What!" exclaimed the Magnificent Potentate, "They have to *swim* to catch fish? This is to see who can catch the most fish?"

"No," said Hco, "It is to invent ways of seeing who is at the top of the pecking order. They jump in the air, dive off boards into water, play with balls – they invent every way to see who is at the top of the pecking order. Then they give the best a golden medal, and the winners walk around where everyone can see them, while the losers suffer pain and disgust with themselves."

A huge mental sigh swept the great Hall.

Thoughts hammered out from every direction. "Death! Death! Death to them."

154

The Magnificent Potentate said, "I have not words... no words..."

He turned to Mark.

"What sports do *you* play, earthling ?"

"None," stuttered Mark. "I like riding my bike by myself, on the moors, or walking. When I grow up, I might be a mountain-climber. But that means it's me against the mountain."

Profound silence filled the Hall as all eyes stared at Mark.

A thought came from the 5,000 – "And why climb a mountain?"

"Because it's there. Because I would like to see the top. I would like to see the rocks and plants or the snow, which I couldn't if I flew up. It's sort of – kind of – the poetry."

Mark was sweating. His thoughts were too complicated – he wasn't sure of what he was saying, or where he was going with what he was saying.

A Grubble came into the building quickly, and went to the podium.

"There are now 54,000 space ships overhead, and they are suddenly flashing lights. The lights are so strong you can see them despite their coming from 500 miles away."

Clackety Hobo spoke: "They are signalling that they approve of Mark's answer."

Mark tensed all his muscles to stop trembling.

"You can go up the mountain in a craft – fly up?" said the Magnificent Potentate, all at a loss.

"Not flying. You walk. Every step you take, you see something different, sometimes something beautiful," said Mark, squeezing out the words from a strangled throat.

Another silence filled the Hall.

A Grubble stood up among the 5,000.

"Let it be known that I am Jbú, and I have been twenty-five years on patrol on earth. Nations on earth also wish to be the best. A nation called Germany lost a war, called the First World War. They were very humiliated – "

"What is 'humiliated'?" whispered Mark, urgently.

"Make you feel you're no good, that you're less than the others, that you're left crawling on the ground," Ethelinda told him.

Clackety Hobo said, "To make you bite the dust."

Jbú went on, "Germany believed it was the richest, cleverest nation, so it went to war again, the Second World War, and 50 million people died."

A gasp rocked the Hall.

"The Germans killed more than half of them. There is a race of earthlings called the Jews, and they say they are The Chosen People. This maddened the Germans, and they killed six million of them. The Germans said *they* were the Chosen, Master Race."

155

"Chosen by whom?" asked the Magnificent Potentate, amazed.

"By their God. They have a God who is the same as the God of the Christians. They believe this God is an earthling who lives in space."

"An earthling who lives in space!"

"They have a Holy Book called the Bible, which says that God created man in his own image, and that God lives in Heaven, which means up in the sky."

An angry murmur filled the Hall.

The Magnificent Potentate said, "It is clear that these earthlings are not Beings of the Higher Spirit."

Mark wracked his brains, trying to remember what they had taught him. He squeezed his mind up very tight, and then said in a shaky voice, "What they mean is that God is Spirit, and he created man in his own image as a Spirit."

Five thousand faces stared at him for about three minutes.

What had he said? Had he got it right? Why did he never bother listening to that stuff!

Jbú said, "Another country is India. They have built nuclear bombs because it feels that the world doesn't recognise it as the nation with the world's oldest culture. Half its people are starving, but its leaders prefer to kill earthlings in other nations to feed its own people."

The Council was thunderstruck.

All eyes swivelled to Mark.

Mark gulped, and said, "My mum says all politicians are the worst people under the Sun."

"Politicians?" echoed the Magnificent Potentate, confused.

"The leaders in India are politicians," said Jbú. "Either politicians or cruel tyrants rule the nations on Earth. Tyrants kill a lot of people. In some countries, politicians kill a few people if they get in their way."

The thought rippled through the assembly. "Death to the earthlings! Death! Death!"

Mark said, "Some countries are better than others. In my country, they change politicians all the time, and they never kill anyone. They look after the old people and the sick. A country like mine – you can't compare it to most of the others. My country is England – then... ah, there's Europe that's like England, and Canada and Australia and New Zealand."

He couldn't remember any more names.

He said, "Ah – well – er, there are other countries that will be like us in a hundred years time."

Jbú said, "The richest country with the biggest army is America – the United States of America. Everyone has a gun, They're always shooting each other – even children go to school with guns and shoot other children."

Before the gasp from everyone had died away, Mark said angrily, "That's not true. Only some people have guns and shoot other people."

The Magnificent Potentate said, "I close this meeting..." when Hgiulbu writhed into the chamber, his long snake-body moving swiftly on the floor, the front part with his big head rearing upright.

His thought went out like thunder.

"I am Hgiulbu from the planet Xiucheu, where I have devoted my life to studying your awful activities on Earth, reporting them to the Science Council of Xiucheu. Greetings! Ethelinda, my dear, greetings! Mark, greetings! Ethelinda, how wise you were to call up all these space ships which I see fill the heavens of Khrooval Measddaa –"

He stopped to read Mark's mind.

"Or as Mark would say, *Grubble Narstee.*"

Ethelinda said, "Mark called up all the space ships."

"Mark! How well we did to make him an Honoured Citizen of Xiucheu!"

The whisper ran around the Council.

"An earthling – an honoured citizen..."

Mark sagged in relief. Joombo had arrived from the planet Choo Choo.

"When I got the message from... Mark? I left instantly, and have been travelling without stop. As I say, I have been watching the way you people have hounded the earthlings, causing their planes to crash, capturing them, taking them on your space ships to cut them open, hypnotising them so that they would not remember afterwards... My reports have horrified everyone on Xiucheu. I am also glad we have finally discovered the mysterious planet from where all your ships came. You have a technology far ahead of ours and of other planets near us – how do you power your craft?"

Silence.

"You do not use jets. You create a field."

Silence.

The Magnificent Potentate spoke.

"Earthlings are dangerous. They kill. In the last century, they have killed 175 million of their own."

Joombo said, "But they are not out in space."

"But they cause untold suffering to their own kind. And they are polluting a truly beautiful planet, which we could give to Beings of Higher Spirit."

He paused.

"I have declared this meeting closed. We will come together tomorrow."

Joombo talked so much, that Mark got sleepy.

"These Grubbles are disgusting and shameless. No earthling is a more reliable man to listen to than a military pilot, but they jump in and out of hyperspace. So, the pilots report they just vanish and then reappear. The other earthlings say they are crazy. All the passengers on one side of an airliner see them – then they just vanish. So all those passengers are crazy too. The politicians say they're crazy too – and you know what a low form of life are politicians. Then the Grubbles can come and go as they please – when someone sees them, they don't believe what they've seen."

Mark tried not to yawn, but couldn't help it. He'd had a wonderful lunch with roast beef and ice-cream as a special treat because everyone was so pleased with him. He knew perfectly well he'd made a mess of things, *and* he didn't really believe it was all happening. Besides, these things *never* happened to children – it wasn't *allowed*. Then he remembered black kids being cut up by machetes in Africa, and Palestinian kids being shot by soldiers, and kids in poor countries dying of hunger...

His head spun.

Joombo said, "In England, Flight Lieutenant Saladin from N° 604, County Middlesex Squadron, Royal Auxiliary Air Force, took off from his airfield at RAF North Weald in Essex at 4:15 in the afternoon, in a Meteor Mk8. He climbed to 5,000 metres, and over North Foreland, he reported:

'...I saw three objects which I thought were airplanes, but they weren't trailing (i.e. leaving white trails of condensation across the sky). They came down towards Southend and then headed towards me. When they got within a certain distance two of them went off to my port side – one gold and one silver – and the third object came straight towards me and close to within a few hundred yards, almost filling the windscreen, then it went off to my port side. I tried to turn around to follow, but it had gone.'"

Joombo was furious. "Whipped into hyperspace, making Flight Lieutenant Saladin look a fool. *Schkluukluk* those Grubble Narstees!"

"What is *schkluukluk*?" asked Mark.

Hettie Hobo said, "It's a very terrible curse, and someone as young as yourself is not to say it ever, or even *think* it. You shouldn't even *know* that word, so forget it, right now."

Joombo said, "Saladin went on to say:

158

'It was saucer shaped with a bun on top and a bun underneath and was silvery and metallic. There were no portholes, flames or anything.'

"They're using a force field! But what sort of field and what sort of force! It's enough to drive you mad! And they play this vanishing trick with the radar stations too. The radar operators see it on their screens, then they don't, so earthlings call them stupid too. But, of course, the radar operators are telling the truth. They call them 'fallible'."

"What is *fallible*?" asked Mark.

"Likely to make mistakes, not very clever, not good judges."

Joombo said, "In August, 1956, a lot of different radars in England tracked Grubble craft. A lot of radars: But the earthlings weren't convinced. Poor earthlings – it's the poor brain they've got in their heads. Not you, Mark," Joombo added hastily. "But look what happened – they ended their report saying:

'This is the most puzzling and unusual case in the radar visual files. The apparently rational, intelligent behaviour of the UFO suggests a mechanical device of unknown origin...'

"Then these earthlings say:

'However, in view of the inevitable fallibility of witnesses, more conventional explanations of this report cannot be ruled out.'

"*Schkluukluk* Grubbles and their dirty tricks!"

"What does all that mean?" asked Mark.

Ethelinda said, "It means that although expert, highly trained men saw the craft at the same time in different places, they can't be sure they didn't all have screws loose and they had just seen birds, or boys flying kites, or something..."

Mark 'sent' the thought to Hgiulbu, "Have a lot of passengers on a plane really seen them?"

Hgiulbu said, "Lots and lots. Ah – ah – on November 11, 1979, a super-Caravelle jet was flying from Salzburg, in Austria, to Tenerife, in the Canary Islands. It carried 109 passengers, mostly German and Austrian tourists, when they neared Barcelona, in Spain. Air control at Barcelona called Captain Francisco Lerdo de Tejada to switch to an emergency radio frequency, but the Captain couldn't hear anything except buzzing. Then he saw two very intense red lights, which seemed to be on the same craft. They flew at the Caravelle with an absolutely incredible speed that numbed the Captain's mind. He first saw them about 10 miles away, and in an instant they were 'playing with us' as the Captain said. It was whirling around the plane in a way no earthling machine could. The Captain said it was as big as a jumbo jet. An elderly man on board collapsed as he watched the crazy manoeuvres through a porthole. The Grubble chased the plane from Barcelona to Valencia, where the Captain put the plane into a steep dive to land. At

159

Valencia, the Grubble stopped over airport buildings where everyone saw it. The Spanish Air Defence Command Headquarters ordered two Mirage FI jets to scramble from Albacete. When they got close, the Grubble dived at the fighters."

Joombo stopped for a bit. Then he went on sending thoughts. "Funny thing, exactly one year later, on November 11, 1980, the Grubbles visited Barcelona airport again. The Caravelle I've just told you about – that happened at about 11 o'clock at night. In 1980, it happened in the late afternoon. More than six Spanish airliners reported seeing it. One Iberia pilot, Commandante Ramos, said he was 108 miles from Barcelona when 'it' appeared. It came straight for his plane and looked like 'an enormous soap bubble.' He said it was green, but sending out other lights... he said 'another plane radioed me... it was Transeuropa (flight 1474)... I told him what had happened to me.' The other plane had seen it and also radioed Barcelona about it. After the Iberia plane landed at Barcelona, the Grubbles came back. They buzzed the runway, and when Commandante Ramos flashed his landing lights as a signal to it the craft 'went out'."

"Went out!" said Mark.

"Like you switch off a light. It jumped to hyperspace."

Mark sent the thought, "Wonder how fast they go when they're on earth?"

Joombo said, "Well, going back to that business in England in August, 1956. Nearby, at Brentwaters Ground Controlled Approach radar, they got several Grubbles on their screen. But one huge one crossed 90 km on the scope in 16 seconds, which gives us 19,000 km an hour."

Mark cried, "In our atmosphere! And it didn't burn up!"

Joombo said, "I imagine it didn't even get hot enough to fry an egg on its hull."

Hgiulbu looked around the room in the flat the Grubbles had given them. Mark found the thick coils of his body comforting. After some thought, he 'said', "Up to the 1960's, they were pretty cautious, really shy. But in Germany, back in 1914, in late spring, a baker called Gustav Herwaeger who had his shop on the outskirts of Hamburg went outside for a breath of air at 4 o'clock in the morning. He saw this cigar-shaped craft, close by, hovering just above the ground. He saw windows, lit up inside. Five little 'humans', as he thought of them, all about 1.20 metres tall, all wearing the same sort of tights, stood beside the craft, and went inside up a ladder. The ladder disappeared into the hull, a door slid closed, and the cigar rose straight up without a sound.

"There's another interesting story from Germany about forest inspector Enst-August R. (he wouldn't give his surname), of Hemer in Sauerland. In the summer of 1948, he was looking after some sheep in a lonely grassy gap in the forest, when suddenly all the sheep ran in every direction. A spaceship about 30 metres long and three metres high landed on the grass. The man walked slowly to the 'object', which was of smooth metal. He touched it and a powerful electric shock knocked him unconscious. When he came to, he was about 80 metres away, and Grubbles stood around him, about 1 metre tall with very big heads and short stiff hair, as he described them. He said they had boxes on their chests, with tubes they sometimes sucked. So, they needed breaths of oxygen every so often."

Mark protested, "If I can breathe the air here, they can breathe the air on earth."

Joombo said, "The stronger gravity on earth might tire them. And they'd have to suck in more air than you do here to get the same oxygen. I suppose it must be that."

Everyone sat in silence, thinking.

Joombo said, "An electric shock. The field they use to make their ships fly must somehow involve electromagnetism. They must suck up electromagnetism from the air and from the earth.

"Just think of the case of the Nato base in Aviano, in north-east Italy. All the Italian and American soldiers saw it. At three o'clock in the morning, a very bright light appeared at 100 metres height. When they got a better look, it was a disk spinning very fast, about 50 metres across. It had a dome on top that didn't spin, but changed colour from white to green and then red. All their lights went out, all electricity failed, all engines stopped. After five minutes, it moved away without any hurry, and then vanished. All the electricity came back on.

"If they did this every time they flew near an airliner, they'd crash them. But they don't. When they 'played' with that young Australian pilot in Bass Strait south of Melbourne, in Australia, at first they didn't. Then they suddenly sucked away all his electricity and his engine stopped, and killed him. That was vicious. Frederick Valentich – only 20 years old. October 21, 1978. They made his Cessna crash."

Next morning, after a big breakfast, they called Mark. A young Grubble was at the door. He was about 85 cm tall.

He said shyly to Mark, "Do you want to come out and play?"

Mark looked at Ethelinda.

"Go on," she urged. "We'll come and watch."

They went outside, and the Grubble said, "I'm Mbi."

"I'm Mark."

"I know. *Everyone* knows about you. Are you any good at throwing spears?"

Clackety Clack had taught Mark to throw spears, using the metal cap he put on Mark's head to make him learn faster. That was just before they went down to the planet Bingo Bango Bongo, where the murderous devils were.

Mark said, "A bit. But what are we going to spear?"

"We don't spear anything," said Mbi. "The spears are blunt. Look, come over here."

Mbi picked up a large hoop, threw it spinning high in the air, then threw a spear through it, and before it fell, two more spears. He moved like greased lightning.

Mark stood three spears in the ground, threw up the hoop, and put two spears through the hoop. His third spear went over the hoop as it hit the ground.

"Not bad for an earthling," said Mbi.

They threw spears for a quarter of an hour.

Mark had been too frightened to look at the Grubbles properly, or to stare. Now he saw that Mbi didn't have a neck, and to turn his head, had to turn part of his body. His arms reached down below his knees and were so long it helped him throwing spears.

"Is it true that they're going to kill all the earthlings?" asked Mbi.

"The other planets won't let them," said Mark airily, with a confidence he didn't feel.

Mbi said, "I didn't know there were all these other planets. I only knew about earth which is dangerous and full of evil. I thought we were the only two planets – ours is heaven and the earth is hell. Do you want to play at *plidj*?"

"Leaping?" said Mark.

"Come over here."

A tall rod was fixed in concrete. Mbi pressed a lever and it bent over till it touched the ground. Mbi squatted by it, and pressed a red button. The rod snapped up, throwing Mbi seven feet high. He let go, and sailed through the air to a sandpit, where he landed in a cloud of sand.

Mark was really scared. If he didn't land squarely on his feet –

The rod jerked him into the air, but as he was heavier, he didn't go so fast. He came down with his legs stuck out and skidded along the sand.

"Hey! That's great!" shouted Mark.

162

Mbi went to a second rod.

"We can do it together, at the same time."

After half an hour, Mark was laughing and joking.

Mbi said, "You don't seem like a proper earthling. I like you. Do you really kill people? How many have you killed? Don't you know it's wrong?"

"I haven't killed anybody and never will," said Mark angrily.

"Oh, good," said Mbi. "Then we can be friends. Do you want to come for a ride?"

They walked some ways, and came to what looked like small cars without wheels and no top.

Mbi showed him how to sit in the padded seat. He had a bar with a crosspiece in front of him.

Mbi said, "You pull the yoke towards you to go up, and push it away to go down. You twist the crosspiece to one side or the other to turn. You push that pedal in the floor to go faster and the other pedal to stop."

"If that's a brake, how can it work when I'm flying?"

"It reverses the force field, silly," said Mbi.

Mark's jaw dropped.

Mark's car was green, and Mbi got into a yellow one.

Mbi's car rose in the air and moved forward.

Mark pulled back the yoke, and pressed the pedal. He was flying behind Mbi.

They flew fast towards a forest, then slowed down and Mark followed Mbi weaving in and out through the trees. Once Mark made a wrong move and headed straight into a tree trunk. The car stopped by itself.

On the other side of the forest, they flew over more miles of lawns, then came to an gigantic spaceport, with hundreds of spacecraft, but these spacecraft were half a mile across, not like the craft that went to Earth.

Mark signalled Mbi to land, and he 'asked' Mbi mentally, "What are these ships?"

"They're for trading."

"Trading! But you don't have anything to do with the rest of the planets."

"No, we trade in a parallel universe."

"There aren't any planets in hyperspace," said Mark, scornfully.

"This is *another* parallel universe," said Mbi. "You earthlings don't know *anything*."

"Oh," said Mark, very taken aback. "And what do you trade for?"

"Two chemicals. If you brought together several tons of these two chemicals, the explosion would destroy most of our galaxy. Our spaceships carry a microgram of each one, vaporise them into atoms, and fire the individual atoms at each other. That would produce a terrible explosion, but

163

we spin molten metal alloys at very high speed to create an electromagnetic 'bottle' to contain the explosion. Instead, it creates a Kx field, which frees the ship from the Higgs bosons in our universe, and also controls the Dark Energy of our universes."

"The Higgs bosons give us mass," breathed Mark. "The Dark Energy slows us down. That means you could travel at 10,000 miles an hour, turn at right angles, and gravity wouldn't smash you to death. And your hull wouldn't get hot if the field holds away the air?" he added.

"For an earthling, you aren't entirely ignorant," admitted Mbi. "One of the chemicals has an atom called *Bex*, which has a proton 26,000 times heavier than our protons in our universe. *Bex* holds about 200,000 *Vetus*, and the second chemical from the other dimension coaxes the *Vetus* to leave the *Bex*, one by one. When each *Vetu* escapes, it releases enough energy to lift 20 tons up into orbit 200 miles up... or to propel a spaceship, if you want to."

"If you only need a few kilos of the stuff, why are these ships so *big*?"

"To generate the energy to break through the membrane into the next universe."

"What is a membrane?"

"A very thin, fine skin, like you have inside your nose."

Mark was awed. "And you need all that energy to break through?"

He thought, then asked, "*Molten* metal means 'melted' metal, that right? And what is an alloy?"

"Different metals melted together."

"And how do they break through the membrane?"

"By vibrating a field zillions of times a second. You aim the vibrations on the membrane to make a big enough hole to let the spaceship through."

"That's what they do to get into hyperspace," ventured Mark.

"Ah, but this is much *harder* to get into. And it needs a different sort of field."

Mark asked, "Are there vortices from this parallel universe?"

He was thinking how he first got into hyperspace, thanks to a whirlwind vortex out on the moors.

"Hyperspace has vortices in our universe, but not this parallel universe. We build special crystals which vibrate once a femtosecond –"

"Once a what!"

"A femtosecond is ten thousand million millions of a second. Comparing a femtosecond to a second is like comparing a second to 32 million years of your time. Putting it in numbers, our crystal vibrates 10,000,000,000,000,000 times a second, but it's easier to write it as 10^{15}. That means 10 followed by fifteen zeros. But," Mbi worried, "Your earthling numbers! Ten to the 15th power could mean only a thousand million million times."

As Mark had said once before, a long time ago, "It's not possible for so much to happen in one second."

And as he had before, he waggled his finger. It waggled about three times a second.

"That's not fast enough, said Mbi, seriously. "You won't be able to push your finger through it. You see, we take that crystal and speed it up by a about a million million times even faster, which makes a field that we narrow so it makes a hole big enough for our spaceship to go through. Then the membrane closes again."

"But if you need so little of these chemicals, why all these ships?"

"Because in the other universe, about 500 planets make one or the other of these chemicals, but only in tiny, tiny bits. And we never carry more than one of these chemicals on any one spaceship."

Mark's head was spinning.

He said sulkily, "Well, it's a lot of trouble to go to just to come to earth and want to kill us."

"If you had this energy on earth, no one would be hungry and no one would have to drink dirty water full of germs," said Mbi solemnly.

Mark asked him, "Are you a boy or a girl?"

"We don't have boys and girls. Our babies are born in bottles."

Mbi had astounded Mark. He tried not to show it.

Mark said, as casually as he could, "I suppose we have to go back."

"Did you like playing with me? Or do you like the Dreadful Council better?"

"I'd like to play with you all day."

"What's it like in the Dreadful Council?"

"I don't understand anything, and I don't know why I have to go in there. It's not fair, dragging me in there. It's much, much worse than going to school. I don't know what they want me there for."

Mbi looked at him with awe.

"The Council was summoned because of you," Mbi said.

"That's silly," said Mark, decidedly.

Mbi said timidly, "Is it true that you have called up the 72,000 space ships that are overhead?"

"Now up to seventy-two thousand!" exclaimed Mark.

"But is it true it was you?"

"Well, sort of. I don't know…"

"It was, wasn't it?" said Mbi.

Mark shrugged his shoulders uncomfortably.

Mbi asked, "And you still like playing with me?"

"Oh, yes!" cried Mark.

165

"You have called up all those spaceships and you *really* like playing with me?"

"I'd play with you all day," said Mark, very firmly. "It's the best time I've had since I came down into your gravity well."

Mbi walked up to him, and put his arm around him and squeezed it tight.

They walked slowly to the cars, and Mbi said, "We can play another game. These thick posts are driven into the ground that we can dodge around. Robots chase us. They're very fast, but they turn badly. If they catch you, they pick you up and carry you back to the starting line. If you reach the finishing line, you get a prize."

Mark said miserably, "I don't have enough time. What is the prize?"

"The robot puts a cap on your head and teaches you mathematical games. You've got a lot of isosceles, obtuse and equilateral triangles of different sizes. How can you best fit them into a circle? It's thrilling."

"Sounds real exciting," said Mark, absently. They got into their cars.

Back at the house, Ethelinda hugged Mark. "I'm so proud of you," she cried. "You've made real friends with a Grubble. You've played with him."

Mark held Ethelinda tightly, but finally let her go.

"I've found out how their ships work;"

"What!" yelled Joombo, making Mark's head reel under the power of the thought.

Mark explained.

Joombo cried, "You're amazing! You're wonderful!"

Ethelinda hugged him again till he could hardly breathe. "I'm so proud of you, Mark, just so proud, and you're my best friend."

"Ethelinda, I'm astonished," said Joombo. "Back on Choo Choo, most people were alarmed and worried and whispered that you had no judgement, choosing Mark. But your mother and father defended you, and said how Mark had brought Choo Choo knowledge about Bvunmbvdva for the first time in history. Little girls are really much cleverer than most of us think."

Mark thought with longing of the planet Poompbah, and his friend Xküoghy – Chuck – who had a very big brain floating inside a shining cloud of gas.

Joombo said, "When we get back home to Xiucheu, we will call the Great Assembly of Science, and you can report this, Mark. This will also go towards your All Schools' Blue Medal for Science."

Inside the great hall of the Dreadful Council, Mark took his place on the podium, sick at heart.

Among the 5,000, a Grubble stood up and said, "Let it be known that I am Khá, and have patrolled the Earth for 91 years.

"Hear me! Earthlings have small brains, and they decide themselves who they are. A little girl will decide she wants to be pretty and nice, and asks her mother and grandmother is she not pretty and sweet, and they tell her it is so. When someone comes and says she is ugly and nasty, she weeps. Luckily, she is too small and too weak to kill the person who says this. A boy decides he is a good runner. Another boy says he can't run to save his life, so the two boys will fight to hurt each other.

"A man decides he is tough and smart. In a bar, another man says he's dumb. So he tells that man that he's a soak and a drunk. But *that* man always tells others how well he can hold his liquor. Then one punches the other. Then they pull out knives, and one stabs the other to death."

A gasp went through the hall.

"Earthlings judge each other by how others treat them. When one person lacks in respect, slights another, that means he has attacked the man's idea of himself, and lowered him in the eyes of his watchers. So that man pulls out a gun and shoots the other to death – perhaps just then, or perhaps later, when no one sees him, to avoid arrest and prison."

Another gasp went through the hall.

The thoughts came in a storm. "Death to them! Death! To the vote! Let us vote!"

A disturbance from the gigantic arch of the doorway drew all eyes.

They looked like two gorillas, seven feet tall, with arms and legs like tree trunks. They had long necks, braided with thick muscles, and huge heads like balls, with eyes and a mouth, but no nose. Short, stiff, grey hair covered their bodies and heads. They carried language-translator boxes hanging on their chests, and two Grubbles hurried alongside, each with a microphone connected to the boxes. They stormed to the podium like two tanks, making it shake. Mark saw they wore two red leather aprons, but he couldn't decide whether that showed their rank or covered their private parts – supposing they did have any.

The bigger creature's voice box boomed out – in English!

"Hail! I am Bhëzh Pezhsuüp, Anointed Keeper of the Sacred Codex, from the planet Bhoobhcgemn."

The Magnificent Potentate said sharply, "Are those your spaceships filling our skies?"

Mark said, without thinking, "Wise Bishob, from the Pumpkin planet."

Bhëzh Pezhsuüp turned to Mark and said, "*Wise Bishob!* What lamentable pronunciation. You must be Mark, the Earthling. I have come many light years to you, my child. Greetings! And greetings from all Bhoobhcgemns."

"Hello to all Pumpkinoneans from Earth," stuttered Mark, out of his depth.

Wise Bishop turned to the Magnificent Potentate.

"There are now 79,000 starships above your planet, but only 44,000 of them are from Bhoobhcgemn."

"Are you threatening us?"

"They have come out of joy, at finding a planet with life of the Higher Spirit, only 17 light years from our own. In aeons of time, we knew not that you were here, so a happy moment it is. We are traders, so all of us want to know about the chances of trade. Also, we are drawn here from curiosity, summoned here by an Earthling child, because you are debating the death of all upon his planet, which our Sacred Codex tells us –"

And suddenly his face screwed up in a frightening glare

"– tells us is wrong and against sacred usages."

The Magnificent Potentate asked, "You have followed all the televised broadcasts?"

"All of them."

"They do not alarm you?"

"They don't."

"Do you trade with earth? Do you land on earth?"

The round face of the Anointed Keeper of the Sacred Codex broke into a big smile. "Not a good idea, that."

"So they are dangerous, the earthlings?"

"Indeed they are. But any of our ships could crush them. As our Sacred Codex forbids us to attack or crush anyone, we stay away."

A deep silence filled the hall.

After two long minutes, the Magnificent Potentate said, "Khá, please go on."

Khá said, "Earthlings themselves decide how good or how bad they are. So other earthlings must try to show that they think of the other as the other thinks of himself, although they probably think nothing of the sort. It's hard for earthlings to lie over a long time – without wanting to, they can show what they really think by the wrong tone of voice, or by an expression on their faces they can't stop in time."

Silence filled the hall, and 5,000 faces stared at Mark.

Mark said bravely, "I don't care what anyone thinks of me."

Ethelinda said, "I know Mark, and on earth, in his country, life is lonely. Mark is lonely, and has almost no friends, but many enemies. So Mark does not have a proper character yet, and he doesn't think very much about himself at all. He thinks about other people. Most people on earth are like him – they are poor, frightened, hungry, alone, in countries that are poor, where they die young because their bodies are weak."

A long silence followed, everyone staring without blinking at Mark.

A deafening thought boomed through the hall.

"Are the Grubbles frightened of beings like these!"

Mark swung around and, unbelievably, saw the Bvunmbvdvan, Xküoghy, his great brain in a ball of shining gas, twenty feet across. The gas rested in a silvered box that floated into the hall, and electric sparks snapped up into the gas from deep in the box.

"Chuck!" shouted Mark in joy. He turned to the 5,000. "This is Chuck from Poompbah! He is a Poombahoomph! Chuck, how did you get here?"

"The Bhoobhcgemns have robot ships that can go down into our gravity well –" he turned to the assembly "– which is an exceedingly deep well – and climb out of it again. Until this Bhoobhcgemnian ship came down, in millions of years only Mark here had come down to visit us. Mark, how is your mother?"

"She is much better. All those diamonds you gave me seem to have cured her depression."

"I'm sure. Our computers tell us that diamonds and women have a special affinity."

"What is *affinity?*"

"Oh, dear," said Xküoghy.

The translation box hanging around Bhëzh Pezhsuüp's neck squawked, "Means nearness, attraction."

"Thank you, Wise Bishob," said Mark.

Xküoghy said, "You will be the Anointed Keeper of the Sacred Codex, Leader of the Bhoobhcgemns. I thank you for bringing me here."

He turned to the other gorilla with a long neck.

"You will be the Consecrated Priestess of the True Galactic Way, Bzzh Mnmömnm. My most respectful greetings."

169

Mark said, "Wiise Nun, hello from the Earth and from myself."

"Thank you," she said. "You are a regal young man."

Mark said, much worried, "What is *regal*?"

Wiise Nun said, "Kingly."

Chuck said, "On Bvunmbvdva we called him the young god," and a murmur rose through the hall. "It would seem we didn't exaggerate. He seems to be handling you Grubbles, and brought together the greatest fleet of spaceships ever seen in the history of this galaxy."

The Magnificent Potentate sneered, "You pretend to know the history of the WHOLE GALAXY!"

Chuck said modestly, "Over half a million years, we have sent through hyperspace our satellites to all planets in this galaxy which have life forms of the Higher Spirit. We have hundreds of thousands of computers which collect all their messages."

"And very inquisitive satellites they are too, "said the Wiise Nun. "They stick their noses in everywhere, at least on our planet."

Chuck went on smoothly, "We did not know Grubble Narstee was here. May we have permission to send satellites here?"

"No one will stop you. Can we send a satellite to access your computer banks?"

"You are most welcome."

The thought came from the 5,000, "Thank you."

The Magnificent Potentate said, "The more we hear of Earth, the worse it gets. I suggest we put it to the vote."

The Wise Bishob interrupted. "I am sorry, but the Sacred Codex says you may not kill, and may *not* kill all life on a planet. No Higher Form has enough wisdom."

The Wiise Nun said, "The True Galactic Way says that you must live by love and goodness. While Earthlings are a most unfortunate form of life, you must treat them with love."

A Grubble ran into the hall.

"Lights are flashing from all the spaceships, oh, Magnificent Potentate!"

Clackety Hobo announced, "They all applaud what the two High Pumpkins have said."

Silence filled the hall for five minutes.

The Magnificent Potentate said, "You agree that the Earthlings cannot be allowed into space?"

The Pumpkins and Chuck said, "That is clear. They cannot."

A Grubble stood.

"Let it be known that I am Lcê. Can we not take two million earthling children in space, teach them, and then return them to earth?"

170

Another very long silence.

Another Grubble stood, and said, "Let it be known that I am Phè. What says Lcê is good, but how do we choose them? Do we choose children like Mark? Where do we find them? If we choose children who grow up to think of themselves, or to think themselves better, or who want to be rich or are bullies who become... what is the word –?"

The word surged out from thousands of minds in horror. "Politicians!"

"Suppose they want to be politicians!" Mark said, "When we grow up, we might be different politicians to those who have gone before."

Lcê said, "They say on earth, 'A leopard can't change its spots.'"

Phè said, "It's impossible to choose. Most of them, perhaps, would not want to come. Suppose most of them didn't like it and wanted to go straight back home."

Five minutes passed.

From thousands of minds came the thought, "We don't know how to choose the children."

The Magnificent Potentate said, "We must vote. Kill them? Yes, or no."

For long minutes, the air was a terrible jumble of confused thoughts.

Slowly, as a river over hundreds of miles collects water from small stream after stream, and grows wider and wider, deeper and deeper, the thought came forth.

"We know not enough to decide. We will never let them come out into space."

The Magnificent Potentate said, "Two decisions. We will not kill them. We will not let them leave their Solar System. So be it!"

He turned and looked at Mark.

"As Mark is an Earthling, he must return to Earth forthwith and not be let out into space."

Ethelinda said, "Mark is a citizen of my planet, Xiucheu, where we are both going now. As a Choo Chooean, he can roam space when, where and how he pleases."

Xküoghy said, sparks flashing up and down inside his huge ball of shining gas, "Mark is also a citizen of my planet, Bvunmbvdva, and as such let no one stay or hinder him. He is a free wanderer of space, a Poompbahoomph from my planet, Poompbah, as Mark chooses to pronounce it."

He turned to Mark, "No one on your Earth will ever know what you have done. Curious it is, but no one will know."

"I'll tell my mummy," said Mark.

"That will be hard," chuckled Chuck. "I wonder how much she will ever follow of what you are saying. Your planet, Earth, owes you everything,

171

but you will be unknown. However, we have satellites all over this galaxy, to its farthest reaches, to a million planets, and already we are speeding the news through hyperspace to each and every planet of what has happened here, so they will greet you with honor should you ever land."

He turned to the Magnificent Potentate.

"Let every Grubble know this, that Mark is free to wander space, and every planet will know of him. Let no one offer him let nor hindrance."

A long silence followed.

"So be it," said the Magnificent Potentate.

* * *

Outside, Wiise Nun, Wise Bishop and Chuck gathered with Ethelinda and Mark beside Ethelinda's canoe. Hgiulbu was writhing across the grass to his own canoe, when he saw them, and came over.

Chuck said, "I suppose you all pick up the earthlings' television. What the Grubbles didn't mention is how those earthlings never admit they are criminals when they murder."

Wise Bishop said angrily, "Those Nazis killed millions and millions of Russians, but said they were innocent because the Russians were subhuman – *untermensch*, or some word like that."

Hgiulbu said, "Those Serbs were killing Muslims, and talking about what the Turks did to them hundreds of years earlier."

Wiise Nun said, "In Israel, soldiers killed a hundred Palestinians and two small children a few days ago, and when the Palestinians killed two of their own soldiers, they rent their raiment. To kill Palestinians was nothing!"

Mark was looking at them dismally. Soon, he would say goodbye to Chuck, the Wise Bishob and Wiise Nun.

He asked, "What is *hinder*?"

"To get in the way, to try and stop someone."

"And what is rent raiment?"

"Tear your clothes. In ancient times, the Jews tore their clothes to show sorrow."

Chuck said to Mark, "What helped was your calling up the fleet of space ships. How long did it take you to think of that – *how* did you even think of it in the first place?"

Mark looked at him unhappily. Soon they would be saying goodbye. He said, "The idea just popped into my head."

"Just jumped into your mind!"

They all looked at him in amazement. Ethelinda hugged him.

Chuck said to the others, "He is the only earthling in space because he is a young god. That is what we think."

Mark said, "I'm not half glad to get out of there. I hope nothing like that happens again. Those Grubbles had me scared. Do you know something – I think they would have killed everybody."

Bhëzh Mnmömnm said, "You can be sure of that."

Back in their spaceship, Dumple Doo boomed, "Welcome home. Mark, you are a hero."

"Ethelinda and Clackety Clack are the heroes," said Mark. "Ethelinda had some things to say to them, and Clackety Clack just rolled in there, when they didn't want him, and broadcast everything."

Clackety Hobo made a sound like ball bearings bouncing inside a saucepan.

"Now you have made him happy," said Hettie Hobo. "But I stood outside and relayed everything."

"Without you, we would have lost it," said Ethelinda.

Dumple Doo lowered his voice like a conspirator.

"Some spaceships have seen *another* planet."

Everyone swung around to stare at his screen.

"It's hidden behind the *second* gas giant. It suffers darkness six months of the year. They saw two cities. It's full of erupting volcanoes."

"Take us there," said Ethelinda excitedly.

"We'd better go through hyperspace. If not, we'll take a week and a half."

When they came out of hyperspace and went into orbit over the unknown planet, they saw thousands of spaceships had come before them.

"It's not really a planet," said Ethelinda. "It's a moon going around the gas giant, like Grubble Narstee."

Dumple Doo said, "Some moon! It's half as big again as the Earth."

Mark said wonderingly, "One-and-a-half times as big as the Earth, and it orbits a gas planet. I'd weigh one-and-a-half times what I do on Earth!"

They looked down, and saw glowing red lights.

"Those lights are the volcanoes," said Dumple Doo. "They're awfully close to the cities. And smoke keeps rolling over the cities..."

He stopped, then said, "Bhëzh Pezhsuüp has told the Pumpkin ships that no one can go down there. It's too dangerous. And the leader of the Choo Choo ships had given the same order."

Mark looked, and the red lights weren't very big.

"Let's go down!" he said.

"No!" said Clackety Hobo.

"Ethelinda?" asked Mark.

"Oh, let's!" she said.

Dumple Doo connected with Hgiulbu, and his 'voice' came through Dumple Doo, roaring, "You both stay where you are!"

Mark said, "I'm going, Joombo."

Hgiulbu said, "I can't stop you, Mark. Why do you insist?"

Mark looked at the red lights, and reckoned they were pretty tiny.

"I'm curious," he said. "I want to know what it's like down there. And I want to get that Dreadful Council out of my mind. Give me something else to think about, y'know?"

"Curiosity killed the cat," snapped Hettie Hobo.

"What cat!" cried Ethelinda, very annoyed.

"It's an earthlings' expression," said Clackety Hobo. "Their top scientists say they are descended from monkeys, who are very curious, so they are curious too."

"I'm not descended from a monkey," said Mark, angrily.

"That's what your top scientists say," said Clackety Clack, sulkily.

Ethelinda threw her arms around Mark. "It's not fair," she wept. "You can go and I can't."

Mark told her, "When I see it's all right, then they'll let you come. But if neither of us go, we'll *never* get to see it."

Ethelinda squeezed him tightly.

"Be quick," she sniffed. "I'll come right after you."

The immense hangar door swung up, showing empty space beyond. Mark flew the canoe down to the planet, to the nearer city. He saw a huge building in the centre and dove towards it.

Now he could see the volcanoes spewing flames and red-hot lava high into the sky, and vast clouds of thick smoke, grey and black, rolling over the countryside.

His tummy tightened in a knot, he sweated, and he knew he'd have to go up to the spaceship.

The canoe computer said, "They're signalling you with lights."

Out the window, Mark saw nothing, but on the screen, he saw a square in front of the big building, with people waving lights wildly.

He gulped, and feeling sick, said, "I'll go down to 50 feet."

There the canoe hovered.

"Can I breathe the air?"

"No. Put on the tank. The air will not hurt your skin. You will need more oxygen because you will weigh much more. Adjust the oxygen to 130."

Mark strapped the tank on his back, put on the helmet, and strapped his talking box to his chest.

He gently lowered the canoe to the square, and the people scattered with amazing speed from the flaming nozzles. He got out, and a crowd surrounded him. They looked like kangaroos, with enormous muscles at their hips that let them leap several feet. An upright body rose from the hips, about three feet across at the shoulders, with thick arms, big hands and fingers. A very short, thick neck held a head like a big tube sideways, about three feet across. The face was almost flat, with two eyes about two feet apart, no nose, and a long mouth in the middle. They had tall, square ears. Whitish hair covered all their bodies, except their faces, which had a bluish skin.

The kangaroos stood aside to let one taller than the rest come up to Mark. He carried a square voice box on his chest, and his voice shouted, "Do you understand English?"

Mark was so surprised he couldn't find his voice.

He stared, refusing to believe his ears.

He swallowed a couple of times, took a deep breath, and said, "Enligh is my own language."

"Enligh!"

Mark knocked the voice box with his fist.

This time it said, "English" properly.

"English is my own language."

"You are from Earth!"

Mark cringed. "I am an Earthling," he confessed.

"That is wonderful! We know of no other planet than earth. We get your radio and television signals. They take 24 years to reach us, and they first came about 50 years ago. Thousands of years ago, other planets sent radio and television signals, but after about one or two hundred years, they stopped. You have travelled 24 light years to reach us. What an enormous fleet. We need your help."

"Help?" said Mark, weakly.

"In this city, we have a Gate to the Convoluted Parallel Universe, which lets us travel to another moon around a giant gas planet 50 light years from here. We are evacuating everyone from this city, through the Gate, but we need your spaceships to carry the people from the other city to here."

"How many people?" asked Mark, frightened.

"Only one million."

One million! he thought.

He supposed "evacuate" meant to get the people out.

"They must come quickly, because the volcanoes will kill them with red hot lava and the gases will poison them on their skins."

Mark went back to his canoe, his heart pounding.

"Connect me up," he said to the on-board computer.

"Spaceships are needed to evacuate one million people from the other city to this. Red hot lava and poisonous gases are about to kill them."

He stepped outside, and stared up at the thousands of lights in the heavens.

They hung there motionless.

Suddenly, they moved, curving downwards in a vast waterfall.

"May the Perfect Awareness bless you all your days," cried the tall kangaroo.

Mark gulped. "What planet is this?"

"Vvudol Vvaagyyn. We are the Gruunoz people. My name is Gruundku, and I am the Leader of my people."

"Do you know about the planet around the fifth gas giant, Grubble Narstee?"

177

"Nothing."

"Have their ships never come here?"

"Never."

Mark went back to the canoe, and spoke to the spaceships.

"This planet is called Wobble Waygone. The people here are called Goners and the Leader's name is Gonnto."

"My name is Mark. Tell me about your Gate, er, ah, please, what does *Convulted* mean?"

"*Convoluted!* It means twisted up, or folded up tightly. In the Convoluted Parallel Universe, space is so folded up that if you cover a very short distance in it, you cover light years in this universe."

Mark looked at him dumbly.

He looked over to his right, and saw the spaceships coming in to land, then disappearing beyond the curve of the planet's horizon.

He said hesitantly, "Could I see the Gate?"

Gonnto led him into the big building. It was a palace, all the walls wonderfully carved, with curving passageways lined with abstract sculptures. Water ran along the floors, and down the walls – a fine mist filled the air. Halls rose almost out of sight, their walls glowing, and moss and ferns hanging around the edges.

"We need wet air for our skins," explained Gonnto. "Our houses are full of mist. Six months of the year, we don't see our sun, and the hot mists keep us warm. The other six months, the water and the mists keep us cool. Now we are in darkness, and it's cold, but the volcanoes have made the air hot and melted the snow and ice."

"Will you be able to come back here?"

"I don't know. This has never happened. But our wise men warned us it could happen, so we built the Gate to another moon. But they didn't tell us that it could happen so fast that we wouldn't have time to evacuate our people."

They left the palace, walked through some streets, and came to open country.

A tall pink arch with thick, straight sides, and a curved top, with such a brilliant light Mark's eyes ached, stood in the middle of nowhere. He saw a queue of Goners stretching for miles, moving up quickly as they leapt into the Gate and vanished, twenty at a time, side by side.

Gonnto said, "They have to cross about a mile in the Convoluted Universe to reach the other planet."

Mark's head spun.

"This pink arch – it vibrates zillions and zillions of times a second so the membrane breaks inside it?"

178

Gonnto's glinting, silver eyes stared at him. "I thought you earthlings knew nothing of parallel universes and membranes. There is not a word on your radio or television."

"They don't. Do you know about hyperspace?"

"Another parallel universe? How interesting. Ah! Is that how you got here? You are extremely young, and 24 light years is an impossible distance to cross in this universe."

"Can I go through the Gate, and then come back?"

"Most certainly. You must wear one of these belts."

Mark saw a high pile of belts, stretching for about half a mile.

Another Goner had followed them at a distance, but said nothing. Gonnto turned to it, and beckoned.

"Mark, this is Gruunkzxeu. Gruunkzxeu, meet Mark. Would you take him through the Gate to the other Gate, let him see the other world, and bring him back?"

Mark said, "Gonnyzo, I'm pleased to meet you."

Gonnto said, "Gruunkzxeu is young like you, a young girl."

Gonnyzo also wore a talk box.

"I can talk to you in English," she said, through the box. "It will be a great honor for me to take you. You are the Earthling who has saved our people."

Mark blushed. "That's silly," he said.

"Look," she said, and when he followed her arm, he saw hundreds of spaceships slowly settling to land, and others already unloading thousands and thousands of Goners some 20 kilometres away.

"They're a long way from the Gate," worried Mark.

"We can leap at 40 km an hour," she told him. "The queue is 20 km long so they are joining at the end."

A whistle blew, and the queue stood aside from the Gate. Suddenly, thousands of belts flew out, piling up on platforms, that moved quickly to make room for more.

"The belts come back by themselves," marvelled Mark.

"Soon you will understand," promised Gonnyzo.

When the Goners went into the Gate again, Gonnto strapped a belt around Mark's waist, and they went up to the Gate.

The Goners stood aside. They walked into the arch, and Mark felt dizzy.

He found himself in a dome, the roof almost out of sight, so that everywhere he looked ended in a shimmering skin. He could see outside, and saw the gas giants, and distant stars of his own universe. Inside, curved folds of a sort of soft, transparent satin twisted this way and that. Before them

179

stretched shining, silver disks, about two feet across and a foot high. They advanced towards the first disk, when Mark said, "Stop!"

Gonnyzo moved him to one side of the line of disks, and then he saw Goners speeding by, from one disk to the next.

"Can we go back? I want to send a message."

They walked to a gentle flowing slope of brown, transparent satin, walked through it, to another line of disks. They lined up with the disks, and an unseen force drove them swiftly back through the Gate.

Mark saw Gonnto talking to other Goners, and he hurried across.

"Please, Gonnto, could you tell my canoe to collect Ethelinda, and bring her here to the Gate?"

"You are the saviour of our people. You may ask what you wish. Your message is – 'tell the canoe to pick up Ethelinda and bring her here to the Gate'?"

Gonnto's talk box impressed Mark. He had said "collect", and the voice box knew enough to say "pick up".

They went back through the Gate, and sped along the line of power disks that pulled on their belts.

Outside, he could see stars racing towards them and then falling behind. They came to a star and went straight into it, the outer skin of the dome dazzlingly bright.

"Why didn't the star blind us?" Mark asked.

"Ordinary light from a planet comes through as it really is. Brighter lights can't get in properly, and the brighter they are, the less light gets in. Only so much gets in, and never any more."

Mark shivered. Inside the star, lights writhed and stabbed.

"How hot was it inside that star?"

"About 300 million degrees Centigrade."

"How could you find planets, if they're so far away?"

"We built robots which could fire beams that vibrated zillions of times a second. That made a hole they could get out through. You see, if you see a planet, you walk towards it, and the skin of the dome moves with you. Look, step over here."

They got off the power line of the disks, and walked to the edge of the dome. Faintly, Mark saw a sun. They walked through convoluted folds of space, and the sun appeared to race towards them. The dome moved forward as they did. Soon, the star was close and they saw planets, some gas giants, and two rocky planets.

"If you keep walking towards one of those planets, you come to its surface. Then a robot cuts a hole through the membrane right onto the planet, and explores. So we know whether it is inhabited, or is no good for us to live on because of the air or it's too hot or there's no water or no earth for growing food. The robot comes back here, cuts another hole to get back in, and goes over to the disks we have laid down to get back to our Gate."

They walked back through the brown folds of space to the line of disks, that swept them across the dome, and Mark found himself standing on rock, in sunlight, with a Gate behind him.

The rock was reddish, and stretched away to a river. Beyond the river lay a forest, that rose to hills, and beyond the hills rose snowy mountains.

He turned, and saw the sky filled by a sun like that on Earth, and a vast gas giant planet, orange and red, that filled one half of the heavens.

"This planet goes behind the gas giant for three months of night; and then we have nine months of day. This is almost as big as Wobble Waygone, but it has a different atmosphere. The atmosphere doesn't matter, because it doesn't hurt our skins. Goners have been living here almost 500 years, building two cities and planting food, so we will all have somewhere to go. But we won't be able to get Earth's radio and television until next year. We are about 75 light years away now. Next year, we'll get the programs you broadcast on the radio 75 years ago. We don't know how good the reception will be. So far, no other planet is broadcasting. Planets are either too advanced, or too primitive."

Suddenly, Gonnyzo asked, "When do you have to recharge your breathing tank?"

"I've got about 40 minutes."

"Let's go back."

Inside the Gate, they went to a second line of disks, that drew them in the opposite direction to that of the thousands of Goners they could see going to the new planet. Hundreds of belts were floating in front of them, going as fast as they were.

They came out of the gate, to see the canoe hovering.

The gale noise from the nozzles deafened Mark.

It landed, and Ethelinda rushed out and embraced him.

"I'm so proud of you, Mark," she cried. "Wherever you go, everyone's safe!"

Hgiulbu came up and said, "Mark, Choo Choo's proud of you."

"Joombo," exclaimed Mark breathlessly. "See this Gate here. It goes into a Convoluted Parallel Universe, and in a quarter of an hour you come out at another planet FIFTY LIGHT YEARS AWAY!"

Joombo looked at it in horror. "That's wonderful, but you'll never get back. Forget it. It's time to go."

"Joombo," cried Mark, "I've just been there AND COME BACK. I'VE JUST BEEN WALKING AROUND ON THE OTHER PLANET."

Ethelinda hissed, "Oh, Mark, take me in."

Mark said, "We've got to wear these belts."

Hgiulbu stared at Mark. "This is true?" he whispered, so excited he was shaking.

"It's true," said Gonnto. "Here are two belts."

Mark said, "I need more oxygen."

On the planet 50 light years away, Hgiulbu searched the skies. "I can't see a thing in the sky with this sunlight. Where are we? Where are we?"

They went back, and Gonnto explained where the planet lay.

"I know! I know!" said Joombo, happier than Mark had ever seen him. "Now I know where it is. We will come and visit you. Perhaps we can trade."

Gonnto said, "I don't know what we have to offer."

Joombo said, "You have knowledge we don't. We can help you buy or build spaceships. We can search your planet for you, and tell you what riches it might hide. You can teach us to build Gateways."

Gonnto said, "We have not thanked Mark. He must come so we can have a Ceremony of National Gratitude for him. Mark, you have forgiven us? For paying so little attention to you. We have to save two and half million lives."

Mark said politely, "I have been very happy to meet you and Gonnyzo, and nothing else matters. You have made my stay truly happy, and I don't know how to thank *you*."

Tears came to Gonnto's glinting eyes.

He walked them over to the canoe, and then leapt away to a safe distance, his hands held up in farewell.

The canoe rose swiftly, and they could see the smothering clouds of smoke, the volcanoes belching red-hot lava and tall flames, and the lights of the spaceships in their labour of love to carry the Goners to the Gate.

Back in the spaceship, Ethelinda said in awe, "A Ceremony of National Gratitude! Mark, aren't you lucky!"

Mark shuddered. "They've spoilt it all. Now I can't go back there ever. It would be as bad as the Dreadful Council."

Snuggled up in his bed in the spaceship, as it zipped along at zillions of miles an hour through hyperspace, to Choo Choo, zillions upon zillions of miles away, Mark thought of Milton Mudwallop. He'd like to go home, and pretend none of this had happened. But he was lonely there.

Yet, there he knew where he was, and who he was. Out in space everything was at sixes and sevens. He wasn't lonely. He had *lots* of friends. But they were all much cleverer than he was.

Out in space, people spent all their time thinking really complicated things. You couldn't stop and *play*. And in Choo Choo, they wanted to *teach* him. Mark twisted about in his bed. How could he get out of that!

He'd been playing with that Grubble boy, and what games he knew! What good was all this science if they didn't invent new games to play?

He wanted to go back to Milton Mudwallop. And he didn't want to.

He wanted to stay in space. And he didn't want to.

What were you supposed to do when you wanted two different things?

He fell asleep. When he woke up, he was starving. But he felt much better – dying to know what the future held.

Halfway through a big breakfast, Mark felt a terrible nausea, and struggled to keep down the food.

They were leaving hyperspace to go back into the ordinary universe.

When he was sure he wouldn't throw up, he said, "We've reached Choo Choo? It isn't possible."

Ethelinda said, "Joombo travels *very* fast. We've kept up with him, with our engines opened to three-quarters full power."

"We've been pouring on the gas," said Clackety Clack.

"*Pouring*," exclaimed Ethelinda. "Pouring what gas?"

"It's an earthling expression," said Clackety Hobo, very self-satisfied. "It means to floor the accelerator."

"*Floor*? *Accelerator*?" demanded Ethelinda. "Clackety Hobo, do you feel all right?"

"More earthly expressions," said Clackety Hobo, smugly.

On that day, months ago, when Mark met Ethelinda, when she pulled him out of hyperspace and took him on board, he remembered she had told him that her father didn't like her speeding, so she never used more than 20% of the force of her engines.

"We're back at Choo Choo," said Mark, wonderingly.

"No, we're at the second planet of the Goners – the one they crossed to. Wobble Waygone planet number 2, I suppose we'll call it."

Hgiulbu's face appeared on the screen.

"Good morning, Mark," he said cheerily. "We've found the planet. I wasn't sure it was here, or somewhere else, but here it is."

"How do you know?" asked Mark. He looked at the screens and saw the three gas giants and several rocky planets.

"We explored this hundreds of years ago, and saw the rocky planets were lifeless. We didn't bother about the moon around the gas giant planets. But this is it. We've photographed the second Gate – look."

Mark saw the Gate on the screen.

"How far up are we, Joombo?"

Joombo told him, "About a thousand miles."

"You can take a photo as good as this a thousand miles away?"

"Mark, that's easy. Well, now we can go down, and they can have their Ceremony of National Gratitude for you."

"You go," said Mark. "I've got to finish my breakfast. I'll wait for you up here."

"Mark! You *have* to go."

"Wild horses won't drag me down there," the boy said firmly.

"We can't make you do anything, Mark," said Hgiulbu. "But you should go."

"Who they have to thank are all the pilots of the spaceships."

"We wouldn't have known without you."

"They would've radioed."

"They don't have radio and television. They can receive your programs from earth, that's all. They have some fantastic technology, but in other things, they have nought."

"No radio –!"

"They thought they were alone in space with earth. Other planets had stopped broadcasting centuries ago."

"But they needed radio among themselves!"

"Mark, they used landlines."

"I'm not going down."

"Mark, I'm disappointed. It would have been a wonderful Ceremony. Well, now I know it's here and not somewhere else. I'm going back to Choo Choo. Ethelinda, are you coming?"

"Yes, Joombo," she said.

Joombo's face vanished from the screen, and on another screen, his spaceship winked out of this universe.

Dumple Doo reported, "We have a steep curvature of space on our port."

"On our port!" exclaimed Hettie Hobo. "*Away* from this solar system."

"*Away*," affirmed Dumple Doo.

"That's not possible," said Ethelinda, searching the screens. "There's nothing out there to pull it down."

"There's a deep gravity well, about as deep as that of planet Earth, and space is curving down towards it, a couple of million miles away – no, 20 million miles off."

"Put us back into hyperspace and cross over there," said Ethelinda.

They came back into the universe, and on the infra-red screen, saw the pale glow of a completely darkened planet. The nearby sun of the solar system they were in was a small point of light, not giving much light and no heat.

Dumple Doo said, "I'm working out its direction and speed… er, er… it's NOT in orbit. It's speeding out of this solar system. It must be a planet that some solar system expelled and it's flying through empty space all alone. There are some lights – it looks like a space port. It could be inhabited, but they live underground. It's dark… can't be any vegetation… just rock…"

Mark said, "Is this possible?"

Clackety Hobo said, "In theory, yes."

"And what will happen to it?"

"If it flies close to a star, the star could capture it and pull it into an orbit – if it flies *too* close to the star, the star could pull it straight in and swallow it. If they have starships, they might have engines, sunk into the rock, that could change the planet's direction when they fired."

Dumple Doo said unhappily, "I have hardly anything in my data banks. This is most unusual, most irregular."

They put on their space suits, and took the canoe down.

At 100 feet, they hovered. A space port stretched away for miles but they couldn't see one ship. Lights stretched away in grids, and beyond, a rocky, harsh land lay in blackness.

To one side rose a hill, and a vast hangar door pulled up to show a well-lit hangar inside, crowded with ships.

Hettie Hobo said, "We go into that hill and they shut us in."

They thought about it.

"In for a penny, in for a pound," said Mark.

Clackety Hobo said happily, "I didn't know that one. I'm going to put it in my memory bank."

"Enter," Ethelinda told the on-board computer.

The canoe slid forward, went into the hangar, and settled beside two ships, each about three-quarters of a mile long and a quarter of a mile wide.

The on-board computer said, "Air pressure is about that of earth or inside any Choo Choo building. You can't breathe it. It has a bit of sulphuric acid, so it will burn your skin perhaps – perhaps not. You can take off your deep space suits, and put on light suits for your skins, with a breathing mask."

They changed, looking out the windows all the time.

No one came, not even a robot.

They climbed out of the canoe, and a robot on four wheels hurried up to them.

It turned and led them for ten minutes to a wall with a door.

A voice boomed from a loudspeaker.

Ethelinda said, "It's a computer, so I can't read its mind."

Mark said through his voice box, "Do you speak English?"

They waited five minutes.

The metallic voice said, "Excuse my delay. I have been searching my memory banks. We passed near your Earth one and quarter million years ago, but in recent years have captured your radio and television signals. Fortunately, they travel at relativistic speeds, and so overtook us."

Mark frantically searched his memory. They had taught him that word in space. Ah! Relativistic meant the speed of light, the fastest speed allowed in his universe.

"You are Earthlings? Welcome. I will announce your presence."

The robot opened the door, and they crossed to a lift.

The lift dropped, with lights flashing very fast.

Mark said, "Computer, how deep down are we going?"

"Five hundred metres deep."

Ethelinda worried, "It's going to be hot."

When they stepped out of the lift, it was a pleasant temperature.

They were in a chamber about 50 metres high, with the walls smooth, covered in rich, intricate paintings.

They stood at a crossroads for five broad roads, with four wheeled lorries moving in every direction. The robot motioned them to an open cart, which took them at about 50 mph down one of the roads.

They came to fields, that rolled away farther than they could see. Huge, yellowish slugs, each about the size of an elephant, grazed on the long grass and bushes. Everywhere, huge trees rose to the brilliantly lit roof about 50 metres above them, making a forest.

Ethelinda exclaimed, "They're not trees. They're rock columns, carved to look like trees, to hold up the roof."

They drove through fifteen miles of grazing land. The road sloped down a ramp, and brought them to a lower level, where they drove alongside a lake, filled with a forest of rock trees. The water stretched out of sight, and they saw boats, with robots fishing from them.

Robots moved along the sand, some with four wheels, others with two, three or four legs, and with two, three or four arms. All the robots were of shining beige or gold.

The 'sunlight' from the roof was very bright. They drove for about 25 miles, then went down another ramp into a another plain, with a forest of rock 'trees' holding up the roof. Here they passed hundreds of factories, twenty stories high, with thousands of lorries on the roads. They saw thousands of robots loading and unloading machinery, big boxes and strange shapes in plastic, metal and glass.

After five miles, they turned sharply left, and drove for 20 miles before going down another ramp, to another plain, with soft, yellow light. As they drove along grassy fields, they saw thousands of small churches or cathedrals, each with a spire or carved tower reaching to hold up the roof.

Thirty miles on – the fields filled with richly coloured flowers among the churches – they came to great open space with a huge, wonderfully carved cathedral.

All the 30 miles, they saw not a robot, not a soul.

Now, in the open space, stood thousands of beings.

Their bodies stretched about twenty-five feet, with twelve feet or arms on each side. Their bodies looked about three feet across, and halfway along, they reared straight up, with six arms with hands. In the upright part, Mark saw a powerful ridge of thick muscle at the back.

Their heads were about three feet across, but about four feet long, like an upright tube, flat in front, with two enormous black eyes, and a wide mouth without teeth. He saw flat ears like dinner plates; and short, bright green hair covered their bodies.

One of them came forward when they got out of the cart.

He spoke a long sentence.

Mark felt Ethelinda's mind reaching to his. He suddenly understood what she understood. She didn't understand the words, but she understood the thoughts behind the words, and she 'sent' them to Mark.

The creature 'said', "Welcome. Welcome beyond what words can say. You are the first strangers to set foot on our planet in millions of years – the first ever. You are earthlings, but from your television programs, we believed you did not have space capability and had no intelligent earthlings like… like… ah! Ethelinda! We understood from your television that you did not have telepathic powers."

Ethelinda sent to him, "I am from the planet Xiucheu – what Mark here calls Choo Choo."

Through Ethelinda, his next thought reached Mark.

"Where is that?"

189

Clackety Hobo rolled forward, and projected a hologram in the air, showing bright clusters of stars.

"I know where that is, but our planet never passed near there. We *did* pass very close to earth."

The metallic voice of the computer said in English, "Please hold that a moment, as I wish to copy it... thank you! Most kind."

"Ethelinda, Mark, it is a great joy to have you here. This is the planet Pbeuxla Gbuezxz –"

"The 'Bolter Hoss'," interrupted Mark.

"When gravity collisions threw us out of our solar system, we changed our name to 'Bolting Horse', so Mark has come close. Our people are called Tpapbuekdatd, 'The Devoted Ones', and my name is Gheirbruevfuamxl."

"'Hierophant'," said Mark.

"Of the priests'," admitted Gheirbruevfuamxl. "Yes, you can say that I am a hierophant in the priestly orders. How did you find us?"

"You are passing through a solar system. A people called the Goners have just occupied a planet. Their own planet is blowing up with volcanoes. Of course, space was deeply curved with the planets and gas giants. But we saw a steep slope AWAY from the solar system and decided that only a gravity well could be pulling space down like that."

"You are advanced enough to measure the curves of space? We can't. Is your ship from Choo Choo or from earth?"

"From Choo Choo."

"Ah, because earth is backward. How many earthlings are in space?"

"Only me."

"Earthlings back on your planet are savages with small brains. We see all their programs. They are frightening, and fill us with pity. Yet you are different."

"How did your planet turn into a runaway?" asked Mark.

"Three million years ago, we orbited in a solar system, with a bright, warm sun. Rich vegetation covered our planet, with seas and lakes. A warm, wonderful world. We orbited with four other rocky planets, when asteroids hit one of them. Its orbit changed, and its gravity tugged at the other three. Over thousands of years, the gravity fields of the other three were pulling us further and further out. Then one year – oh! At the end of winter, the summer didn't come, but the winter went on for three years, while the sun got smaller and smaller. We knew what was going to happen, and were already digging. Snow, ice and blizzards covered our world. Then the sun got bigger and bigger – we had three months of summer. Then winter returned, and the sun grew smaller. After five years it was tiny and finally it disappeared. The night of space covered us. Our planet carried us into the empty black reaches of deep space."

He paused.

"One and a quarter million years ago, we passed close to your solar system. We saw that this could happen to your earth – in fact, we thought it had already happened, until we received your radio and television programs some years ago. We had our space ships out in your solar system, when huge asteroids smashed into your planet Mars, stripping away the top two or three kilometers of its northern hemisphere."

Mark thought frantically, "Hemisphere?" He had learned that word. Ah, yes! The bottom half, or the top half of a planet.

"The asteroids hit the *southern* hemisphere, but the shock waves blew the top cover off the *northern*, into space. What you call the Argyre crater is three km deep and 630 km across. The Hellas crater is FIVE km deep and nearly 2,000 km across. You should have seen the impact! They're in what you call the Valles Marineris. They were the two biggest, but another thousand asteroids hit leaving craters of 50 km across and smaller. Mars changed its orbit, and we wondered whether earth would be sent flying out of the solar system. It didn't, but as you have millions of millions of asteroids and comets in or close to your system, it will happen in the end."

Mark's heart was beating so hard, he thought it would burst.

"How… how… many people did you have, how many Devoteds, when the other planets pushed you out?"

"About ten million. We stopped having babies, and then had so few, today we number 700,000."

"How long do you live?"

Ethelinda said, "You're always asking everyone that."

Hierophant said, "Now we never die, unless we want to return into the Perfect Awareness."

He studied Mark.

"Your solar system grew from a cloud of gas around your sun. The bits of dust joined up to make gravel. The gravel joined up to make pebbles. The pebbles made stones. Stones grew to boulders, and boulders to asteroids. Asteroids came together to make small planets – planetoids – and the planetoids grew into your planets. All your orbits should be *circles*, but they are much longer than they are wide. That's because asteroids have been knocking you around. A few more hard knocks on Mars or Venus – and off flies earth! But we think it would be a good thing. No one would survive. There are six billion of you, and you would all try to look after yourselves instead of working together. We can see that the earthlings you have left behind, Mark, are a murdering, ignorant lot of thieves, and it's not good to have creatures like that in the galaxy. It would he for the best, Mark," he said, compassionately. "But you would remain."

"No thank you," said Mark, firmly. "I'm no better than anyone else."

191

"When it's going to happen, you will know. Choo Choo can send spaceships, and save two million boys and girls like you."

He looked at Ethelinda. "You could send a quarter of a million to us here, and we will bring them up to know the Perfect Awareness."

Mark shuffled his feet uncomfortably.

"And suppose asteroids hit *you*," he said.

"That is why we are so deep underground. But we search space around us, and when we discover asteroids, we fire thermonuclear bombs at them."

"And suppose you run straight into a star?" Mark challenged him.

"Twice that was going to happen. We have great engines on our surface, which change our course millimeter by millimetre. Over thousands of years, we pass millions and millions of miles away."

"Oh! Could I see one?" cried Mark.

He looked around at the thousands of Devoteds. Not one had moved. They only blinked as they watched.

"We will get back to your canoe. You cannot wear these suits in the vacuum and cold of the surface. It is *the* emptiness of deep space. Do you have space suits?"

"Oh, yes," said Ethelinda.

Dressed in space suits, they drove the canoe out of the hangar through an airlock.

Hierophant explained, "When we saw your canoe, we waited till it got in the hangar, and we closed the door. Then we filled the hangar with air and heat, before you got out. Your on-board computer saw this, and told you to put on your light suits with breathing apparatus."

Their small craft flew at about ten feet, very fast, and five hundred miles away they saw a tower with a nozzle. The tower was about a mile across and half a mile high, and the nozzle looked 300 meters long.

Hierophant said, "Towers like this stretch every ten miles right around the planet. Accelerators underground produce anti-particles, which are contained in a force field – if the anti-particles touch space, they would blow a hole in the planet. The force field carries them up the tower and into the nozzle, where they shoot out, little by little. The bang when they come into contact with this world – you can't imagine. But – our planet is spinning on its axis. So, after a few minutes, the spin of the planet has carried the tower to the wrong position. We switch this tower off, and switch on the next one. The spin of the planet has carried the next tower to the right place, and then we fire that one for a few minutes.

"And so on."

Mark stared and stared.

Hierophant said, "We can go inside."

* * *

Inside, Mark saw it was just like inside the engine of the black spaceship they had boarded so long ago, and found no one inside. Cables and cables lined the curving walls of the empty cave-like space.

Mark asked, "You need the cables to make the force field?"

Ethelinda asked, "Is it an electromagnetic field?"

"Goodness, no," said Hierophant.

He said, "Trying to contain anti-particles with an electromagnetic field would be like protecting the flame from a blow torch with a piece of cardboard."

Mark asked nervously, very apologetic, "Please, what is an anti-particle?"

"All our universe is made of particles of every sort, yet the same energy fills them. Anti-particles can't exist in our universe. There are all sorts of them, but they are *all* the opposite energy of our particles. When they meet, they instantly destroy each other, changing all matter to energy. In an atom bomb, only a tiny fraction of matter is changed to energy, but have you seen *what energy* when an atom bomb explodes! That's just a firecracker to when a particle and anti-particle go off. Anti-particles belong to an anti-universe."

"Is that a parallel universe?"

"Earthlings don't know about parallel universes. How do you know?" Gheirbruevfuamxl stared at him, unbelievingly.

Mark lowered his head, and didn't answer.

"Parts of our own universe, could be made of anti-particles. So long as the different galaxies never meet! Poor spaceship that flew into an anti-galaxy! As to parallel universes – we believe they exist, but no one has ever crossed into one. Perhaps on some other planet, they have found a way."

"Do you use anti-particles in your spaceships' engines?"

"Of course."

"But I thought accelerators measured five or ten miles across – aren't accelerators rings that accelerate particles to rel... rela... relativistic speeds?"

"A spaceship doesn't have the mass of our planet, Pbeuxla Gbuezxz, please! We only need a small accelerator ring and a small engine."

Back in the wide park where they had first met Hierophant, they found that all the Tpapbuekdatds had gone.

Mark said, "Everyone has gone back to work."

"We don't work," Hierophant said. "We have robots. We meditate."

Ethelinda looked at him wonderingly, then took Mark's hand and held it tightly.

From the magnificent cathedral in front a Devoted came out and walked towards them slowly. He had white hair all over him instead of bright green. Four others followed, with dark brown hair.

The white-haired one stopped before them and said, "I am Gheirbruevfuamxl. Thrice welcome are you to our planet. Allow me to lead you into our Temple of Meditation."

"'Exalted Pontiff,'" said Mark.

The Pontiff smiled a wide, toothless smile.

"Gheirbruevfuamxl," he corrected Mark gently. "But if you can't pronounce it properly then by all means call me Exalted Pontiff."

He said, "We have 3,000 Temples of Meditation, but this is the most important. The four people with me –" and he gestured to the brown-haired Devoteds – "are my Synod."

Inside, Ethelinda and Mark gasped. Light columns rose airily into hundreds of thin arches, interwoven in great beauty, and so intertwined were they the eye couldn't follow.

The walls were carved densely, but gave a sense of quiet and peace as Mark had never felt. Over all the vast floor sat Tpapbuekdatds – perhaps two thousand of them – unmoving, heads bent, in rapt meditation.

They walked down an open aisle in the middle to a carved alcove at the end.

They stopped, and Mark said, "Our friend who took us outside has the same name as you, but he is called Hierophant."

"We pronounce it differently. But before the Perfect Awareness, what does it matter?"

He looked at both of them.

194

"What do you know of the Perfect Awareness?"

Ethelinda said, "They have a God on earth, or gods. On Choo Choo, we know only of Spirit who has not made itself known to us."

Mark tried to escape the question.

"What do you meditate for?" he asked.

"To join our minds with the Perfect Awareness."

Mark said, "Awareness is knowledge. We are aware of this planet, but this planet is not aware of us. On earth, we are aware of red, but red is not aware of us."

The Exalted Pontiff, "We do not see red, although from your television programs we know what its wavelength is, and we realise you must see it where we don't."

Mark felt easier. He had changed the subject.

The Exalted Pontiff asked him, "And you, Mark, what do you know of the Perfect Awareness?"

He wouldn't let Mark go!

Mark tried very hard to remember what they had told him on other planets. Out in space, it was always the same! Thinking! Racking your brains! You got no rest.

He stammered, "That is God, isn't it? Sir. God, who enters this universe in the Present, in the present moment, which never changes."

Had he remembered that properly? He felt the palms of his hands grow damp.

The Exalted Pontiff gazed at him in disbelief.

"Child, who are you that you know these things?"

He looked at Mark for a full minute.

Mark remembered some teachings on earth. "God created us and the world. Is that right, sir?"

"The Perfect Awareness *does* nothing," said the Exalted Pontiff sweetly. "God *IS*. Just *IS*. God does nothing. God – or the Perfect Awareness – is *Love*, is the entire energy of all the worlds and universes that are. God *KNOWS* everything. God is aware of your every thought, because He is already *in* you, is aware of all the dust around the most distant star, aware of the farthest galaxy, of each and every colour and radiance that fills it."

"Please, sir, what is *radiance*?"

"Shining light."

After a pause, he went on, "The Perfect Awareness is aware of every word ever spoken or written, of each microsecond inside an engine, of each and every star that explodes –"

He stopped and waited.

"Do you both understand?"

Ethelinda said, "We shall take this back to Choo Choo."

195

Mark said, "And He is only in the Present, only in the very present moment?"

"Very good. We live in a world of change that never stops, but it is unreal. The only real thing is the present moment. We live in our change, that races through the present. But what happens to us vanishes, because it never was real. We remember it as the past."

Mark remembered. "And the past doesn't exist?"

"Exactly. But we must remember this unreal past, to learn from it, so we can better live in this unreal world we do. We can leave this unreal world when we join our minds with the Perfect Awareness."

Mark said, "Then where does everything come from, if God does nothing?"

"Have you seen a fire throw off sparks, and start other fires? It doesn't mean to. It just *does*. A volcano throws out rivers of burning lava, that in millions of years become rich land for crops. God is the pure energy of perfect love. Energy escapes from Him, to make universe after parallel universe, to make Angels who create every form of life. It all just happens.

"The Angels, full of God's energy and love, *do* create people and things."

Mark felt a little bit dizzy. He thought he understood it all, but it was so strange and new.

He looked at Ethelinda. He wanted to run away.

Ethelinda said, "I shall carry all these teachings to my planet. We thank you. You are wise beyond measure."

"Go back into space in peace, my children," said the Exalted Pontiff.

He stopped, and then asked, "How many earthlings now are in space?"

"Only me," said Mark.

"What!"

The Exalted Pontiff recovered. "How did that happen?"

"An accident. A complete accident."

"There are no accidents. On earth, you believe most of what happens is by chance. But what is chance in one universe, is part of an order in another place. Probably, you were chosen by an angel."

Ethelinda and Mark looked at each other.

"You don't believe in angels?"

"No," they said together.

"Mark, back in Milton Mudwallop, if they had told you about this planet, Bolter Hoss, would you have believed it? What would you have said?"

Mark shuffled his feet, and bowed his head.

"Although you have not seen something for yourself, that doesn't always mean it's not there. And as to your earthlings' ideas of chance – once, on your television, I saw a mine, and at the pit head a machine went Thump – Thump – Thump – Thump, once every second.

"Now suppose you were two miles away. With the wind, mist, the sound of waterfall or of traffic, you might hear, Thump – seven seconds silence – Thump – two seconds – Thump – twelve seconds… and so on. You would have to walk to the machine to find that it was regular – Thump – Thump – Thump. But standing two miles away, you would say the sound was random."

"What is *random*, sir?"

"By chance. Happens without any order. So, you must think you have been chosen."

"That's *silly*," exploded Mark. "No one's going to choose a boy or girl! We don't know *anything*."

"We must say farewell," said the Exalted Pontiff sadly. "Fare thee both well, and know that, everywhere, you go under the blessing of the Perfect Awareness, even when this unreal world makes you suffer."

Mark recognised Choo Choo instantly, from his last trip. The bare, black, rocky surface, lit by patches of light. No sunlight. The sun was a distant point in space. Everywhere, buildings rose a mile into the vacuum.

As before, they docked at one of the ten-sided buildings, each side a mile wide. And, again, they walked the long way to the front docking port of the canoe, to find themselves inside the building, in a brightly-lit corridor with yellow walls, just as Mark remembered. They went down in a lift, strange figures whizzing on a tiny screen. At the bottom, they got into one of the small, open cars, and it raced along golden corridors to stop at another lift.

The lift rose, the numbers blurring on the tiny panel. They stepped out into another passage that ended in a fantastically decorated dark glass door, set in a high arch.

Inside, they found the same immense room, with vivid, amazing colours twisting and entwining in slow movements over all the walls – golds, orange, greens, blues, reds purples – every tone of colour changing every few seconds.

Mark saw about 30 great snakes waiting for them, and Hgiulbu hurried forward to welcome Mark to the planet.

Another snake glided forward, and Ethelinda put a mental spell on Mark's mind, and Mark suddenly saw Ethelinda's father as an older human with white hair and grey mutton-chop whiskers. Her mother hurried to her daughter, and Mark saw her as an elderly earthling in a voluminous light blue dress.

Hgiulbu said, "Mark, honored citizen of Xiucheu, welcome home."

Mark mumbled, "Joombo, I thank you. And I greet all the people of Choo Choo."

He looked up worriedly, but he had clearly said the right thing.

198

Ethelinda's father, Trajáncheu, said jovially, "We have missed you. And how can we thank you enough for keeping such loving company with Ethelinda."

Mark said, "Thank you, Grouch'n'chew. I'm the lucky one. It's me who has to thank Ethelinda. No one, ever, has had a friend like Ethelinda. She's the most wonderful girl in the whole world –"

He corrected himself.

"In the whole galaxy."

Ethelinda embraced him, and then embraced her mother, Biulbiul.

Mark said to her mother, "Hello, Boo Boo. I have missed you too."

Her mother gave him a joyful hug, and filled his mind with thoughts of happiness and love.

Trajáncheu asked, "Are you tired? We have called the Great Science Council. They are our 5,000 most important scientists."

Mack remembered that this planet had 3 million people, who never died.

Mark's watch showed it was ten o'clock in the morning.

He said, "We stopped sleeping two and a half hours ago."

"Wonderful. Let us go."

They crossed three halls, rising up to high domes, all of wonderfully worked glass, with fantastic, dancing colours weaving strange pictures.

They stepped into a huge chamber, the walls beautiful in worked glass, that shone with a steady yellow glow. Then Mark saw the benches rising up away from a podium, filled with Choo Chooean scientists. He thought of the Dreadful Council on Grubble Narstee, and broke into a sweat.

They sat at the podium, and a great snake said to Hgiulbu, "Speak."

Mark listened to Joombo's thoughts, as he radioed them.

"We crossed through another parallel universe, *not* hyperspace. They called it Convoluted Space. In a short time, we went 50 light, years to another planet. On the planet Vvudol Vvaaguun they have built a Gate. This planet is a moon circling a gas giant planet in the solar system, Kgdxikh. We had mapped Kgdxikh, from a distance, and thought it held no life. Kgdxikh also holds the planet, Grubble Narstee."

He paused.

He said, "Grubble Narstee – called Khrooval Measddaa, to be exact – is the home of the Unidentified Plying Objects which plague the planet earth."

Mark felt the great mental gasp from everyone.

He went on, "We went through the Gate thanks only to Mark. The planet was full of erupting volcanoes. Only he risked his life to go down. He went through the Gate, and returned. Then he sent us a message to come."

Five thousand heads turned and considered Mark in silence.

199

"Mark knows of a third parallel universe."

Thousands of scientists half rose up, stupefied.

The president nodded to Mark.

Mark had trouble explaining things by just *thinking* them. He supposed that if he talked, he would be *thinking* what he was saying. They could read his mind that way.

He told them about playing with the Grubble, and how the Grubble boy had told him that the Grubbles went into a parallel universe to get fuel for their spaceships, and that in the other universe there were planets and things like

in this one. He told them about the *Bex* atoms and the *Vetus* inside.

The president said, "Ethelinda and Mark have proved a remarkable combination. Remarkable. You bring us news of two new parallel universes, and an extraordinary atom, which could change our future."

On the long journey to Choo Choo, Mark had been doing arithmetic, with the help of Clackety Clack and Hettie Hobo. So now, thanks to them both, he knew what to say.

He said, "In Convoluted Space, each step you take of one meter seems to be eleven light days."

"The distance light travels in eleven days. In one day, light travels almost 26,000 million km," Clackety Clack told Mark, adding, "I might be wrong. I don't understand km."

"A little bit more than 30 meters means about one light year, outside the membrane in our space. You go through the Gate on Wobble Waygone planet."

Another shocking mental gasp filled the council.

They all stared at Mark in silence. Mark got very uncomfortable. He should have shut up. He fidgeted, crossed his legs, then uncrossed them, and didn't know what to do with his hands.

The president said, "We have heard these reports. We already have Ethelinda's report on her *personal* visit to the planet earth, which no one dares visit except the Grubble Narstees. And they are *very* careful. I think these two have earned the All Schools' Blue Medal for Science. What say all of you?"

Mark's head buzzed with the thousands of thoughts saying, "Aye!"

He thought, but I'll never be able to show the Blue Medal at school in Milton Mudwallop.

The president said, "I suppose these two youngsters are anxious to begin their lessons. Mark has come all the way from earth to study."

Mark's heart sank, he wasn't going to get out of it.

The president said, "Ethelinda will take you to the school," and a despairing, miserable Mark stumbled after her.

The schoolroom had white, metal walls. Forty or so Choo Chooeans sat coiled on the floor, and they all looked at Mark. Their thoughts flooded his mind. "Welcome!" "Welcome! "Isn't he ugly!" "Isn't he weird!" "How does he stand up and not fall over?" "Isn't he puny! How can something as puny as this earthling make all this fuss!" "What short, skinny runts are these earthlings!"

Mark asked Ethelinda, "What is *puny*?"

"Weak. No muscles. Short."

The teacher, a very big snake, roared out the thought, "Stop it! Silence!"

He turned to Mark. "You do me a great honor to let me teach you. I shall be the first man in all space to teach an earthling."

"The honor is mine," said Mark, uneasily. "And I don't deserve it."

The teacher looked at them all. "We Choo Chooeans are stay-at-homes. We have our merchants who drive their spaceships to the stars, but the rest of us –! Yet, Ethelinda here is different. She does not trade, but she explores planets so it is not surprising she has made friends with Mark, who has left earth to explore with her. But Mark, the earthling, not only explores; he lives dangerously. Where no one else goes, he goes."

He paused, looking at them.

"So, then, we will begin by studying cosmology – the study of stars.

"We all live inside solar systems – that is, a sun with rocky planets or great planets of gas, orbiting around the sun. Wherever we look, we see neighbour stars, some with planets, the other stars without. Thousands of millions of these stars make up a galaxy – great dishes of stars, gas and dust, that slowly turn like a wheel. Outside of them, we find empty space for vast distances, till we see the next, lonely galaxy.

"Earth has given our galaxy a poetic name, The Milky Way. Here, in the Milky Way, we belong to a local group of neighbour galaxies... several dozen dwarf galaxies including these in the Magellanic Clouds and the Great Galaxy of Andromeda. The other big galaxy is Triangulum.

"Our Local Group is poor, small fry compared with our nearby cluster, the one in Virgo, which has hundreds of galaxies of all sorts. It has giant galaxies each 50 times bigger than our Milky Way. Fifty! Imagine the life in that cluster!

"This cluster lies 50 million light years from us, and holds 60 shining galaxies and hundreds more that don't shine much. They all form a ball more than 10 million light years across.

"Now, while empty space surrounds most galaxies, sometimes we find bridges. Between our Milky Way and Andromeda we find a long thin haze of stars reaching out from one to the other.

"As I say, galaxies join up into clusters, like that in Virgo. Clusters usually form balls, and inside the balls we can find hundreds or thousands of galaxies.

"These clusters form Superclusters, the ball-like clusters stretched out like beads on a string. The longest Supercluster is 1000 million light years long. Between the Superclusters lie vast reaches of almost empty space.

"We belong to a local Supercluster which is some 60 light years across, and it looks as though we sit at one end of it.

"Now, you have to think that the whole universe is expanding – everything rushes away from everything else. But the Superclusters travel at 700 to 1,000 km a second (we're travelling at 700 kilometers a second), all in the *same* direction that is different to the general rush!

"Why is that? We don't know. Perhaps the Superclusters we see are on a wheel – a gigantic wheel – that we can't see.

"So, what blew the universe apart?

"On Mark's planet, earth, they say it was a Big Bang. Our scientists say the universe has no end, but on earth they say it measures 15,000 million light years only – because the earthlings' Big Bang took place 15,000 million years ago. We say that as the universe has no end, and that energy only, without any matter, filled one certain, local place. Something stirred up the energy and it all rushed together. It exploded, to make all the matter in our universe in an instant, and hurled all the particles of matter outward everywhere. So we can call that a sort of Big Bang too.

"Any questions?"

Mark asked, "Is there anti-matter in our universe?"

The teacher said, "In nature, you usually get six of one and half a dozen of the other. In our universe, everything tries to balance. If you've got one on the right, you've got another on the left. At the first explosion – the Big Bang as you call it – there must have been equal numbers of matter particles and anti-matter particles.

"Did the anti-matter particles vanish? Are there whole galaxies of anti-matter? Or whole Superclusters? Space is so empty between them that there is no danger of ordinary galaxies or Superclusters touching the anti-matter ones.

"But Choo Choo is bombarded by gamma rays, as is earth. If there *is* anti-matter, then when an anti-matter galaxy touched the thin dust of matter at its edges, the explosions could produce pions – a tiny particle – which could produce the mysterious gamma rays.

202

"What are gamma rays? They are electrons which are shot into space with incredible energy. When a positive electron meets an negative one, they destroy each other, producing a wave that races forward. When the wave hits an atom, two more electrons appear out of nowhere – one positive and the other negative. When they reach us, they go through us – a negative hits a positive one inside our bodies, vanishes, makes a wave inside us, that hits part of us, and two more electrons appear from nowhere inside us. And so on."

Mark felt around his tummy and waist with his hands, but didn't feel a thing.

Mark hated going to school, and hated sitting in a classroom, especially back in Milton Mudwallop, but this wasn't bad, not altogether bad.

Another 'boy', a long snake coiled on the floor, with a huge head, asked, "Why do the galaxies turn around and round?"

"We don't know. Maybe the whole universe turns around, and pulls on the galaxies. We don't know."

Mark asked, "This Big Bang thing? Could the membrane from another parallel universe get a hole in it, and stuff pour through? You know, a really violent parallel universe."

The teacher said, "We don't know. Personally, I like that idea more than any other. That *would* have stirred up the energy in this universe and helped make it turn to matter."

Another 'boy' asked, "What are quasars?"

"Ah", said the teacher, moving his coils. "Who have you been talking to? Or what screens have you been looking at? Very good!"

He stopped, and thought.

He said, "Quasars are about the brightest things in the universe. They are at the very edge of the universe we can see, 10 or 15,000 million light years away, yet they shine as strongly as a nearby star. The brightest quasars are a hundred times brighter than the giant galaxies quite close to us... I'm talking about the light from a *whole* giant galaxy! A quasar can be only 30 light years across while a giant galaxy can be 30 *million* light years across."

Another 'boy' asked, "How far across is our Milky Way?"

"About 100,000 light years across. A giant galaxy can be 300 times bigger.

"I say a quasar could be 30 light years across. But some quasars could be only light-months or light-days across – the distance light travels in months or days. Some quasars flicker – they change their brightness very quickly, so they must be only light-days across. You must think that the solar system – Choo Choo's solar system – is 17 light-hours across and the earth's solar system is 11 light-hours across.

"So where does the incredible light come from? From thermonuclear explosions? That's a joke. That could give only one percent of the light they give. So, imagine something 100 times brighter than a thermonuclear explosion covering at least about 30 million km, and often thousands of times bigger.

"Perhaps they are supernovas, all exploding together.

"Perhaps they are black holes. Back on Mark's planet, most scientists think that, but we must remember that earthling scientists are ignorant and don't have much imagination. If we have a black hole, we have gas and plasma whirling around and falling bit by bit into the black hole. The black hole compresses and heats this whirl to huge temperatures. But for a black hole to be big enough to do this, they would have swallowed 10^7 or 10^9 suns like Mark's sun – have swallowed up to 1000 million suns, that is; and are gobbling up an entire galaxy – all its gas and its entire stars. Then the bright flashes could be when the black hole swallows an entire star.

"One quasar – on Mark's earth, they call it S50014-81 shines 60,000 times more brightly than our Milky Way, as earthlings call it, and it's 15,000 million light years away."

Mark thought of his bike and the moors around Milton Mudwallop. He'd go out on his bike any day before sitting in a classroom; but this wasn't half bad, and it did make the Mudwallop moors look *awfully* quiet.

Mark said, "Could it be a rip in the membrane to a parallel universe of unbelievable light?"

"I like that *very* much," said the teacher.

The big snake teacher went on, "But it's not just the quasars. We also have what they call on earth Seyferts – there're one-hundredth as bright as a quasar, but they're still *bright!* Their light changes over minutes so they have a tiny centre turning out this incredible light. Seyferts are galaxies, but quasars are probably galaxies too – they're too far away for us to see. Seyferts are closer, and we *can* see their galaxies. They shoot out light like 10^{12} suns – like a million million suns, or a trillion suns – from a place about 100 light seconds across… about the distance from Mark's home planet, earth, to his sun.

"Again, we could have a black hole, with gas and stars whirling around it at 100s or 1,000s of km a second before the hole sucks them in.

"Or is there some incredible star at the centre?"

Mark asked, "Could there be a gash in the membrane to another parallel universe?"

"*Very, very* good," said the teacher.

"Now, there's another sort of quasar called a Blazar, from one of them called B lizard, or B Lacertae. In 1975, a Blazar flared up and was the brightest thing in the whole universe. Blazars' light gets brighter and dimmer. Imagine 10,000 million suns from the earth's solar system inside a place as small as the earth's solar system."

Mark said, "Please sir, what about a tear in the membrane of another parallel universe?"

The teacher said, "Now that *could* be. That's something to think about, it certainly is."

Mark knew *all* about holes in membranes. Hadn't he walked through one, with his bike?

He thought, well, perhaps space is a bit exciting, more exciting than earth is. Visiting planets *is* exciting, he decided, but maybe all this stuff is exciting too.

The Teacher said, "Blazars lie in galaxies and they're like *violent* galaxies. You have to think of 100 times the energy of a giant galaxy stuffed into a place one million times smaller. In one month, that Blazar called B Lacertae, I just mentioned, went from the light of a giant galaxy to the light of TEN giants.

"We have found 30 or 40 of them, and they seem to stretch, each at the centre of its galaxy, about 30 or 40 light years across with a violent centre of only light days.

"What produces this incredible energy? There seems to be *no* gas for a black hole to gobble up. Quasars, we know, have *lots* of gas. Perhaps Blazars shoot out light like a searchlight beam, and we see only those that are pointing to us. Is there a cut in a membrane? What must that parallel universe be like!

"It could be that at the centre of a Blazar we find non-stop supernova explosions.

"Or it might he a ring of energy, working like a laser of 10 watts followed by 41 zeros! It is impossible for the minds of Higher Life Forms to imagine. Only the Spirit, which creates all, can take it in."

Mark said, "But a hole in the membrane to a parallel universe?"

"Indeed." said the great, coiled teacher. "For our scientists on Choo Choo, that is a new idea. Our scientists think that the unbelievable gravity well of these giant black holes drags down the membrane separating us from a parallel universe and rips it. Energy pours in from a violent parallel universe to produce unimaginable, cataclysmic explosions in our world."

Mark sat back. He was off-world for another eleven weeks. They didn't teach you any of this stuff at the school in Milton Mudwallop.

He could be in far worse places.

He put his hands behind his head and leant back contentedly.

THE END